CHLOE'S COLLAR

CHLOE'S COLLAR

Blackthorn:
Book One

R. F. DEANGELIS

R. F. DeAngelis

This book is dedicated to my daughter Raven.

It's been five years since I started, maybe more. It's been a long, strange road. Thank you to August Gates for saving me from homelessness. Thank you to my husband Jayson Spencer who looked after me when I got sick. Thank you to all my beta readers who offered suggestions and help with flow. A special thank you to my editor Kerys Ash, who as a beta reader fell so in love with my work they offered to help, without them my work would be unreadable.

Thank you all.

CALENDAR

Darkest Night
Tywyllwch
Geni
Gwledd
Deep Winter
Cynnydd
Medwch
First Thaw
Cariad
Winter
Aros
Spring
Gwynt
Fall
Heliwr
Summer
Blodeuo
Cryfder
Cryf
Ymuno

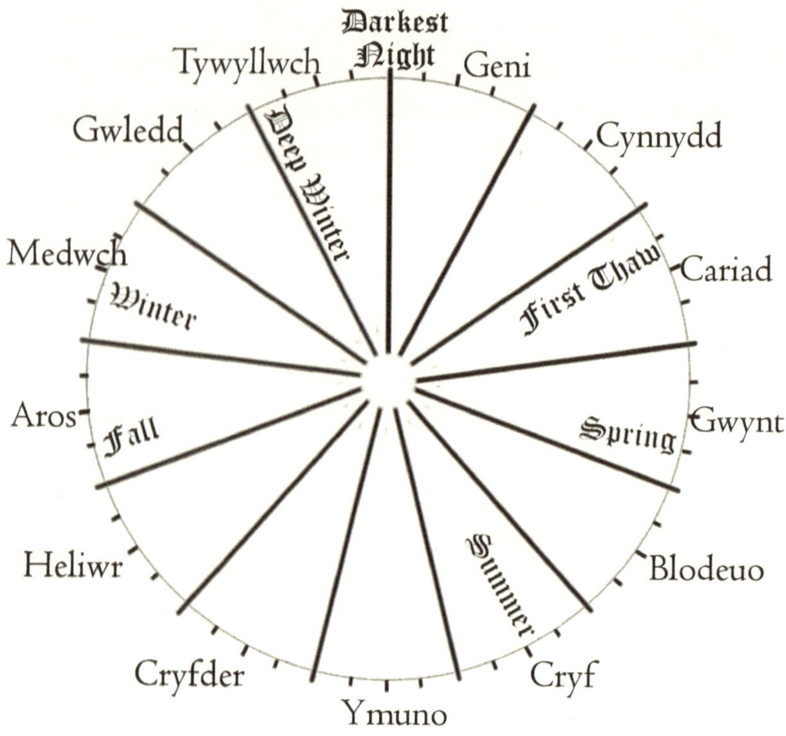

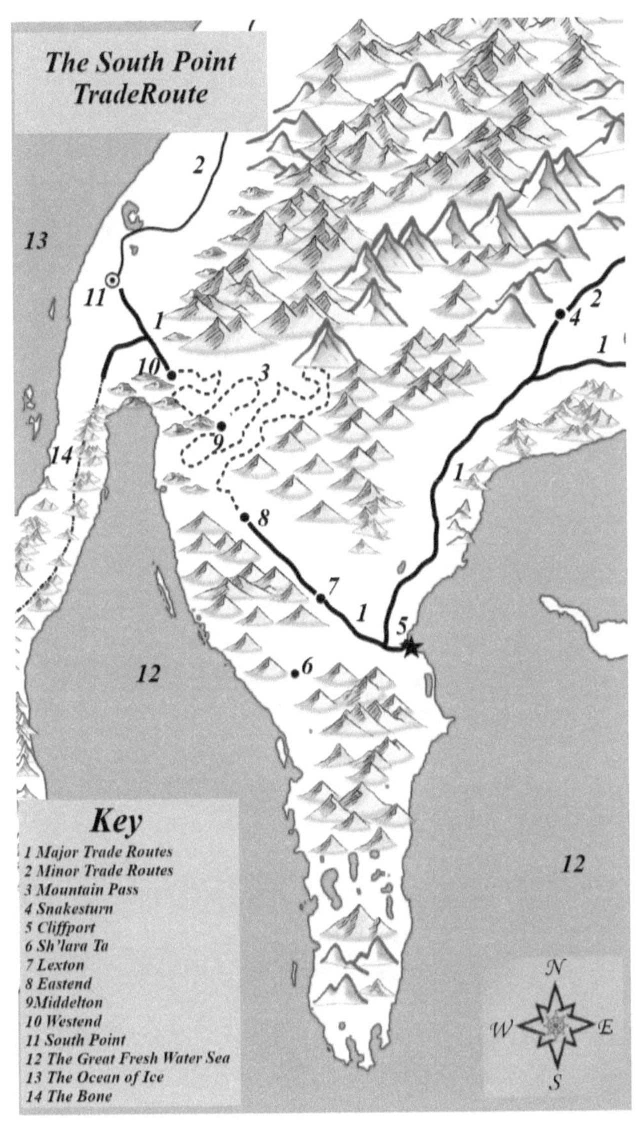

The South Point
TradeRoute
2
13
11
1
10
3
9
14
8
7
1
5
12
6
4
2
1
1
12
Key
1 Major Trade Routes
2 Minor Trade Routes
3 Mountain Pass
4 Snakesturn
5 Cliffport
6 Sh'lara Ta
7 Lexton
8 Eastend
9 Middelton
10 Westend
11 South Point
12 The Great Fresh Water Sea
13 The Ocean of Ice
14 The Bone
N
W
E
S

Prologue

My name isn't important, there is no one left to mourn me, let alone carve it on a stone to set above my head. It's amazing how quickly things can go from "on the right path" to "complete shit". Less than a year ago I was a master thief, at least in my own little mind. Now? I was huddled up against the back brick wall of a fireplace in an alley with a demon standing over me, realizing too late that I had frozen to death. It was over.

Back then I, no, *we* had plans. *Big* plans. The fire that cost us everything also convinced us it was time to move on. To do that, my best friend Piper and I had been trying to put things together. We were going to be rich and famous. We were going to be adventurers. Those were simpler times, and oh how I wished things were still that easy.

The reality of it was that by summer a war had broken out. War meant that the beautiful people were more aware of their surroundings. That wasn't good for someone used to making money by being ignored. Piper got caught saving my life on a job gone bad, and the Count's men took her hand instead of mine. She was gone now, and I was alone.

By fall, I barely had enough money to keep up with what that pig of a landlord was charging me. He had offered other methods of payment and I...*declined*. I had once tripped a trick, and while I found no shame in the work, it wasn't for me.

I kept thinking, *Everything will be better. At the Harvest Festival people with too much beer in them and bellies full of free food will be celebrating their boys coming home from war after a victory. They will be easy targets; fat, drunk, and slow.*

Only, there was no victory. The Count said that the battles had not gone well and that the men would not be coming back yet. It was up to the women to do the harvesting as well as keep up with the daily running of their homes. So, the Festival was somewhat...*lacking*.

What should have been a seven day Festival with so much food even the poorest of people could eat their fill, never came. Instead, it turned into two days of slim pickings and somber faces that almost no one attended. Worse, there was no food left over to be begged or stolen.

Our once proud town of South Point, with its rich homes and buildings boasting as many as three stories, began to feel run down. The cobblestone streets and alleyways started being dirtier than I had ever remembered them being. Sickness spread through town, even up to the merchants' districts. All three town squares saw their market stalls first lose their colorful banners and decorations as such frippery was sold off to pay for the rights to even set up. The tax collectors did not care what you sold, only that they got paid. Then, the merchants lost the stalls themselves as the cost of doing business became too much. New regulations and taxes on the poor, new ways for the rich to avoid those taxes, meant that a lot of people soon joined the ranks of the destitute. Only the wealthiest merchants could afford to do business anymore.

Soon winter's cold had set its teeth in hard; it was a bitter time to be out on the streets. I had been turned out of every church and boarding house in the county in favor of those that needed it more: wounded soldiers, children, the sick, and the elderly. I was "a woman who was into her third year of adulthood who was perfectly healthy". It was a health that would not last thanks to the cold and starvation.

When I heard the beating of wings in my alley, I thought for a moment that Ca'talls had sent an angel for me. Instead, I opened my eyes to a white skinned, winged, horned devil staring down at me.

It was tall, taller than a man I think, but I *was* laying down. The look on its face was feral. I would like to say unreadable, but I understood it all too well: hunger, loathing, anger, and lust. Its opened mouth showed fangs that dripped with spit. Its hands were clawed, and as it reached for me I tried to fight, but I could barely raise my head, let alone defend myself against this monster from myth. I knew that I, Chloe, small time pickpocket and one-time whore would be dragged to the Hells where a thief like me belonged. I didn't believe in such things, never really had, but when you are that cold and sick rational thought doesn't really enter your mind. I knew that there was no fairytale being coming to comfort or damn me...yet here one was in front of my eyes.

Awakening in this world again never entered into my mind.

Chapter 1

My first thoughts after my death didn't sit well with me. The world around me was wrong. In death, I had been cold and alone, and then a devil had come for me. Why then, was I now warm and comfortable? More than that I was being held and something savory was on my tongue.

That could not be right. I was obviously still fever drunk. Yet...

The warm broth held a taste I could not place, but it soothed my throat as it rolled down. My stomach was the part that wasn't having any of this and rejected it immediately. When my body was done convulsing with the rejection and I had gotten the slimy yuck everywhere, or at least all over myself, a cool hand cleaned me up.

Something, no, *someone* with kind and gentle hands, who was much stronger than I, held me close. They helped me and made soothing sounds to calm me. Between the weakness that came from hunger, as well as the fever I had had for weeks now, I was trapped drifting between the world of reality and the landscape of dream.

In some of those fevered dreams, I was held by an angel. She was holding me, helping me. Her touch was soft and warm, yet cooled my fevered skin. Her words were in a language I did not know, and though I didn't - couldn't - understand, the tone soothed me. I felt at peace.

In others I saw a devil waiting just out of reach, but always when the angel was gone. He was achingly beautiful, each time I saw him my pulse quickened with fear, fear and something else. His skin was the color of fine porcelain, his hair was like pure snow, and his eyes were of deepest lavender. All these things he had kept from me when he was serving as an angel of the All Father, and the horns on his face were the marks of his betrayal and his fall. So were the bat-like wings on his back, his clawed fingers, and his legs like those of a dog. *No, not a dog.* Dogs do not have feet that look as if they could grasp things to fly off with them, taking some poor soul to the fires of damnation.

Yet even there the skin was still so perfect, so flawless.

The horns did not mar his face as I thought they would, three small things just above each eye ridge, and three down the middle of his forehead, nine in all. He wore a loin cloth with a metal ring belt, and his tunic of black fur set off the paleness of his skin. A flat tail that came down to his knees twitched and curled as the creature watched me.

I had thought the devil was a woman, but the thing in front of me looked like a man. One of her Dukes perhaps? That tail looked like it had ribs and the underside was like the hood of the monk snake. When it relaxed its tail, the result was as vulgar as what you expected from a fiend such as this. If this was the form of a devil, no wonder sex was so poorly looked upon.

In my fevered state I begged the angel when she was with me not to let that devil take my soul. I pleaded and confessed every sin. I asked what penitence I should do to avoid that fate.

These thoughts wore heavy on me when I woke in the furs after the fever finally broke. I had long given up believing in the gods or the soul. It was nothing more than a fairytale to keep people in line and not something that was real. Fever madness was apparently very real. The fact that these thoughts had created such a vivid hallucination in my mind let me know how much they had screwed up my world with their lies.

The first thing I did was take stock of me and my surroundings. It took a moment to rebuild myself and get my bearings. I was Chloe Blackthorn. I was a girl who had run away from an orphanage of Ca'talls and turned to a life of crime in desperation. I have awakened to find myself in a body aching and weary from long bed rest due to sickness. I hurt far too much and in too many places to be in Heaven, but the pain was not severe enough for me to be in even the nicest of the Hells that I was taught about as a child. Once again, reality trumps pretty lies.

Every muscle in my body was sore, a dull ache that comes from being in one position for too long. I was warm, a glorious condition I had not known for... I had no idea how long. I felt and smelled animal fur. A deep brown coat of cured fur lay before my eyes when I opened them, one below me and another above with the smoothness of a properly tanned hide against my skin. That and the lack of the smell of urine and refuse was further proof I was not in the alley that I had tried to find shelter from the cold in. Obviously, I had left that far behind.

My lungs no longer burned with each and every breath, and there was no wet rattle on my exhale nor popping sound on the intake. Though I could feel that my strength had yet to return, I knew I was no longer starving. My insides did not feel cold like they once did, and the burning and emptiness were gone.

I turned my head and looked around to be greeted with more unfamiliar sights. I expected to be inside a house, or a church, as someone had obviously taken me in from that alley. Instead, I was inside a womb of hides, which was comforting in a slightly disturbing way. It was a dome made of sticks and poles with tight stretched hide keeping the outside out and the inside in.

The dome was tall enough that an Orc could reach up and brush his fingertips along the ceiling and could lay down with its feet at the center and brush the round sides, yet somehow it felt cozy; not small or confining, just kind of homey and close.

To one side was a strange collection of stick frame work and rope to make a sort of hammock, but one with three points of contact at the top making for two V-like cuts in it, and one point at the bottom. The entire thing, frame and all, had the look of something that could be taken apart easily and put back up with little fuss.

There was also a tree trunk near the center pole with its limbs cut off but the bark still on to make it easier to move. Looking around, it seemed it was used as an anchor point for racks, odds and ends, and various other things. In addition to the iron pots and other cookware that hung from it, there was a backpack of strange design, a staff, and a silver medallion with a leather lanyard. At the top, suspended on a wrought iron rod to keep it well away from the trunk, hung the lantern that was the only source of light in my new world.

The floor was covered all around with furs of various colors and thicknesses; bits and pieces of different lengths and from different animals, from the close short hair of a deer, to the shaggy pelt of a sheep with the fleece still on it. Though the pelts were thrown around, there was definitely the suggestion of harmony, almost like the owner of the furs was worried about them clashing with the decor. I had seen high society people in town worry about such things, but to find it here in a barbarian's hut was strange indeed.

That thought brought me back to the here and now. Someone who was obviously a barbarian, a wild-man of some sort, had found me and had brought me here. They often came in to town to trade, mostly bringing goods up from the south.

Up that way were wild lands with no government...well, not any as we knew it. Those southern barbarians claimed that further up in the cold reaches of the Deep South, was something called "The Empire of the Five". They said this in such a way as if it was a fearsome force and something not to be taken lightly. To hear them talk, it was a land ruled not by men or law, but by monsters, and breaking what few laws they had was always a death sentence. Yet, they claimed to be treated better there than in most towns they visited down in the North.

The priests often pointed to these men and their strange ways as a bad example, talking about their lack of civilized behavior, but the visitors treated me well enough. They just didn't seem to care about ranks like Lord and Lady. I had to admit that their ideas on fun, sex, and how men and women should interact were distressing, and the way they dressed and their mannerisms were sometimes frightening.

Armed women were nothing new to me, but their women often acted and dressed no different than their men, and the men drank, fought, and bled more than even *I* was used to. Life seemed cheap to them. They were always looking for the next wenching, even if they had their wives along with them. The stories I had heard of how the women of these people like to lay with dogs or stallions for the sport of it always disturbed me.

Now I found myself in a place that looked like one of their tents, owing my life to them. If half of what I heard was true, one of the Hells may have been a better option. At least I would deserve what I got there. Again, small comfort in a fairytale.

The flap that acted as a door way opened then. As soon as I heard it I dived and grabbed one of the black iron pans off the post. Sitting there clutching the weight of it, I knew it had been a very long time since anything this heavy had been in my hands.

A dark outline entered from the brightness of outside and light flooded the near dark interior, blinding me. I lost sight of whoever it was. How long had it been since I had seen natural light?

A gentle hand took my new weapon out of my grasp before I even realized anyone had moved. Not that I could have really done anything with it, but it had felt good to have the illusion I could protect myself and not be at this stranger's mercy. Maybe I could have dropped it on their foot and crawled away quickly, or maybe they would have been so stunned I could have gotten outside the tent still naked and crawled away into the darkness of this obviously bright day ... Yes, and maybe I could sprout wings and ascend to the Heavens. Both were just as likely to happen.

As my eyes adjusted to the light and my mind grasped what was in front of me, I went numb in terror. Before me stood the devil that I had dreamed of, his skin still like porcelain, and his eyes still as beautiful.

Maybe this was a Hell after all? Then he opened his mouth to speak and my world came crashing down around me. His voice was that of the angel that had held me and nursed me back to health. All I could do was shake as the shock ran through me.

"Vanti Dawn," he said softly, then again in TradeSpeak "Calm, peace. No harm do I mean to you." His smile was warm but his words warmer. I could smell him, smell his breath and a scent of lilies was coming off of him. This was no dream, and my mind could not come up with a nightmare like this. I realized how much trouble I was in, how terrible things were about to get for me, and how truly screwed I was.

This wasn't a devil. It would be better for me in the long run if it were.

I was alive. If it had been a devil it would just kill me. Maybe not fast, and it would probably do horrible things to me first, but it *would* kill me. I knew that for certain. This, though, this was going to be worse than anything I could imagine. This creature in front of me may not be *a* devil or *The* Devil, but it was one of her mortal southern followers. One of the monsters of the so called Empire of the Five.

"I know you not know my tongue, but might I know yours. Speak and let us see if my tiring studying has paid me off." His words were soft and he had a voice meant to sing songs to loved ones on cold nights.

This could not be happening; this could not possibly be real.

The word softly escaped my throat unbidden. It was both a muttered curse and a prayer of salvation from the path before me. A prayer I did not know if even Ca'talls could have answered if he existed.

"LeatherWing..."

Chapter 2

"Ah, good! This language I know, and it is a full and rich one with many fine ways of speaking." A smile spread across his face showing dainty little fangs; four on top and four on bottom. The canines looked wickedly sharp, as did the teeth directly behind them. "Now to begin explaining to you. I am in your debt!" He said this as proudly as if he had just announced the Count having picked him to lead the men off to war.

Confusion halted the terror in its tracks, and I hesitated. OK, *that* was not something I expected to hear, not at all. Maybe this guy was not as good with speaking Northern as he thinks he is. There was no way those words could make any sense within the context of what had happened. His slow approach and calm mannerisms confused things even more. The fear in my mind was retreating, as it found no purchase on the demon – no, LeatherWing's back. When faced with a world gone mad, instincts are useless.

"*What?*" It was the only thing to fall out of my mouth, the question a product of my numbed mind. Not the greatest comeback, but come on, this guy just said that water was dry and fish flew in the sky, for all the sense his words made. *He* had saved *my* life. I was in debt to *him*, not the other way around. Not that I wanted to be, mind you.

The ridiculousness of his words chased more of the fear out of me. His smiled widened. It was as if he found joy in my confusion.

He proved that point with his next words, "Your life, I have saved. Now I must feed you, clothe you, see to your shelter, teach you, make you comfortable, fulfill you, make you happy, and let you always be you." With each word he seemed to vibrate with excitement. He showed such delight in this absurd idea that it was infectious. In spite of the fact that I still had no frame of reference for anything here, I felt myself smiling a little.

"You mean you are going to take care of me, in all things?" Disbelief still filled my voice, but as a kid I had dreamed of someone coming and taking me away to a life of ease and grace. Hadn't we all? So what if it was a LeatherWing?

He let out a slow sigh, nodding, "As if you were my most prized possession." The relief on his face was comical. This guy was going to be playing Prince Charming for me and you would think it was all he ever wanted to do with his life.

"All right, what do I have to do?" No offer this good came without a price, so better to ask now than find out later.

"Mind me, do what I say. Do chore I give you. Learn what I teach, and for seven years I will do these things for my slave." Again, he beamed and the pride he felt was plain to see in his face; pride at what he said, and what he offered.

Warnings bells went off in my head. I saw two problems with this; one was *slave* and the other was *seven years*. "Sev... Seven *years?*" I pulled back away from him, "*Slave?* Have you lost your mind?" Definitely not my day for witty comebacks.

"Yes, no... uh..." His confusion seemed very real. "Seven years, um, twenty-eight seasons, ninety-one moons, and... sorry, I do not know how many weeks, my math is not that good." His face showed a hesitance that had not been there before.

Dear stars in the sky. Did this guy think I would *like* this offer or something?

The slaves of the world were fed, housed, and looked after. Suddenly the possession part of his statement made sense. He thought he owned me, and moreover, he thought I would be happy about it.

"Now see here..." my voice raised itself with all of the fear and outrage I felt. This was not good, and I wasn't going down without a fight. At the very least I was giving him a piece of my mind. "I am a free person, in no debt, beholden to no one! I am Chloe Blackthorn and yes, I am poor, but you have no proof I have broken any laws." The more I spoke the further back he drew. "I *belong* to *no one*!"

Two things happened at that point.

First, the beast of a man was horrified. He understood he had offended me, and from the looks of him, that was not his intent. He looked to be on the verge of tears. How could a guy who just announced he was going to throw me into a life of servitude as less than a person make me feel bad because I broke his heart?

Second, my legs gave out.

I hadn't realized I'd stood up for my little rant. Pride had driven me, pride and indignation. It also kept me from feeling the pain that standing brought with it... until now. Now, fire raged through my legs, making my muscles feel like they were going to pull themselves apart, and in the process pull one bone from another. It was a good reminder of how much I was at this devil man's mercy.

As I fell, he gently caught me up into his arms. The lily smell couldn't be cologne; it was coming right off of him.

He took me back over to the bed of furs and laid me in it like my mom used to do when I was sick. He was saying something, but I couldn't make it out. The pain was like a sound in my ears, blocking out everything else - or maybe I was just screaming.

The sound of his voice soothed me, and all the while he worked he kept talking. His hands were tender, but insistent that the knots I had tied my legs in were coming out. If you've never had someone with soft hands work on a cramp in your leg, I highly recommend it much as I recommend everyone take a rock to the face. It is one of those "must have" pains of life. It felt like he was breaking my bones, but there was no venom in his words as he talked to me.

I just about made the poor boy cry, and obviously this wasn't going as he planned it, but still, I heard no sting in his tone. Of course, he could have been calling me a whore or worse for all I knew. So, is this what it feels like to be a dog?

A look of genuine grief and concern stayed on his face the whole time. He massaged my legs until the pain subsided, then he brought me water. As soon as I could uncurl, he left me alone with my thoughts.

Slowly, the truth of the situation dawned on me; what I said was no longer true. I *did* owe this strange man something. I owed him my life, and that, at least as far as I was concerned, meant that I was beholden to him. "I'll be damned if I am going to be some slave, I'll work it off." That muttered phrase was the last thing I said before exhaustion caught me. As I was drifting off, I heard another voice. It was a woman's, and it was the same sing-song tongue he had used.

Great, there are more of them.

Chapter 3

I woke at the sounds of him coming back in. Night had fallen outside; if you are used to it, you can smell the difference. I rolled over and sat up to look at him. What I saw was sadness in the way he held himself, and frustration was plain in his eyes.

"Look," I started, but the word sounded more of a sigh than I meant, so I took a deep breath and tried again. Strength was needed here, a firm hand, but I had to be careful not to make it an attack. I still had no idea where I was.

"Look, I appreciate what you have done for me, really I do. And yeah, even in my book it means I owe you, a lot, but I don't relish the idea of being in chains." It was a good start, and made him look me in the eye. When you are being robbed, if you can make the person doing it look you in the eye they might back down because it reminds them you are a person. You become more than just someone in an alley to them. Since I was being robbed of my freedom, I hoped that would work here.

"I will work off whatever fair debt you think I owe you. You let me go, and I will follow you but I will take care of my own food and shelter." I didn't want to owe him any more than I had to, "It isn't that I don't trust you..."

I hesitated for a moment, and thought about what I just said. I decided to go with honesty, "OK, so it *is* that I don't trust you. I don't eat other people's table scraps and I don't even want to think of myself in a situation where I can be forgotten. I don't like slavery." Now I was on solid ground. He hadn't hit or threatened me, so maybe I could make good headway here. Slavery may be legal in the Kingdom I grew up in, but I completely disagreed with it. The only thing that kept me talking to this guy was the fact that he had obviously treated me very well and that counted for something, damn it.

"I think it is wrong to treat another person as property. I am not yours to own." I knew too many that had been dismissed because they were of a different race, and, superstition aside, all he was, was just a different race. Piper always had it hard that way, being an Orc. Everyone looked to me because I was the human, so I was the smart one, and I would be dammed if I was going to do that to anybody. Piper was also the reason I felt the way I did about slavery. She had told me the story of her family's past where a human woman had been force bred to a True Orc slave.

Now I waited for the worst, as I had finished saying my piece.

He didn't seem mad. No, instead he gave me another of those sad smiles. At some point I was either going to punch it off of his face, or admit it made him attractive. No bets on which or when. I would have no idea what to put the money down on, anyway.

He held out his hand to me, offering, not commanding, "Come, I want you to see."

I took the hand and he helped me up so we could carefully walk outside. He didn't try to carry me, and only gave me as much help as I took. I bundled my naked form up tight in the furs I had been covered with, since even in here I could feel the chill of outside. Winter was still upon us. For the first time since my rebirth I was going out into the world again.

The dark was punctuated with torches and fires lit all along the stone walls, glistening off the snow that seemed to coat nearly everything. What I had taken to be a tent was actually a permanent home on an out of the way cliff ledge, a spur that jutted off from the mountainside town. It looked like a basic village, stone walls complete with a Watch, but it was built *into* the mountain's side. It looked like they had used an existing network of caves and, much like Dwarven settlements, used dirt and stone dug from expanding the caves to make flat places to build buildings, and we were on a small one of those. I saw more permanent buildings and parapets, watchtowers and pickets, and as I kept looking around to get my bearings I realized I was in a town full of LeatherWing.

It took a few moments for my mind to catch up with what I was seeing. "They're all different colors."

He smiled at me, "Of a kind. In truth there are only four by four different colors; Red to Orange, White to Green, Blue to Yellow, and Purple to Black. Female to male." He said these words with pride.

Sure enough, I looked around and saw that all the Reds I could see were female, while the Oranges were male. Two things struck me as funny, however. One, he had put the female first. I had never heard anyone do so in my life. Two, he was white.

"Does that mean you are a girl?" Okay, so I was being coy. I was also testing the limits of what I could get away with him.

He laughed, and for a moment I thought I had it wrong, Greens were female, and like any guy he had simply put his own color first.

"Reds and Oranges typically are fighters, guards, hunters, and warriors because they are stronger. Blues and Yellows are leaders because they can see farther than most in their understanding. Whites and Greens are different and yet not. Whites are priests, where Greens tend to be storytellers." He chuckled as he looked around, explaining his world to me, a stranger in his lands, "But you are right, Whites are normally female. I, however, am not a woman." He sighed, and it was an almost sad sound, "It is called the Empress' Touch when you are born a different color than you should be. It is often seen as a great honor."

I could hear the pain in his words, but I also heard something I wanted cleared up. "What about Black and Purple? Does this mean what you do is decided by your color?"

He chuckled "Purple and Black...they are of Imperial blood. It is kind of like Blue and Yellow. It means that the Empress herself runs in your veins, or I have been told so. And no, being a color means you have leanings towards one thing or the other, but not that you must be it." Chuckling and shaking his head like he was remembering something with fondness, he continued, "I have an Aunt, a Red, that cuts herself anytime she picks up a sharp object, and she can't hunt for..." he paused, and seemed to be searching for a word, "*Dalist*." He turned to me and smiled, "I don't know your word for it, but I want to mean 'not very well', but she can make foods and breads better than anyone I have ever seen." His tone shifted then, and his next words were serious, "What happened to you would not happen here."

"What do you mean?"

"What I did for you would have been done long before it got that bad. Someone would have taken you long before you got to the point of curling up to die, forgotten."

"Oh," Cold disappointment crawled across my skin, "You're a slaver culture."

I turned away from him to look back out over the cliffs. We were in *his* city. I was a prisoner and knew I had no chance to get away from him at this time. There was always the cliff... but I couldn't be sure it would do more than hurt like Elie herself had gotten a hold of me; not killing me, but only leaving me crippled and helpless. No way to tell until I knew what was down there. Besides, death meant I would have no other option. If he was good to his word, I would be free in seven years. Surely, I could survive that long.

"Not the way you mean it." His words were quiet.

I turned back to him at that, and looked straight into those lavender eyes again. Though his words had been slow, there had been anger in them. An anger so deep it chilled me. One that if it was directed at me, I may have tempted the cliff and taken my chances, but I had long learned how to read people, and this anger wasn't directed at me. So I waited.

"Eleven generations ago, one of my ancestors joined the war against Unstoma to stop the type of slavery you mean. Most of our families did."

I was all too familiar with this tale. The last great Empire of Man, Unstoma, was the greatest bastion of freedom and justice in the world, an artistic and cultural center that had become corrupt in its later days. I knew of some of the sins of that

Empire. Piper could trace her family back to their slave pits. Before Unstoma fell, no one had ever heard of the Empire of Five, or of the LeatherWing, then one day they came boiling out of the southlands slaughtering every fort, waystation, and port that housed any of the Grand Army of the Empire. Men, women, children, it didn't matter. If the LeatherWing landed everyone and everything there died. That was what I had always been taught.

Piper had told a different story. She said that in every slave pen the LeatherWing found they cleaned up the slaves, took them in, fed them, and then released them as free peoples. That even the most violent of the True Orcs were tended to and given their freedom.

Then it was over, and as quickly as they came with their rain of blood, they left. They took no land, treasure, or anything else. They left everything behind, except the ruling families of the Empire.

"Why?" It was the only thing I could think of to say. After all this time, after three centuries of speculation, and here I was with a real live LeatherWing to ask, and I wanted to know. If not for gold, or land, or food, why come and kill so many?

"We have rules, rules on how to treat slaves. I can think of no other word for it." He shrugged, almost apologetic that it was the same word that offended me, "It is a privilege to own a slave. They are your most prized possession. You feed them before you eat, clothe them before you clothe yourself. You see to your needs only after you see to theirs, and you teach them your ways and learn from theirs. Mistreat them at your peril." With his last words he looked at me. "That is part of the Third Law."

I found myself smiling at his naiveté. "Hun, no law on any book can stop someone from being a jerk. If people actually treated slaves that way, I might be willing to listen."

"If you break the Laws, the penalty is death."

I went dead still. I was, by trade, a lawbreaker. It is how I had fed myself for a very long time. It was no wonder his city would not have let my situation happen; I would have been dead a long time ago.

I licked cracked lips with a tongue that had suddenly gone dry, "Cheery thought, that. You must have a lot of people to bury, I mean, if you kill people every time someone breaks a law." The cold was starting to claw at my skin, it was still winter and, though a fire was near, I didn't think it could do anything for the cold caused by true dread.

His laughter interrupted my thoughts as much as it did my words, and I was instantly angry, "Hey, now! You made me a slave without asking, and just told me if I break one of your laws I die. What in the hells is so funny?"

He was shaking with real mirth, "Realized," he started, nearly strangling himself on his own laughter before he could continue, "Your laws, hundreds you have. A death trap you must think you are in." His Highland wasn't so good when he was laughing fit to burst. I still didn't see the joke, though him thinking my grasping the situation of the crap I was now neck deep in was funny was *really* starting to get on my nerves.

"Five we have," he finally managed to get out between fits, "Only the Five Laws." After that, if he said more I completely missed it.

Chapter 4

Around the edge of the outcropping we were on was a line of stones. Probably the top of the wall that made this terrace. The spur of land we were on was jutting off just outside and to the left of what looked to be the main part of the village. Its outer wall was a line of pine pickets carved into wicked points. It was not vertical, but was angled slightly outward, it meant the wall would offer no support if you wanted to climb it. At its base of the outside it was propped up with a finely made, small stone wall at the opposite angle to give it stability. That only went up about three feet. A Gnome child holding up a massive Orc, but it looked like it worked.

Between each tooth of the picket line was a short shaft of wood with what looked to be blacked spear heads each with a silver edge that danced with the reflected light from the fires along the walls. They looked wickedly sharp and had serrated edges. Simply throwing a ladder against the wall during a siege would mean having to get past those blades.

At the top had to be a walk way as I saw armored Leather-Wings, both Orange and Red, walking back and forth along the wall. Their patrols went from one small wooden enclosure to another. Each of these were about as far apart as it took a man to walk about twenty paces. These outposts were dark inside, with the torches and watch braziers being along the unseen walk way to give light to the patrols. Along the wall the creatures never stopped moving. Inside the window openings the light from outside showed faint glimpses of darker shadows. Some moved, some didn't. Out in the dark a bowman would have an easy shot at the patrols, but inside those posts they would have a hard time hitting their targets at night.

These people had a strange set up. Back home I could get over almost any of the walls there without too much risk of being seen. Here I would be spotted. It would take a much craftier person than I currently was to get past that wall at night. I didn't want to go in. I wanted to get out and we were already outside of the town proper. Maybe if I survived I could sneak out and away.

Until then the one before me was still laughing himself silly. I watched as he tried to get a hold of himself. Something obviously amused him to no end.

Why? I could hardly guess at this point. I was still trying to deal with two distressing facts, on what was a very disturbing day.

Three, if you counted the fact that I was leaning on a large boulder on a manufactured plateau on the out skirts of a heavily armed town peopled by the demons who had destroyed the greatest empire mankind had ever seen.

Fact one; to break the law meant you die. Given how I had seen justice carried out my whole life? It felt kind of like it was only a matter of time. I would never make the seven year mark. Fact two, if I understood him correctly, they only had five laws.

The concept was disturbing. Even at basics, you needed more than that. Laws against murder? Okay, so I could see that one not being too big around here. Yes, I could see murder not being a big deal.

Laws against theft? Those were always my very best friends when it came to laws. We meet up so often. I had also never heard of a barbaric society that put up with it. The more that I thought of it, however, most laws were a variation on those.

Then there were things like obeying the Kings and Lords. Yeah, definitely in the "death sentence" category, even for back home. I had had enough of this. My life was in the hands of a man who was laughing too hard at his own joke.

"Are you done?" I made sure the irritation showed in my voice. The chill was still creeping up my spine and his humor over the situation was not helping. I had to find some way out of this.

"A moment, moment more pleasing."

He straightened, took a deep breath, and let it out slowly. "Yes, we're are only having-" He stopped and started again "Yes, we only have Five Laws. And yes, you will be expected to learn them and obey them. Not only for our protection but yours as well"

I thought to myself, *Of course, so my head doesn't wind up on a block.*

"Alright, you said that part earlier was part of Law Three. So what is Law Three?"

"Law Three is the law on slavery. We recognize there will always be a need for slaves, but we also recognize that slaves do not have good lives. Rather than stop calling it slavery and simply paying people less than it takes for someone to feed and clothe themselves we chose a different path. That is, our Empress decided to change the way slaves were treated. Law Three is broken down into what an owner and slave are to do, as well as their responsibilities for each other."

"Let me guess. Whatever the master tells the slave to do?" The sarcasm was thick in my voice.

"No, no guessing, you do not need to. All LeatherWings are taught the Five Laws first, and we all memorize them and live by them. As you are mine, it is my responsibility to teach you. It is not your life that is threatened, but mine."

Was he serious? Would he die if I broke a law? It had possibilities. I forced that thought out of my head. If he dies, I would wind up on someone's to do list. Besides, he was dumb, but dumb didn't deserve to die. I may not like the situation, but I didn't want the poor guy dead. Out here, on more even footing I looked him over.

He looked almost my age, maybe younger. So basically, he was still a kid. He was small and slight of frame for the most part, and he definitely had the hips of a girl, even if it was a young one just starting her bloom. His skin and lips were, well, pretty. So was his hair, it was as white as the rest of him and hung between his shoulders. His wings were like hands with very long fingers with skin stretched between them. A small thumb stuck out on top with a thin veil of skin coming off of it, but it wasn't part of the rest of the wing, more an afterthought of the webbing, just like those of a bat, dragon, or demon. His chest was deep, but it would have to be to get him off the ground. His torso was wrapped, the cloth of it peeked out from between the gaps in his fur tunic.

Then it hit me, it was wrapped like he was binding small breasts. He really was bodied like a woman, even if it was a young one. Over all the kid was built like a twig, like one of those young scribes back home. All books and ink in dark rooms with candles for light, no real time outside or exercise. If I was healthy, I could have broken the boy like so much kindling.

The tips of his fingers and toes had very long and sharp looking claws. They looked sharp but also dainty. Each one had a kind of natural shine to them. All in all, despite his monstrous appearance he was far more pretty than handsome.

The hell this poor boy must have put up with for looking this much like a girl, I actually felt sorry for him. "Alright, tell me. I will do my best to memorize them."

"The Third Law: The Law of Slavery. To masters; it is a privilege to own a slave, and they are your most prized possession. Feed them before you eat. Clothe them before you clothe yourself. See to your needs after you see to theirs, teach them your way and learn from theirs, mistreat them at your peril."

He let that sink in for a moment then continued. "For Slaves; Serve your masters in all things and trust they will care for you. Learn from your master. Teach your master. Ease the life of your master."

I could tell he was not finished, but I so badly wanted to ask for clarification on some of that last bit.

"Together, no slave shall be a slave for more than seven years. Slaves are to be paid and may buy their freedom early. A slave shall have a signal that temporarily suspends slave hood so the two can be equals and converse as needed. Masters may discharge slaves at any time, for any reason. They may not take new slaves until one year has passed. Slaves wishing to serve more than seven years may do so, but they shall be offered their freedom again in seven years. Do not neglect your family for your slaves."

It sounded better than what I had said to him only a few moments before. Hells, it was what I had offered to him before but with more freedom than I had originally tried to bargain for. If I was in a trap, this one at least had well marked exists and a comfy bed, as long as I didn't get used to it. If I understood what he was saying by his law I could refuse an order I didn't like.

"Let me get this straight. You will feed me, clothe me, and pay me, and I can buy my freedom?"

"Yes." was his only response.

Chapter 5

"That... it," I thought for a moment. It sounded wonderful. Well, as wonderful as things could sound in the circumstances. "It sounds...frankly, it sounds too good to be true, and like horse crap." I finally got it. It may be the law, but if he decided that a loaf of bread was sufficient, and as long as I ate that first, he could dine on succulent meats, and sugar breads.

"Don't get me wrong; it sounds like every other justification I have heard people use. It sounds great and wonderful until you look at it closely. I have seen orphans stripped of what little they had with honey words, and those same children thank them for it."

The White cocked his head to the side slightly, tilting his chin more toward me and my words. His upper eyelids came down to cover half of the black slits that were his pupils and stopped, but the skin above continued to move down making it bunch and crinkle. His lower eye- lids pulled away from the nose, getting tight. It was an oddly animal look of confusion, but still very understandable if you watched his eyes. The rest of his face was completely placid. It was as if this emotion had none of the normal facial clues I had seen out of all the other people I had ever met. Even Orcs held their mouths open in a dumb founded way. It was the first utterly alien expression he had so far.

Everything else showed on his face as if advertised. Sadness, joy, amusement, but confusion only showed in the tilt of his head and set of his eyes.

"How? Who? Who would do something like that?" His voice slowly filled with quiet horror it was as if he could not conceive of such cruelty in the world. This man, who was trying to talk me into being a slave for seven years of my life, was appalled that something bad had happened to motherless children. He was making it hard to hate him.

The question caught me off guard. I found myself talking without meaning to. "Um, when I was a kid, my mom died. I was given to the church. They sent me to their orphanage about a mile outside of the city."

I stopped for a moment and swallowed down a pain. That happened a long time ago and for all intents and purposes to another girl.

"I was there for a year or two when we got a new head priest. He spent a few months getting to know us and being our friend. Then, in a sermon one morning, he talked to us and told us that we were going to be donating all of our toys that had been given to us, all the clothing that had been donated by the nobles and such to the needy. That the Gods had saw fit to take from us what was given, our parents, and that it meant that we were strong and needed to carve our own way in the world. That we would be given tools and supplies to make our own toys and clothes. That we would no longer be used by the rich to ease their troubled mind. That all we were to them was another thing to use, something so that they could point at and brag about how good they were as people. He was going to take that lie away from them and show them real charity, the charity of such hurt, lost and lonely children as they made their own toys, their own clothing, and toys and clothing for others."

I stopped. It was a catch in my throat. A silent sob that had stopped me. I fought it down. I kept working hard to make that story not about me. It was about a girl too young and too dumb to know any better. Too young to know how the world really worked. It wasn't about me. Not anymore. After all, I had gotten away.

"We cheered." I felt something wet on me and looked up. The sky was clear, and yet I had just felt water drop on my throat.

I reached up and wiped my face, covering and hiding my shame and embarrassment for having cried about something that happened so long ago.

"See, the stuff they had been giving us was all old rags and broken toys; most of it we had to fix anyway. It was always a joke to us kids that we were wearing the rags that the lords had used to wipe away their sins. It was a black humor kind of thing."

I joked. *Divert attention. If he sees me crying he will use it against me. I am not some weak willed simpleton.*

"So when this priest said we were going to be sticking it to them, we knew, *just knew* that we were going to be showing them!" I smiled and straightened up. See, I can do this. I am tough. I can play the tears off with no problems.

"Of course, we all went to work and did just that. I did it for over a year. Then, one day while in the Fathers office, I heard him talking to a man I had not seen before. It seems that the 'Good Father' was selling what we were making at a profit. He was calling our stuff 'angel made.' Those same Lords were wearing our meticulously crafted clothing that they were buying at outrageous prices and getting to feeling good about it because they were helping out the local orphanage. It seems that the little fingers of children made for smaller stitches. He was selling out stuff at the cheapest at a Small Crown apiece."

The smile on my face was crafted to show I knew better than that now. That I was someone that had learned the lesson early on, that anyone could be used.

I came back from that place of so long ago and looked at this strange little man with his soft voice and soft manner. I needed to read his face in that moment. Shock meant he was naive. Pity, I could use that. Perhaps a knowing look, if he was a little bit wiser to the world than I thought.

His features were twisted into a cold and murderous rage. Lips pulled back from bared teeth, his tongue testing the gaps in his skull's smile. It was beating against the ivory bars of their cage, ramming into them again and again like a beast desperate to get out and kill its prey. His nose crinkled, his face set into a snarl, and his eyes; his once warm and expressive eyes were now cold and feral. I was staring into the silent face of madness.

The change was so complete that I knew I was dead. I felt my heart freeze in my chest. If you have never been that scared before then let me tell you; it hurts. My entire body went cold and I could no longer feel the fire's warmth or the night's cold breath. Every muscle I had seized and went rigid.

I have worked hard all my life. Ever since I hit the streets to avoid danger, to move when it happened. To fight when I could, run when I couldn't. And I froze. I was sick, had no strength, but still, I could have done something. Should have. I didn't, I couldn't even really think looking at that. My mind was utterly blank and accepted the bad that was about to happen.

Calm words left his mouth, so quiet and so smooth I missed them entirely. Fear of this man had consumed my previous courage and bravado.

I thought I could break this boy like a stick? No, this animal would simply eat me, tear me limb from bloody limb, and if I was lucky I would be dead when it did.

Oh gods, *it* had spoken.

Answer it quickly, and correctly, and it might let me live. I had played this game at the orphanage too, find out what was said first. "What?" I ask carefully, just as carefully as if he had been holding a knife to my throat.

"I said, what became of this?" Again the words were quiet and calm and very out of synch with his barely held back fury.

I finished it as simply as I could. I had no idea what the right answer was, so I went with the truth. With as steady a voice as I could muster, I told him. "He... I." Started, then stopped, and started again. "I called him on it. I was mad. I asked him why. He said that we had eaten better than we ever had, that we had more than we ever had before. Why should a child care if they saw a hundredth of it or any of it? He pointed out we were happy. All I could think of at that point was that we were lied to. So that night I ran away and never looked back." See? I could still talk calmly, without my words shaking too much.

He quickly turned from me, his shoulders seem to sag. "Then it is this man's fault you nearly starved to death in a back alley."

The wild creature was no longer looking at me, nor was it so close. "Well no, it was mine. At least for the most part." Granted if any of those good, Gods fearing people had bothered helping me I would not have been there for him to find. "I take responsibility for me. I made the decisions that got me there."

He turned his head and looked back at me then. His face and expressions back to being open and not as frightening. "You, and your brothers and sister were his charges; he lied to you, used you. All the choices you have made since are based on these lies. You may have guessed part of the truth, but you still thought of the Lords as entitled brats did you not?"

"Well yes. They are. They don't know what hardship is." He was calm again, keep him that way.

"He used a system set up to make you hate them, an 'us versus them' way of looking at the world. Did you ever think of them as being part of your own?"

"Own what?"

"People."

Relax, if he still thinks you're keyed up it might set him off again. "No, not really. Most of them would not know an honest living if it bit them. Most of them just sit around and congratulate themselves on how good they have it. Besides, they think they're better than the rest of us." Nice safe ground here. He obviously didn't have much of that. There was no telling what would set him off again.

"So, not human, not people." His words were soft again, but not with anger. It was like he was leading a man delirious from lack of water to a cool spring. Go careful, or it might attack you. He was treating me as if I was dangerous in a way. The man just proved to be a literal beast, and he was talking to me like I was crazy.

"Well, I didn't say that," but I had. And as I thought about it, in a way it was kind of right. Think about it; they didn't have any right to tell me how to do things. People were literally starving on the streets outside of their opulent homes. What did they care? All the suffering they passed daily. And all of them with the money to make every single one of our lives better if they just gave a damn. Didn't that make them somehow less than human, less than people?

As if he had followed my thoughts inside my own head. "No, they are people just as you are. Your world has taught you to be enemies. They were taught that you were where you were because you would not go and get a real job. That people like you would rather steal from those that had anything, take what they wanted and giving nothing back to the world. They were taught to hate you, just as you were taught to hate them. To each other you became less than people."

His words were so close to what had ran through my mind, I had to ask. "Did you just hear what I thought?" I had heard of such things being done, mind to mind speak, but didn't know if the LeatherWings could do it. It would explain so much about how they quickly killed the Empire of Unstoma.

"No, I have just heard that same argument before, and many like them. I was trained a priest of my faith. One of the things we are taught is what the 'sickness' teaches. What you just said in your mind and in your heart is an evil that you had been taught. One that you were taught as a small child." He took a deep breath "That evil is why we killed Unstoma."

All of this and now he answers the question? "What, some devil had taken it over?" Okay, baiting the mad man, not smart.

"Perhaps, but much more likely it is like with anything else the sickness touches. The sickness is a universal truth. No, that is not right. Not truth. It is the universal Lie. Possibly the first lie ever told."

Interesting, I had heard a great many stories on just that growing up. The First Lie, the first sin. I had also heard others' views on them. As far as I was concerned, it said a lot about a person, what they thought and believed that lie, or sin was.

I had stopped believing in such things long ago, so it was more of a curiosity for me. "Oh? And what is that? What is the First Lie?"

"*I am better than you.*"

Chapter 6

"But lots of people are better than lots of other people at plenty of things." I stood before him, the man that styled himself my master. Moments before I had seen him show such savagery, but I was beginning to understand that wasn't aimed at me personally. He seemed sane and rational again. Yet he had just said something odd.

I knew that when it came down to it that no one was better than me. Nor did I consider myself better than anyone else, not really. He came from a slave culture. How could he sit there and tell me *"I'm better than you"* was a lie? He would have to think himself my better in order to own me. Wouldn't he? In a way he had proven he was better than me, at least for now.

"You misunderstand. The lie, the great lie is so wrapped up in what the world says, what it thinks, how it acts, that it cannot simply be stated. I was illustrating it."

"Oh?" I leaned against the boulder at my back, wrapped tightly in the furs and let the fire behind us warm me. *This should be interesting.*

"I," he gestured at himself with one finger, "...own you." He reversed the gesture but didn't point; instead he held his palm up and angled towards me. As he did this, he also bowed slightly at the waist and brought his wing around with the arm but held it cupped as if to encompass me. It was a warm gesture, downright friendly, but it left no doubt in my mind that it was a possessive yet protective gesture. "As such, the common mode of thought and belief is I must be better than you. That is a lie." He straightened back up.

"Once a culture figures that out, they tell a different lie; *all men are equal*." He had just said the basic motto of the Unstoma. A motto they had stolen from ancient days, from the glory age from the time of the Elven Empire, before the birth of Elei.

"But men are not created equal, some are smarter, some stronger, some faster, some have all of these and more while others have less. And yet, I myself have seen such gifted souls do nothing with their gifts, while those with less did the impossible time and time again. The idea behind all men are equal is fair, but it is not just. Blood determines your natural ability, and even the strongest blood lines do not produce fruit worth it. Yet the weakest blood produces spectacular examples of sentience." He took a deep breath and continued. "Blood doesn't make you better, it is what you do with it. Being a slave doesn't make me better than you or you better than me; it is what we do as ourselves that will decide who and what we are."

I thought about it. I tried to get my thoughts around what he said. It made a kind of sense but also seemed somehow wrong. Yes, it should be nice to be judge based on what someone actually did instead of by birth, but he and his people were divided by the color of their skin. It even influenced what they would do in their life. It didn't seem that much different than what I grew up with, the Lords and Ladies at court, and those people were forever thinking they were better than anyone else. "You are White; you are a priest, yes?"

He smiled, "Yes."

"That was decided for you based on your color and your birth. How can you say how we are born doesn't't matter?"

"Because if I had wanted to I could have been a war leader, a potter, or a minstrel, and no one, not my kin, not my people, no one in the empire would have said I was wrong for doing so." He said this with pride. Earlier he had said his Aunt was a Red that could not hunt very well.

"Unless I truly did not have the ability to do so. Such as if I could not hear the differences in the tones of music. As long as I could do it, and I liked what I did, even if I wasn't the best, my coloration wouldn't matter."

"Yet you're a priest." I pointed out, illustrating the predestination of it.

"Yes, and a lot of whites are. Most, however, are not. LeatherWing skin color is like your eye or hair color, two reds get together and have a white child. A red and a green mate and have a black. As such, could you imagine if every white were a priest, or every green a troubadour? Reds and Oranges are the most numerous of our kind; all of them only wanting blood and glory? A nightmare this would be." He sighs. "The Law of Self forbids what you fear."

"The Law of Self? Is that the First Law?" Back to these laws then. There were five, and now I figured it was as good a time as any. Perhaps I could understand this insanity then. "Tell me about it."

"It's the Fourth law, actually."

"So tell me the first and we can get to the fourth."

"Let's go inside and get you some more food first. You will freeze out here if we stay much longer." And with that he scooped me up and took me back in his home.

I didn't flinch. All that rage moments before and I didn't flinch. Was that a good sign or a bad one?

Chapter 7

I settled back down amongst the fur as I held a wonderfully warm stew expertly made with a brown gravy, potatoes, carrots and well cooked beef. I made myself ready for what I was sure was going to be a tedious lesson in the laws of a barbarian culture.

"The First Law, The Law of the Stone: There is a circle of five stones. Within this circle is a sixth stone at its center. At any time, anyone that has any grievance may place their hand on the sixth stone and call for a hearing. The highest representative from each race within range of the Call will hear it and must come to hear that grievance and will listen and judge justly. They will treat the individual as an equal to them in rank, no matter the rank of the petitioner. No harm is ever to come to the petitioner who has laid hand on the sixth stone. No social rank nor class nor age is to ever be denied." He finished and waited.

"So as a slave, I could do this, and my judges would have to see and treat me as an equal no matter what?"

"Exactly right."

"So a little kid could do this and tell the judges all about how her brother stole her dolly?"

"Of course." He beamed.

"What a waste of their time." This was insanity, not tedium. It was the imbecilic ramblings of belief and naiveté, not reason. "It calls the most important people from all the races around just to have them hear about a child's lost doll? First off, there would be like twenty people there if it was all the different races, some of them evil. And they all have more important things to do then hear some brat complain about her lost dolly." How a system like this could have survived this long was beyond me. No wonder they were still barbarians living in huts made out of hide.

He stuck the knife in my heart and twisted. "I bet you wish someone had taken the time out of their busy day to listen to your tale of the orphanage when you were small, a tale of your lost dolly. And there would only be five people there."

That stopped me cold. What if there had been someone there to hear me and had to listen? Would it have changed anything? Then what he said, it hit me. "What do you mean five?"

"There are only five races. LeatherWing, SkyLord, GrassLord, Heard and Man." He said this with the conviction of someone describing the night sky but having the unfortunate task of trying to explain it to the blind.

"Okay, you are a LeatherWing, obviously. I have seen the Sky folk; they are the strange raptor people, birds of prey with arms tucked under their wings." He nodded. "GrassLords are the Cat nomads out beyond the Smoking Mountains." This next one I wasn't so sure of. "I don't know what a Herd is, but you have forgotten the Dwarves, Elves, Liberi, and a host of other races there now."

"Elves, Dwarves, Liberi, Orc, both True Orc and their kin, Gnomes, Goblyns, all of them are part of the race of Man. In the case of the Goblyns, they are part of your race twisted by demons and devils into what you know today, but yes, they are part of you.

I couldn't help it, I broke out laughing hysterically. This was too much. First off, Elves were immortal if stories could be believed, living for centuries. A Liberi only grew to be the size of a toddler. Dwarves and Gnomes claimed a strained kinship despite being very different in looks, that much was true. Orcs however, True Orcs were little better than locusts, eating and destroying all in their path.

As for the dark races, the story was that they were all of the peoples mentioned before, but had been twisted by the dark pacts they had made with devils. "So if I do this, a Goblyn could come to my trial?"

"No, they severed their connection with that ancient magic when they made their deal with Lunavner for their 'freedom'."

The name stopped me cold. I had grown up being told to say her name like that would bring her attention. Lunavner was the undisputed ruler of the Hells. The daughter of the All Father that had decided mankind was a waste of her father's time effort and energy, so she set out to corrupt and destroy them.

The only dark god that did not answer to her was Elei, and Elei was too insane to listen to anyone. Too many years of sitting in a pew and having the stories drilled into me showed through at that moment.

I knew better. The gods, the devils, if they even existed, didn't really care about someone like me. I shuddered anyway. All the reason in the world, all the knowing that mankind was its own devil, that it didn't need any help from the outside meant nothing in that moment. Not after what I had been through today.

"You say that like you believe she exists. Who are you a priest of?"

He smiled sweetly at me and relaxed. He seemed to open up again, as if this was more familiar, more welcomed ground. He simply stated, "The Empress."

Great, I thought. A God King like they use to have. And I was with one of its flunkies.

Chapter 8

"So, you worship a god king like the old human empire had?" I braced myself. I knew how he and his people thought of Unstoma, but I was deliberately testing to see if that madness would come back.

The white smiled. "No, and in a way, I guess yes." He took a deep breath; I think he was gathering his thoughts. He didn't flip out again, so that was a plus. "The Empress was just a woman. She was the first LeatherWing, and the founder of our way of life. She believed in a few simple philosophies that were out of touch with the world she grew up in." He settled down on the hammock. "She was a villain, dyed in the wool murderer, and she deemed herself worthy of ruling the entire world."

I was shocked. Here was confirmation of what I had been told all my life. They, the LeatherWings, really were devils, but I had to know. "And you worship her?" It seemed at odds with what I had seen of this strange man. How could someone so kind worship a monster?

"She was human back then. The story goes like this. To a good man and a wicked woman, a daughter was born. The father was very happy and loved the little girl unconditionally; only he saw within her darkness. She was cruel and heartless in all things, but she had a love for her father. The father tried to curb her darkness and show her the light. The mother wanted more than what the father was giving her. So she had him killed and married a more powerful man. It broke the little girl's heart and eradicated what small light she had." He stopped and smiled at me.

A fatherless child. I wonder if he knew.

He continued his story. "She decided to embrace the darkness, but she hated her mother. She controlled and manipulated everyone she came into contact with. Then she started torturing and killing, not for gain, but because it was fun, and they were less than her."

Again he stopped. This time, however, he looked at me. "She was not a nice person."

"No, she sounds like a brat."

His smile broadened. "Oh she was...she had already decided how to take over the world. She would make people love her. She had started working on that and was one of the most popular people in her kingdom. Then one day, a man came and ruined all her plans. The man came and told her he needed her help. Since part of her plan was to convince the world she was a hero she went with him."

He reached over and pulled a skin to drink and clear his throat. "But he took her to a hell, the nightmare world where he was from. It gave her more power than she had, but it was far removed from her plan." He smiled at me and winked. "She adapted. She found a mage and together they did as the man asked and saved a portion of his world. It gave her money and power. She and the mage went out on their own, and they found a place the man did not care about. He may have been a hero, but he was also selfish. If it was not part of his world, he did not care what happened."

He sat back against the central pole, that pillar of wood and slid down making himself comfortable. "Together they conquered and ruled. No one could oppose her for the gods had given her the ability to heal any wound, and to inflict them by making lighting come forth from her. No vice was beyond her reach and no one could deny her. After a while, she betrayed the mage and killed him. With his last act he cursed her."

Somewhat excited by this I chimed in. Stories such as these often serve as morality tales in any religion. "And that changed her and made her realize what she was doing was wrong." It wasn't a question; it is how all of the stories go.

"No. She continued to rule with an iron fist. It seemed the curse didn't work." He said this in a hushed tone.

"That's a bit of a letdown." The wind left my sails.

"She did so for over two years and wielded absolute authority over these powerless people. Nothing and no one could stop her, and they tried. One day she realized it had been months since anyone had opposed her, since anyone had tried to kill her. She had won." He said it with finality.

"That is the birth of your empire?" If it was, I hoped after the woman's death they had gotten better. If not, I was in real trouble.

"No, that is the end of the beginning. See, she discovered she was bored. And when she realized that, nothing she could do would ever stop that boredom. So she took off her belt that let her heal endlessly, and went and picked a fight she could not win.

She decided to kill herself the only way she could." He settled back down and waited.

I nodded. I think I understood. This was a self-made woman, who, although evil, couldn't just cut her wrist, and as such went to pick a fight; she went to commit suicide by monster. It was the same reason she was bored. No challenge. His god was a *conqueror*. I had heard some stories of these people, and that made sense for a barbarian culture like his. Good and evil weren't the point. Not the best place to find yourself, but it fit. "So what happened?"

"She realized her life was important. Problem was that knowledge came too late. The monster had her dead to rights and was about to kill her."

Okay, he was definitely getting to his favorite part of the story. He was smiling much too broadly. I might as well be nice to the guy. "Go on" I said.

He grinned wider. "A man dressed all in black: black armor, black horse, and black hair, stepped in and saved her. Not only did he take her out of the hell world and home, but he also took her in. He was a guard for the greatest city man had ever built. He was a paladin of good and justice. This was a man who knew bad laws but knew how to make them work, a man not from the city, but from the people that the city dwellers had conquered long ago. We call him the Dark One, and he was the first hero of the Age of Entitlement."

That was a lead in if I ever heard one. This guy missed his calling as a bard or minstrel. I shook my head. "Okay, what is the 'Age of Entitlement'? I never heard of it."

"It is the age where everyone had plenty of food and yet people starved. Where everyone could have had gold or silver to afford anything, and yet some people had no houses. It was the age where freedom gave way to good ideas and security, and people taking more than they needed."

Wow, that sounded a lot like where I grew up.

"People with more coin and more money than others sat outside and protested that the lords were rich and that they were selfish because there were poor people, all while having enough money to feed another person. It was a world where the lie had people believing they were owed everything from housing to food to a job, but where others did not deserve anything unless they worked for one of the great Lords. These weren't bad people; the lie had reached a critical point. And as such, people saw it, but like in most things they could not see it in themselves."

Okay, we were entering into sermon territory here. Time to deflect. "And he was a guard in this 'greatest of cities'?"

He smiled sheepishly, getting to the point. "Yes, and in this city, in the whole kingdom, you were not allowed to live alone. You were still a child even until your second decade."

That stopped me. It seemed odd. I knew of no one still a child by their second decade. Maybe elves, but...then it hit me. If this was actually based on old legends, then this would have to be in the time of the Elves before Elei's birth. I nodded. These were old stories and so full of contradiction no one really believed them anymore.

"As such she found herself living with the guard and his family. All of the guard's children were urchins no one else wanted. For the first time since her father's murder, the little girl found herself in a home. A home where she fell in love with the father as a wife does. Unlike before, she denied herself. Soon she started seeing her sisters as real people, as she did the guard. She found herself in pain and anguish. Too many people who had grown too close, people she cared for. And the guard was doing his job in a world that did not care. So she vowed to care, to show him she was worthy. She became the hero as she had planned, not for conquest, but for love, twisted though it may have been. Then she performed her first act of self-sacrifice. The guard's wife, her new mother was a barbarian, and she had had a sword wound through her stomach. As such she could not bear children for her husband and that was very important to her and her people."

He was up and pacing now, his energy going and flowing. Like a good story teller, he was throwing up his hands and turning to face me. I was really starting to get into this. This was a very important cultural story to him.

"She made a deal with a dragon to give them children. The mother's egg and the guard's seed met in her womb. And the little girl's god saw fit to bless her sacrifice with twins. As a hero, she had made the men with real power in the kingdom mad. After she gave the children to the new parents, she was killed. Assassins had found her, and they were quicker than she was. She tried to turn to lighting and leave, but they struck before her body could change. Her soul escaped into the air. She ran to her most faithful servant, who stole her body from the wicked guards that had taken it to their masters to prove her death. He took and placed her magic belt around her, but he had little hope. They had used fire to try and destroy her body before he got to her. The servant prayed to the god that the little girl had turned her back on as a child. Slowly the belt healed her body, and the little girl's soul slipped back in to it."

"When she opened her eyes, she was not in her body any longer. The mage who cursed her as she killed him so long ago simply said, '*Let your outsides match your insides, vile demon.*' And now she found herself in such a body. She had claws, fangs, and great wings like those of a bat on her back...nine horns upon her face and a tail like that of a cock made into a snake. She wept."

"She had finally gotten what she deserved." I said quietly. At this point in the story I was almost hoping for a happy ending. Some of the parts of his tale were almost a blasphemous rendition of stories from the faith I had given up. "So what happened to her?"

"As she cried, she realized something wasn't right. Yes, she was marked as a demon, but she didn't smell of brimstone. She smelled of lavender. Her claws were wicked and cruel to look at, but she could hold anything in her hands and not leave a mark upon them. Her form was like that of a demon, but it wasn't a demon. She prayed to the god of her childhood. And quietly, she had a one sided conversation with something she could not hear, but found herself responding to anyway. She had turned her life around, and as such was no longer evil, but she was still cruel, still a child of darkness. As she had chosen to enjoy the light she was not turned into a demon, but as she was dark. Everyone would see her and know it. She asked what she was supposed to do and was told to teach others what evil really was, so that it may hide no more among the people. To show them how to once again be good and to stop evil from masquerading as good."

"So, you really do come from evil?"

"Oh yes, but the Empress spent the rest of her days understanding what and why she did what she did and teaching others how to spot evil in the most innocent of acts. As she got better at this, she found others that wished to help and made them like her. Soon there were hundreds like her, her LeatherWings. She learned how she had become twisted and untwisted herself and others. Based on this she made our laws, our way of life."

"So, you worship her for it?" It sounded like a great story, but this woman sounded more like some twisted saint than a god.

"Each of us picks a god to follow. They are all part of the heroes of old. They are more than heroes, but less than the Empress's god. We follow the philosophies of those heroes and as such serve that god. The Empress is flawed. She is still one of us, but she is wise. And her ways are worth following. At least I think so. My sister is sworn to the Dark One."

If he saw this Empress as a flawed being then she wasn't like the God Kings of Unstoma. "The Dark One...that is the guy that saved her, right?"

"Yes, he is the guard from the story; he dressed all in black with a black horse and so forth. He also brooded a lot and wasn't a very happy person, hence 'The Dark One.'"

"Now, before you get sidetracked again, what are the other laws?" This place and he both were fascinating, but he was one of those if I didn't make him tell me now then we would see dawn and not get to what had started the conversation.

Chapter 9

The young man smiled at me. "Yes you are quite correct. If this keeps up, tomorrow will find itself before you find sleep. One thing I am thinking we have not done that is beyond needed. I am Alabaster. Your name you said was Chloe. Is there a last name? I know this is the custom of your people."

Alabaster. He was named after tomb stone. It fit. His skin was that white, and he may yet be the death of me.

"No, no last name. Blackthorn is more of a nickname really. A name I made up. I had one once. When my father died, the local Justicar stripped my mother of our last name. Fairly normal when the woman is of low birth. My mother lived out her last days thinking my father was actually alive and would return. At the orphanage all last names are either Founder, or Grace, depending on if you were a foundling, or if your parents had died. So until I left, it was Chloe Grace. I left that name when I ran away."

He nodded. "Well then Chloe, we have done the First Law, as well as the Third. The Second law is The Law of the Hunt."

I choked. How unbelievably priceless, and it was right up there with these people. "A law for hunting? In the 'break these and we kill you' laws?" The absurdity of it was too much, I laughed.

"Something like that, yes." His voice betrayed his offense.

I quieted down. Odd though it may be, not knowing this was deadly. Maybe not to me, not yet anyway, but for him it certainly was.

He continued his voice gruffer than before. "The Law of the Hunt: The Hunting of thinking beings for the betterment of them and you is a sacred task and shall not be made cheap. The Prey shall be taken alive; you can't learn from the dead. The Prey should be treated with respect, for one day you may be hunted. The Prey may be hunting you, for you are no better than they. And they may wish to learn from you."

There it was. The reason I was here now. He had hunted me and found me cold, alone, and dying. This Second Law of theirs, but it also stated something else. I had to know, so I asked. "Does this mean that if I feel you are not respecting me, I can invoke the Law of the Stone?"

"Yes it does." His words were soft and warm again. "To continue?" It was a question, he was seeing if I wanted to discuss it.

"No," I shook my head. "Let's continue."

"The Third Law is the Law of Slavery. That one we have done. The Fourth Law is the Law of Self." He took a deep breath, and in his teachers voice he continued.

"The Law of Self: No one is inferior to any other being by birth. Rank is an example of training and opportunity. Each person has their own strengths and weaknesses. All are not created equal. Each has their own value and worth. A person's life and death decide that, not their birth. Never interfere with a being's right to choose or to say no. Only protect yourself from having it done to you."

I was thinking hard as I heard it, gearing up for questions and rebuttals as he spoke, that this Law contradicted the Law of Slavery. For them, slavery wasn't about forcing your will upon another, at least no more than any boss would. No, this was about their view point, and their view point is it wasn't right to force someone to your point of view. It also had something to say about both rape and murder. I could easily see where either crime violated this law and was therefore a death sentence.

"That is four, go on." I wanted to see...to understand.

"The last law is a reminder. It can neither be enforced, nor can it be broken. It is the true way of the world. It is how the world has gotten to this point and how the world will move to something even better. It is the Cycle of Barbarism, and how we of the Empire of the Five Races should interact with it, use it and learn from it."

"The Cycle of Barbarism: People become tribes. Tribes become villages. Villages become towns. Towns become cities. Cities become kingdoms. Kingdoms become complacent. They fall and scatter. Those people become tribes. Be good to the Barbarian at your door. You were them once and will be them again."

And there it was, The Five Laws. It was the totality of their justice system in basic. The Law of Self covered everything I feared might happen to me. I had to know however. "Stealing? That isn't covered under your laws. At least not that I saw."

"Theft is only a problem when people do not have enough, or when people take more than their share. The first is handled well by the fact that if nothing else, you can always become a slave and be fairly treated. And the second by the fact it does interfere with the Law of Self. Greed is thinking you are better than someone; that you deserve more because you are better."

"You do not have rich people here?" That didn't seem right to me. Why do something if you couldn't be paid for it?

"Oh, we have rich people, just not rich people living off of poor people." He was quite proud of that fact. And if it was true, I could not blame him.

Chapter 10

So here I was, in the hands of a man who had nursed me back to health...just to be told I was his for almost half as long as I had been alive. If things had gone differently, if I had had a normal life like my mother, I would already be married...probably pregnant. All of that had been taken from me, and now, so was my freedom. I didn't really have a choice.

I didn't have a choice... the Law of Self said I had to have a choice. It also said I was to be respected.

"So, if I have a choice, and I am to be respected, what is to stop me from walking outside and simply leaving?"

He nodded, turned his back on me and walked over to some furs in the corner. He bent down and picked something up. I couldn't see what it was. He turned walked back over to me and took my hand. In it he placed a dagger. "Nothing. If you wish to leave, once you are well, then do so. I will not hold your life ransom. No coin could ever pay it at any rate." He smiled at me then. "I will even take you back to your home city. It isn't far."

Home. He was offering to take me *home.* To set me free before he had even started, but what did I have to go home to? I pushed the dagger back into his hands. "I would like to stay, see this place, and learn about your people, at least for a while."

"You misunderstand. The knife, it is yours whether you stay or not. I bought it for you while you were sleeping earlier." He handed it back to me, turned and went back to his hammock. I understood now what the V patterns were in it; they were for his wings.

I examined the blade he had given me.

I half expected it to be a simple dagger. It cleared its sheath with a slight ring. The blade was a dappled metal of more than one color. I had never seen anything like it. Its edge was slightly wavy.

A Kris blade. It looked extremely sharp and was well balanced for holding or throwing. This blade was mine now. I could have waited until he went to sleep and solve all my problems with a little bit of bloodshed. I might even make it out of town before it was noticed.

I looked up at him. "I could kill you in your sleep, walk out of here and never look back. Why?" I gestured feebly to the weapon laid bare in my lap. I hadn't realized I had set it down.

"It is a poor owner that fears for their life because a slave is armed, and a foolish one that arms a slave abused. To my people, we believe that an armed person always has at least the option of protecting themselves. We arm all of our slaves with the finest weapons we can afford. If the slave does not want this, that is their business. If I did not arm you then it meant I did not trust you. As of yet, you haven't given me a reason to distrust you, and I have not treated you badly to deserve your wrath."

"You just met me. I could be anyone. I might not need a reason to kill you."

"If that were so, you would not warn me. If you are so insane that you would, then I have misjudged you. You have asked questions, paid attention to my answers, and to me at least, proven you are an honorable person."

With that he turned the flame out on the lamp. I watched his shadow get into the hammock. He left me there with the power to end him sitting and waiting on my decision.

I had frozen to fear. Anger made me hesitate. Joy once robbed me of speech. Never before had I been rendered paralyzed by *trust*.

Chapter 11

Over the next few days, this strange man introduced me around to the people and places of his village. The place was smaller than the cities I had seen, more or less arranged as a fort or an outpost. The only thing that separated it from such was the children running everywhere. As it was, you had walls and palisades on the outer part of the village with very few houses outside of it. Most of those were more tents like Alabaster's. Inside were more permanent structures, forges and the like, and large permanent structures. The architecture of those buildings seemed to be a hodgepodge of styles: wooden, stone and wood, fire baked brick, stretched hides and more. Some of the buildings even had more than one story, but they also had doors and balconies. I guess when the sky is open to you, it affects how you build. Towards the back of it, where the mountain once again started to rise up, were cut out caves, simple in their openings, with the smells and lights of homes.

Outside the walls were not only the tents like Alabaster's but other designs, some domed like his but bigger, some long and thin, while others were round like a wheel with a pitched cone roof.

Be it outside or in, all the roofs, on the buildings that had them, seemed to be thatched. Fireplaces were all stone, yet none of the housing looked worn. A lot of them were obviously old, but even the tent housing seemed to be in good repair.

Looking around I realized I was far from the only human here. Most of them had collars like the one I had wrapped around my wrist but not all. There were a few other races as well: a few Orcs, a dwarf or two, as well as the short bird men I now knew were called SkyLords, as well as a deer people I had never seen before, but I had heard about. I found out later they were simply called The Heard. They were the fifth race. They all had collars. What shocked me was that uncollared LeatherWings were deferring to them. Two young, a green and a blue, were watching a Dwarf and learning the secret of steel.

The children were of every race I had seen, and none of them acted as if any were any different. Mostly, they just seemed to be playing games together. Some of those games I recognized while others I did not. No one child was excluded from any group. The adults of the village went about their work but watched the little ones run around as if they were a source of both amusement and joy.

It was the single most diverse group of races I had ever been exposed to in my life. I saw no snide comments, or anyone belittling another. Just because I didn't see it didn't mean it wasn't there.

Other than that, it looked and sounded like the small village it was. Oddly, the smell was not as ripe as it should have been. For some reason that put me on edge. I promised myself I would give the place a decent try though.

My new owner and I wandered from place to place with him introducing me to people he knew, and he seemed to know most of them. They all greeted him warmly, but I could tell some of them were just humoring him. It had become obvious to me he was showing me off as the new possession I was. While they were happy for him, he was like any other kid with a new toy. His excitement was contagious as was his joy over having me.

The majority of the populace of LeatherWings were Reds and Oranges but not so much as to make me think that the other colors weren't here. Purple and Black may have been the rarest of blood lines, but Yellows and Blues also seemed scarce around here.

The biggest difference for me was not the racial mix, though that was there, but the fact that the place felt happy. If you have ever been to a place that lives in fear, hopelessness or despair, you know.

Don't get me wrong; they weren't putting on a show for me. They weren't all happy. I saw children crying. I saw youngsters balking at the work they were having to do. I saw adults who were hurt and laid up, and the sick were there too, but they weren't shunned. People were genuinely helping the sick...looking after kids obviously not their own, the young being taught, not just expected to know.

Al, as he kept telling me to call him, took me to see his best friend growing up, a young Yellow named Shatel. Shatel had also caught a slave a few months ago and had been spending a lot of time with the girl. Al was looking forward to introducing us to each other and me to his friend.

Shatel's home was well inside the walls and was a nice permanent structure that looked to be made out of the rock carved out of the caves to make new rooms for those that lived there.

Al knocked on the thick oak door and said with a loud voice, "Shatel! You perv, put some clothing on and talk in this accursed tongue. I wish to make you jealous of the lady I have found. She wishes to teach me how to treat her and to make me almost respectable!" He was grinning at me and the entire town. I got the feeling they were "those" kind of friends. Sometimes men will do that to each other...insult and pick when they mean anything but.

Sure enough from inside in a voice meant to sing, came the reply "You skinny ass, how could a slow poke like you ever catch a slave? Poor girl must have been starving to think you were a catch!"

I am not sure which got to me more; the fact that this banter sounded more suited to a couple married too long, or the fact that this man was right and Al had caught me while I was starving.

Soon enough the door opened and a long tall man whose skin was the color of butter stood before me. In one hand he had a pipe smoking away, and he was wearing nothing more than a simple cloth around himself. His golden blond hair was down to his waist; his smile was that of a truly good-natured man. His blue eyes danced to see his friend.

"This must be the girl Rowan told me about." He took my hand and kissed it gently as he bowed before me, his friend's property.

"Don't look so surprised girl." He let go with a slight chuckle, "Everyone knows your story. He had several people, including his mother and the chief healer, seeing after you." His mood was infectious. For the life of me I could not remember anyone but Alabaster by my side during the fever.

He turned back to his friend "Good to see her up and about, but she is still too thin. And even wrapped in all these furs, she must be cold. Take her home, feed her, talk to her and let things happen or not as they will."

Al smiled at him and shook his head. "I agree with you. It is why I figured we could go in, introduce her to someone else in the same boat as herself. Someone even from the same town."

At that Shatel tensed slightly. "T'is not the time old friend. I and her have just...finished, and she is still recovering." His unease was plain, and from Al I sensed more going on here suddenly.

"You've had the girl for a bit. Tell me not that she is still body shy. I thought you had boasted in her prowess. We have all seen her tease you to distraction." His tone was still light hearted, but it felt to me, now more than before...something was definitely up.

"No, of course not," he denied. "I just know those from the north of us tend to be a little uptight about sex and nudity. You yourself told me to cover up for your girl's sake. My freshly enjoyed woman might not be the best of sights for her." He gestured with his pipe as he spoke; his body language had gone defensive. Even to me, someone who did not know him, his excuses sounded like what they were.

The look starting to grow on Alabaster's face however made his shoulders fall. With a sigh, Shatel asked, "Your mother sent you, didn't she?"

"Yes, but the smell of fear and rot on you, light though it may be, told me her worries were right. Shae, my friend, what is wrong?"

The man before me leaned against his home, and let loose the sigh of someone whose rescue had come at last. Here was a man who had taken too much of a load upon his shoulders, and now the help he so desperately needed had arrived. "It went great to start with. A High Born of the city comes to you and wants you? How does that happen? I had to deal with the normal air headed drivel humans seem to love to tell their children, throat pregnancies, kissing is sex, the like." He gestured in an offhand way. Do people really teach that to their daughters? What must their sons be taught?

Shae let out a wary sigh and then a gut wrenching sob. "She came to me to have the '*Demon*' ravage her." He looked at Alabaster almost pleadingly. "But I thought I could work with it. And to start with, it was doable. Then one night..." he hung his head in shame, "...one night, I raped her. Not a prearranged normal one, but...like one of those with no self-worth does to degrade others."

He looked up at the sky. "And gods help me, it was the best sex we had had. Don't get me wrong. She was terrified, but she was more responsive than ever before. I felt I was worthless. Then she crawled over, still bloody from the...things I had done." He looked Alabaster in the eyes, pain was starting to break down his good looks and his face was that of a small frightened child. Here

I had learned this man had raped a woman, a woman from my own town who I might have even known, and the look on his face made me hurt for him. I steeled myself for the rest of his repulsive story.

"She crawled over to me," he said again in a whisper this time. "And said 'Good demon. That is what I have wanted from you since I came here. It is what your kind does and is all you are worth.' And I..." He swallowed hard and broke down crying. "And I broke." Tears were freely flowing down his cheeks. "We started doing more, being more. Because if I had not done it like before, it wasn't enough. If I wasn't terrifying her then she didn't like it when it was done." His voice was soft as if somehow saying the words out loud made them more real, but whispers kept them from being too real. "I love her. She is sweet when she is not..." He gestured, searching for words that would not come, "...like that. But then she starts to tease me, and I lose it."

"And every time you do, she reminds you that you are in fact nothing more than a beast, doesn't she?" Alabaster's voice was soft. "Shae, *no one* should ever do that. Not like that, not ever. *You know better*." Those last words were hissed out threw clinched teeth.

Shae looked up at Alabaster quickly "She-" but that was as far as he got. The white priest slapped him.

"She is obviously sick and in pain to think something like this was okay to do to herself and you, but *she* doesn't know better. She was raised with a belief system that told her she needed to be raped to enjoy sex. Because *good girls* don't like sex! Therefore, the only way her urges could be met was to get a demon to *rape* her!" Alabaster took a step back and ran his hand through his hair. "You were in charge of helping her become herself, not feeding her destructive delusions. Why didn't you come to someone for help?" His voice was pleading; his cheeks glistened with shed tears. Apparently, no one had ever told him men don't cry.

He stood there for a moment, looking defiant as if he would swing on my new owner at any moment; his pipe trembled in his hand.

Finally with a scream of rage and heartbreak break he answered. "I was ashamed! She keeps doing it, she keeps getting to me. I thought I could handle it, but every time, every single time I gave in! I hurt her! And I liked it!" Tears of rage and frustration ran down his cheeks. "I liked it, and I was terrified she would go away. She holds me afterward, tells me how much she enjoyed it. She pets me and tells me she understands that I...that I can't..." Slowly a look of horror hit him. It was as if it was a liquid someone was pouring into him. It started at the bottom of his face. Slowly his lower jaw went lax, then the muscles in his cheeks. Finally it reached his eyes. It gave him a waxy and sick look. "That I couldn't help myself..." He said it in a low whisper trailing off at the end. He took a deep breath and used the rapidly escaping air of it to breathe out the words. "She flipped me."

Alabaster merely nodded and let it sink in.

Defeated, he leaned against his house. "Empress love me, what do I do?"

"What you should have done to start with. Ask for help. Submit yourself to a Lord or Lady that can help you. They will take you and the girl. If she truly loves you it will work. If not, she will most likely be dismissed. I suggest a Lord, Shae. You being on the receiving end might do you some good." He said it so smoothly that it took me a bit to realize the implications of what he said. It was if this was common. Later on, I learned it was.

"Actually, I think I will go to Vela if she will have me." His tone was hopeful, but resigned.

A broad smile swept across Al's face. "I am sure she will be happy to. She likes you."

With that the young man walked back into his home, and we left. I looked to this strange man that had both upended my life and saved it. "So what happens to him now?"

"Now? Now, I will give his wishes to my mother. She will make sure he abides by them. If he doesn't, the clan could bring formal charges against him. Hopefully, with help, he will get better. As for the girl? If she can be helped, mom can do it. If not, she will most likely be let go. That I really don't know. She is not a healthy person and needs help, but apparently she is also very forceful in personality."

I thought about it for a moment. Shae and the girl had broken the law as far as I could see. "Isn't this a crime, what was done? Doesn't your law call for their blood?"

He looked at me in slight horror. "The law is meant to protect, enforcing it every time to the letter forfeits the purpose. Killing them means no more growth out of either. No hope. This..." he trailed off, "This is bad and may be worse than even mother knows. But you try helping before you try punishing."

So the law wasn't always the law. It made me wonder how and when exceptions were made. There was something else I wished to know. I needed to understand and start learning the slang these people used. "What is *flipping*?" The word earlier seemed to have more significance than it implied.

"*Flipping* is when the bottom turns the tables on a top who isn't strong enough to hold them." And with that we walked on.

Chapter 12

It had been six days since I had woken up. Winter was still deep. I had been officially back among the living for almost a week, but had no idea for how long I been down. Having met almost everyone in this little village, everyone greeted me every time they saw me, even the ones that didn't speak Highlander or knew enough of the Trade language to at least say hello.

I had at first thought they were being polite, but quickly learned they acknowledged everyone they came across. It wasn't always hello mind you. Sometimes a nod, sometimes just a wave, and if you didn't respond, they stopped and asked if you were ok. This was an honest questioning as well. They actually seemed to care.

My world had been turned upside down. I had thought this place a small village, but it wasn't. The city just wasn't centralized. Some of it was in the cliff face, some of it above us and some below. Other parts of it, like the garrison, was all the way at the top of the mountain. From the bottom, you could not see it, and even if you were up on it, it looked like nothing more than a small fort. That is until I had learned it was nearly a thousand soldiers strong. On top of that, every single LeatherWing knew how to fight and would help with defense.

Back home, the closest garrison was almost half a day's ride away, and it only held five hundred troops at any given time with the local militia of able body men to be called up if needed. Granted, when the call came for war, the fort dropped down to only a hundred people, and the town gave up nearly two thousand able body men. If this place mobilized like we did, the LeatherWing soldiers would number over three thousand.

Now, imagine all of them armed. They were a violent people: swords, maces, war bows, knives, and daggers. Everyone had at least a knife or dagger, and I don't mean an eating knife. Most people carry those, and so did they, but they also carried real weapons of death. They squabbled and bitched almost constantly. Everything was up for debate with these people.

Everyone spoke their own mind, even other "slaves" like me. I saw a slave yell at and pull her dagger on her master, and no one batted an eye. Turns out she was mad because he kept wanting her to cook, and that was not something they had agreed to. Get your head around that, a slave, pulled a knife on her "legal" owner because he wanted her to do what women back home did. Not doing so was grounds for divorce and to be thrown into the streets. Yet, the guard watched it and did not interfere. Oh, but they watched; they watched closely.

I decided to pull at my leash and see how much I could get away with.

So here I am sitting on the center stone of the judgment ring, by all rights a holy place to these people. I sat with a pipe, smoking brown weed. Back home, the moral authorities would have run me off as soon as they smelled that pungent scent. Never mind it did nothing. It offended the "gods" and because of that, even those of us that didn't buy the crap were forced to live by their laws. Granted, if I was in a bar then no one cared, but in public? For some, I might as well have been acting lewdly in broad daylight.

So there I was, propped up and letting the aromatic smoke quicken my heart and relax me at the same time. I prefer brown weed to green weed. Green weed is for making you relax. Nothing wrong with that I guess, but having my reaction time lessened was not my idea of living long. Besides, green always made me so damn hungry.

For two hours, no one said anything. Not one word mentioned about it. Then a woman whom, if she were human I would say was in her thirties, still young but older, sat down on one of the other stones and looked at me. Her skin was the color of wisteria flowers, and her hair was so dark it was almost black. The underside of her forearms and palms of her hands were almost porcelain white.

"You are Chloe, yes?" She looked at me with all the weight of what she had to be, this town's leader, Vela. I had heard that they actually had a Lavender here but had never really seen her. The woman was purple I guess, but more like the mallow flower than the color of fresh lavender, but maybe I was being picky. She smiled at me, and I marveled at her jet black straight hair. The effect of her hair against her skin was striking. She looked at me and asked.

"Alabaster's new toy?"

I jerked my head back at the turn of phrase. "I am no one's toy." The instant rage boiled away in my stomach. So many of these people had gone out of their way to be nice to me, and here was their ruler, their mayor for lack of a better term, calling me a toy. I guess I had gotten complacent in this and had forgotten I was an owned object to these people, no matter how good they treated me.

Her face darkened a little, "You are Chloe, and Alabaster owns you for the next seven years. In this time, he will teach you and care for you, as you do him. Why then does a simple word curdle your voice to anger?"

"Because I am no one's trollop. I am no toy." I almost stormed off. I am glad I didn't. The look of confusion on her face is a memory I will cherish 'til my day's end. I spun back and looked at her, "Trollop, whore, sex toy!" I almost screamed at her. The horror on her face stalled my anger; part of me hoped I had offended her as badly as she had me. Part of me hoped that my testing that leash I had not just popped my head off by insulting a Lady.

"You say those words with such venom. Are those things you are truly ashamed of?" The look on her face told me she meant what she said.

"Of course they are something to be ashamed of." I took a deep breath. How did I explain? Why, here, did I even need to? "Women are not just sex toys and objects for men to play with. We are more than that!" How could a female centric culture not think what men do to women every night for a few coins not be degrading to a woman? And how could she think those women didn't degrade us all? Yes, I had been desperate enough to trip a trick, once. No, I don't think whores are bad people. They, like me that day, have no other choice. I couldn't do it. I could not debase myself like that.

"I see." She smoothed out the front of her loin cloth with her hands. She was sitting with her knees together and placed those hands in her lap. Her breasts were uncovered despite the cold, and yet I felt as if I was standing before a Mother of the Church, the leaders of the Sisters of Light, one of the overly stern women in their fully covered clothing that showed nothing but their faces. Women who had gave up all pleasures of this world for the rewards of the heavens, those women were not to be fucked with, not ever, and before me was a woman that they would have called "base". Yet she was every bit their equal in decorum and power. She, in that moment, seemed as righteous as they pretend. Blame it on the orphanage and the schools ran by such women; she glanced at me and my rage left. She gestured and I sat.

"Young lady," she began as if I was a very young, slightly slow pupil. "You have to understand. Nothing you wear, nothing you eat or drink, nothing you do in sex whether for money or fun, can ever demean you if you hold yourself to a higher standard and way of life."

She paused and took a deep breath. "Some women who marry degrade themselves every night, even if they waited for marriage as your culture suggests. This is because the men they are with do not value them and they do not value themselves." She tilted her head up and looked me dead in the eye.

Have you ever stared at the night sky just before dawn? Her eyes were like that. Dark purple at the center to a light almost blue; it bled into the fiery orange of the rising sun at the outer ring. "And some women spend their lives on their back making the money necessary to help them, their children and others, who know exactly their value. *Toy* to some child who enjoys it is not a curse, nor is whore to the children she feeds. You have let men devalue you with words. Words that have no real power, but only the power you give them." She sat back and watched me for a time.

I had no idea how long I sat there gob-smacked. It couldn't have been long, but it was longer than my wit liked. That wit was getting bruised as I tried to think of a good response instead of a smart ass one. Sadly my mouth won that battle over my brain.

"Last I looked, sluts weren't the happiest people." Okay, so my wounded wit isn't the king of comebacks. Come on, everyone knows that the boys are just going to talk to each other. And everyone is going to know how loose she is, and how she is nothing but a joke to them. "Everyone knows as soon as the guys find out you're loose, they pass you around and you become a joke they share."

"That says more about your men than it does your women." She smiled.

I tried to think of a retort. Of course my wit decided it had taken enough of a beating and slinked off into the corner. My pride looked at it and merely smirked. For once the boys were finally getting the wrong end of the stick.

That left my intelligence, and it was having a hard time coming up with a counter.

She must have seen my discomfort. "Think of it. I have studied your ways. Women are to be pure and chaste. In order to ensure this, you are shamed if you stray. Your men are supposed to be young and virile, sowing their wild oats. If the women don't open their legs, then that only leaves other boys or beasts. Such men are shamed for both. That leaves a culture where men become so twisted in their desire that women get raped. Or they seek out those girls that do not follow the rules, and afterward, they make them pay for it. They reward their friends by telling on her to them, so that they may be virile too. It is an endless cycle to keep women degraded, and it degrades men until they are forced to degrade women."

Ever heard something you knew was wrong, but couldn't understand how? Or should I say it sounded so wrong. Everything I knew said it was wrong, but I myself had decided not to put out and be a slut and got called frigid for it. Most people thought Piper and I were lovers. I was shamed at every turn. My reaction to it was to not do anything, to look down on others who were "sluts". They made my life harder by proving to the guys that women were like that. I had blamed other women. The way she put, it the men were no better off.

I realized guys were supposed to have sport and score. That's just what guys do. Looking back, I could see where guys that hadn't were treated as badly in some ways, as most of the girls around were treated.

As if she were privy to my thoughts, "It is worse than that. Men are so beaten with this that if a man refused to play, refuses to be what they call being a man, he too is raped."

I thought about it, and she was right. I knew plenty of girls that had been dumb and gotten drunk around the wrong guy, or had turned down the wrong alley, but I also knew a guy that had been raped. He had killed himself afterward. I couldn't remember his name. I worked with him, and I couldn't do it.

Shame washed over me. Shame for those I had condemned because they were weak and deserved what they got for being dumb enough to go down the wrong alley or open the wrong door.

She wasn't done. "You think the problem is 'toy', 'whore', or 'trollop'. The problem is not the problem. The problem is your *reaction* to the problem." She leaned back. A smile washed over her face. "Now, I was going to ask you for some of your *towbaka*. I seem to have forgotten mine back at the house."

I blinked at her. The change in tone was one reason, a Lady wanting weed was another. With a shaking hand I handed over my pouch. She nodded her thanks and took some out. She took a piece of velum paper and put it into a small box with the diced herb and rolled her thumb over it a few times. Then she produced a pipe stem of black wood with no bowl. Into its tip, she inserted the cylinder from out of the box, a cylinder of brown weed and paper packed like a scroll. Then she took her hand and made a gesture and spoke a word quietly. A flame erupted from her palm and she lit the tip of this strange tube, igniting the towbaka. She took a long inhale and blew the smoke out of her nose. Never had these people to me looked as draconic as she did in that moment. She held it and herself as if that simple odd pipe stem was a scepter of office.

"Now, child, understand this world has lied to you in ways you cannot even begin to understand yet. And realizing it, which most do, they correct for the lie only to discover later that that correction only feeds the lie more. Like you thinking that you were sticking it to those with more by stealing from them while all you were doing is giving them reason to think all poor were like you."

"Why?" It was the only thing I could honestly think to say.

"Why else? Dear girl, to keep you under control. To keep you doing what is expected. Do you really think your Lords and Ladies care if you *fuck*? Do you think your Priests and Priestesses care? Oh, don't get me wrong, most of them have no idea that is what they are doing. They don't realize they are lying because they believe the lie. It is an old cycle in which you participate, or they punish you."

It all sounded a little farfetched to me. "And how long does it go back?"

"To before The Fall."

"The fall? What fall?"

"The Fall of Elei my dear, all the way back to the Age of Entitlement and probably further still."

The words were a sigh, as if she was talking about something of a great sorrow. Well, it was a great sorrow. Elei ended the greatest age of elves, a dread god that destroyed paradise. It was a myth of course. If Elven kind had done anything like what was talked about in the myth, there would be evidence of it.

Chapter 13

"The Age of Entitlement was before the coming of Elei. Some say she came because of that age. I disagree. Something like Elei goes where it likes with no need to be there." Vela looked around as she drew air in through the stem and rolled weed, exhaling slowly.

"If you believe in the gods and believe in justice, then you must believe Elei was a punishment." One of my favorite arguments was this line of thought. Either there were gods, and Elei was simply stronger, and they could not prevent her birth into this world, or mankind had displeased the gods, and those that had nothing to do with the displeasing were made to suffer with the so called wicked. Or the gods simply didn't care, or they didn't exist.

She chuckled, smoke curling out of her nostrils as she did and each sound being punctuated with little puffs of billowing grayish clouds of the stuff. "It is very hard, isn't it? To think that there are great imaginary parents in the skies above us or ground below, who are not forcing us to behave as we should? That if they were more powerful, more morally right creatures than man, beings of such virtue, how could they possibly allow so much suffering to exist?"

Ever start out having one conversation, and then suddenly you are completely lost? This woman had been talking as if she believed in gods just moments before. Now she was speaking as and had even said that they were imaginary. The shift was so sudden that I think I lost the thread.

I asked her. "So you don't believe in gods?" Never be afraid of looking dumb if you want to learn.

"Oh, I believe. I just don't believe the way your people do." She took another drag. "Think of this. Right now, Alabaster has power over you. He thinks his way of doing things is better than the way you grew up with. Do you follow me so far?" She turned towards me.

"Yeah, and that is pretty much how it is. He isn't an ass about it, but yes." Actually, Al had been great so far.

"Now imagine, just for a moment, that because Alabaster was 'right', and had a 'higher understanding' of the world than you, he made you behave as you should. He didn't ask you questions, didn't seek your input, and just made you do it."

My heart suddenly felt like a lump in my chest and my skin cooled enough I had to wrap the fur tighter around me. "I'd kick his ass."

"Very good. Now, why do you want something more knowledgeable, kinder, more powerful, more understanding than my son to force others to behave 'properly'?"

"Because they're gods. If they exist, then they created us, and they have the right to make us behave, to make people stop hurting people. They don't. Either they don't exist and priestly magic is no different from arcane magic, or they don't care unless you kiss their ass." I took a deep breath, "And that makes them petty and we'd be better off without them."

"They gave up the right to 'make us behave' the moment they gave us free will."

"Then they made a mistake."

"Really? I will admit that so much harm has been done in the name of selfish power. I sometimes wonder if it is worth it myself." Her voice trailed off.

"Don't you get tired of it? Tired of praying to a god that either doesn't exist or doesn't care?" I have issues; I know it. This wasn't me being that person; I honestly wanted to know if I was the only one that had ever felt that way. Felt completely abandoned as you huddled and hid in the shadows. Dodging blows from adults who accused me of things not yet true.

"Frankly? Yes. I sit and watch time and again as one person steps on another in order to grab for something of no importance or that doesn't even exist. I watch as all of mankind fights like starved dogs over a bone that will kill them. Anyone that tells you they never once felt that way simply has never looked at the world...the real world."

"Then how? How can you still follow something like that?"

"Simple. I don't." Her smile was infectious. This I needed explained. I guess she could tell from the look on my face. She continued. "To me, the gods, or more importantly *one* god did do something about that. You see, free will is a double-edged sword. To me, and what I believe, that makes it my responsibility to do something about the suffering I see, not some imaginary beings. The god I follow isn't a god; not like you have been taught. It isn't a supreme being with a plan for the world or its people. No, I follow an idea. The person who exemplified that idea was a screw up like the rest of us. My race is due to her sin. She stopped waiting for others to do what she was capable of. That is what it means to follow our 'gods'. Pray, but act as you pray. Don't wait for someone else to feed the child of the streets; feed them your food. Do not wait for someone to stand up for the hurt, the injured, the stepped on. Do it yourself."

I smiled. I was truly beginning to like these people. "That is my plan. So, why do you still call on the gods?"

"Because I have to believe in a power greater than myself. I may be captain of my own ship, lord of my own house, but I am not the river nor the land it stands upon. No matter how powerful you are, there is always more." She stared off into the distance, her gaze steady. I saw a flaw in her way of looking at the world.

"Something better than you." The First Lie, or a version of it. It was one of the first things that I was taught here just a few days ago. Reason, logic, they are good at seeing things those with faith often overlooked.

"Not better. No, just more, higher on the food chain. A parent is not better than a child, just wiser. A human is not better than an ant; they just have a broader perspective."

"But we discipline children; we kill ants." I wanted to see her point of view, but her arguments were a little over simplified.

She turned her face towards me, joy was in her eyes. "We discipline children because it is better to sting their butts than to have them damaged far worse later. We do this in hopes that they learn wisdom. If you approach it with the '*I am better than this child*', then you have forgotten that you were once a child.

As for ants, only a fool goes to the nest in the woods and kills them. That is their place. It is the ants in the house you kill. Not because you are better than they, but because they are offering harm to you and yours. Taking food they do not realize is not theirs, and territory where they bite and sting, it is an attack, and much like it is not an evil for a mother bear to kill a person in her home, it is not an evil to kill an ant in yours."

"I have to believe we are better than ants."

"Some would agree with you. Ants have no free will, not that we know of. They are instinct only. They would tell you this makes us better than ants."

She stopped for a moment and stared out into the space between here and there, seeing something only she could see. It made a bitter cast come to her face. I watched for a moment as the acrid smoke curled around her. Then she continued, "They are wrong. Free will gives us freedom, yes. It also gives us more responsibility. Ants fulfill their responsibilities to this world and to nature. We shrink from ours. We say it is too hard, or that it is not our problem. This is when we fail." The last words were said not with sorrow, just said with the same matter of fact certainty that one says. An apple is red. The problem is apples are some-times green.

"I'll believe in gods when I can see they have done something in my life, or the lives of others. Until then, all I see is random happenstance. I see cruelty so easily prevented. I see those with god granted magics do exactly what their gods say they shouldn't do. Evidence says they don't exist and do not care if they did. If I see otherwise, I will rethink, but until then, I won't waste my time praying to a thing that doesn't care or can't care because it isn't there."

"Good. That is the right attitude to have for you. I think it might serve you well in life."

Chuckling I looked at her, "What, no attempts at conversion? No argument as to how I am wrong?"

Amused she looked at me. "Why? Would you like me to convert you? To prove you wrong? What would be the point? A god is a calling. If you do not feel a calling, then I am wrong to force it on you. Only those unsure of themselves scream endlessly about how they are right and others are wrong. A person who is right doesn't care who believes them. They care about the truth, and your truth is right, as is mine."

"We can't both be right." I hated when they did this. It was a cop out. I can't convert you, so I will now stop listening to what you have to say. It was a smug, superior attitude that drove me to near madness, and now to hear it out of a LeatherWing?

As she got up to leave she turned towards me. "You misunderstand child. My walk, our way will show you the rightness of what I believe. Or yours will show me. All else is words, and words are easy to say. Besides, part of my way is to accept your way as right for you, if it works."

Chapter 14

It had been days since I had talked to the leader of this town. A couple of things still got to me about her. One, she basically just wandered around without guard or assembly following them everywhere, and that was a little odd to me. I asked Alabaster about it. He said she did have guards; they were just under orders not to be obtrusive. I had always thought protection needed to look the part to deter problems.

Two, she actually seemed interested in what I had to say. She still threw me for a loop that she could understand that the gods were more imagination than fact. Yet she still clung to them like a child to a blanket or doll. Like believing in the Great Spirit of Winter after watching someone else put out your solstice gifts.

Still, at the point of trying to see if these people actually lived what they said or if it was just a facade and normal was waiting just under the surface, I decided to go see her again, this time seeking her out. I spent most of the morning looking for her home. I figured, simple or not, it was probably one of the bigger places. That turned out to be one of the sick houses. Granted, most of the people there seemed injured rather than sick, but I didn't know what else to call them.

The next one turned out to be the local Kirk. Trust me. It wasn't normal. The place was run by five whites and two greens, but lots of people were there. I thought it was a service day, but no, people were encouraged just to come in and mill about if they liked.

I had long since gotten used to the style of dress these people preferred, so I was a bit put off when I saw one red wearing not even the loin cloth, but a simple strip of leather around her waist. Her cinnamon colored skin seemed to glow in the light of the place, a sort of whimsical angry happy kind of thing. A contradiction like most of the things these people were. She had a small stringed instrument with a long neck, in her other hand was a bow. It was a bit bigger than the fiddles I had seen before but looked to be the same type. She was roosted in one of the large opened windows staring out into the day, lost in her own world.

These people were open and not body shy at all, but I had never seen one of them without something covering their lower half, be it male or female. On top of that, this was obviously a very public place, and children were running around, playing both inside and out. No one else was even giving the girl a passing glance. I walked up to her.

As I stood there, she continued to stare out at nothing. I would have to get her attention. "Hello." She turned and looked at me, eyes still completely unfocused, but she smiled.

Ah, she must be blind. Then she blinked and seemed to snap back into the here and now. She tilted her head down looking at me fully. Her eyes and skin color were the same. It made her look utterly demonic.

She smiled at me, showing the barest hint of her fangs. It was a half-smile, only pulling up one side of her mouth, a cocky smirk. Her head was lowered slightly making her peer out from her top lashes. With a simple look from this woman, I was unsettled. I had to take a step back. She had yet to speak, and already she put my back up.

"*Adveal Lok Dan'noy*." Her voice was just above a whisper; it was smoky and dark, befitting the rest of her looks. Had she been the first of these people I had met, I would have run away screaming.

In a volume to match hers "I'm sorry, I don't understand."

She let out a low chuckle, "So very muchings I think. Answers you are looking for, so to temple you come." She shook her head, laughing at some joke only she had heard. "Ask your questions, perhaps wisdom I have for you, perhaps more questions I will giving to you, maybe both."

I cocked my head to the side. Help me, I was starting to pick up their mannerisms. "Are you a Priest then?" I had finally met a Red who was a priest.

She nodded, her smile growing as she responded. It didn't make me feel any better. I felt like a mouse before a hawk.

"Your leader and I spoke a few days ago. She spoke as if the gods were pure imagination, but confesses to believe in them anyway."

As she spoke, her eyes danced. "Ah, you are one of those that do not fall for the god's trap. You see them for the frauds and fools they are shown to be." She slid off the window ledge and looked at me. "Your knowing is just as good if not better than most believings. Why do you not leave it as this and just rest in your understandings?"

Was she serious? Not that long ago my entire town was cleaned out of good strong men, off to war to stop the ungodly. There were hundreds dead for nothing more than the greed of the church and the lie of the gods. "Because men use that lie, that mistaken belief, to control, to kill, to keep those that do not get they are being lied to under control."

Her head ducked once, chin touching her chest then back up 'til her eyes locked with mine. "You seek to save those who have been lied to from the very real hell of the sufferings inflicted by people of power. A noble cause." She looked out the window and nodded. "And one I can agree with."

Confused, I looked at her. "You are a Priest. How can you say that and still be a Priest? If you know it is a lie, then why do you insist on doing it?"

She cocked her head to the side. Softly she spoke, "Let me ask you something. Where you are from, do they still use children as labor?"

I blinked at her and then smiled. It was one of the things I was actually proud of my little town for. "No. A few years before I was born, the count's wife visited some of her husband's holdings and saw the children from the mines. She was horrified and made her husband pass laws that lets children keep their childhood a little longer. No more kids crippled before adulthood. No more dead before they had even lived."

She smiled at me, the predatory look intensified on her face. She seemed to be getting a rapturous joy from this conversation. "Good, you understand the problem of the small being used as coin. As nothing more than a commodity to be used and discarded. So, tell me, how do children fare now?"

I chuckled. "Better than before. Crippled child beggars are almost unheard of now. Don't get me wrong; it is not perfect. Some people still illegally employ children. I myself took a few of these jobs. Trust me; it is not worth it. I rarely got paid what I was promised, and the jobs were all menial and degrading." I shook my head still smiling. The orphanage wasn't covered under the law, being a place of god. All of the children's work was voluntary to make their own stuff. Families still used sons and daughters to do work, and farmhands and inn keepers often did this.

She cocked her head to the side, "And you have less homeless children now?"

"Well, the orphanages take in what they can. Homeless children are still a problem." I frowned...I had been one of those. "Still, it's better than the mines."

"Of that I have no doubt." Her body language said "hunter ready to pounce". These people were beyond odd. In some ways, it was like watching a wild animal when seeing them interact with each other or others, though with others they usually at least tried to rein it in. This one did not. She was a harsh reminder of how alien these people truly were. "Howevers, what of those that have pain?"

"You mean the ones that are sick? The healer houses are there for them. No healer house will charge a child for medicine, and they will take them in when they can and get the guard to find a place for them." I had been here for a while. It was nice to have something to actually brag on my people about.

She shook her head. "You do not understand." She sighed and looked up at the ceiling. Her next words chilled me in a way that did not go away for the rest of the day. "Some, some children, they do not be having a place in their own homes. Father beat them. Mothers ignore them. Maybe sex is forced upon them before they are ready. Or they are lied to about it when they ask, so they think what they want makes them freaks. In your city, they have to stay with these people or starve. They are trapped. You have taken the options not out of the hands of the bad task masters, but out of those that have nothing."

I shook my head; she was justifying child slavery. "No, they can go to the guard; they can tell someone, go to the churches even."

She locked eyes with me, and the jaws of her argument clamped shut on mine's throat. "Yes, and tell me child, how did that work for you? Tell me how many having lives so bad that starvation and begging on the street is preferable. How many more are too afraid? You took away their choice. You should have punished the people who abused them. Should have ground the bones of the child cripplers, the ones that put them in the mines to be chewed up and killed. The job of messenger is vital, and a child can do it with little to no harm. Fetching and the carrying, these too can be done by those still too small to be adults but bigger than those that run tubes from one person to another. As for not getting paid? The child has done something against your law; as such they are terrified and controlled by bullies who know they do not know better. The fear getting turned to orphanage that care not for them or returned to parents that are worse than that and all if they tell the guard if they get shorted. Your law was aimed at protecting, and yet it winds up hurting."

"The guard, they help out children all the time, go in and get them out of bad homes." How this went from me asking about why she and others still followed the gods when it was plain the harm it did to this, I had no idea.

"I have no doubt. How many are missed? How many will grow to do it to their children? Abuse works that way...did you be knowing?" She looked at me and smiled. "And how many were because the way they believed was different from what the churches believed?"

I jumped right back in. *Back on topic, finally.* "Exactly, the church wants everyone to think, act and behave the exact same way." I felt hope that this was her point, and it was. Just not the way I thought.

"The problem is not the problem. It is how you think of the problem. Just as some child suffers right now because they have no other place to turn due to a law meant to protect them. Outlawing religion would do much the same. Instead, let us punish those that force you to think only their way, whom cuts off discussion, whom brook no questing of their authority. Any authority that fears questioning is by nature wrong, no matter how good they say they are."

Her eyes lost some of their predatory sheen. "I have faith that my god is a good god and that god's servant which I follow is good and necessary. I am not so insecure in my belief that I must make you believe as I do in order to feel as if I am justified in my believings. My actions in service validate me, not your belief in my belief. No one can tell you how to live. Question everything and everyone. No matter how much you agree with them, always question, especially if they seem right. Figure out why they are right, how they are right, what makes them right, so that when you are questioned you have understanding to pass on to others."

I had approached this entire conversation bent on convincing this woman, the woman I talked to yesterday, or anyone, that I was right, that something from the way I use to live was right. I needed and craved validation. Yet this entire time, she didn't care; none of them did. They didn't care what I believed. All she wanted was the hunt, a good debate. That something was learned and view point were shared. She didn't care if I believed in her god, or its servant. She cared only that I questioned every-thing...including the people around me, her people.

Twice now, I had heard that the problem was with how I viewed what was going on, not what was going on. These people we so very odd.

Chapter 15

At some point in the life of any person, they begin to realize that there are rules which can be broken, ones that shouldn't, and ones that are inviolable and ubiquitous. One of those rules is as follows, a man alone is brave. Perhaps fool hardy, but brave. A *woman* alone is a target. This is simply a law of nature.

Women, children, and invalids need to be protected. This is the mark of civilization. How healthy a place is depends on how much men violate this natural order in order to protect said people. Inevitably, women, children, and invalids will balk at the idea that they need such protection. In order to combat this, they should be told and shown what awaits them if they deviate from the norm.

I always had a problem with this thought process. I knew of many women that were capable of taking care of themselves. I did have to admit that those women were often unwomanly and that bad things did happen to them.

Another of these little rules was that pain and failure was to be avoided at all costs. That one with which I had less of a problem. After all, if it hurts, don't do it. The woman I was talking to, the red priest with the violin thing, was telling me both of these were not only rules to be broken, but were lies used to make sure I always was in the control of the people I hated.

"Look, it is not that they meant to lie to you. They live under those rules, and if it is good enough for them, why isn't it good enough for you? Do you think you are better than they are?"

She was still naked except for the belt, my new friend, the Red Priest. She reclined on a rock with the last of the snow around her. She should have been cold. If she was, it didn't show as she inhaled the pipe weed she had gotten off of me.

"All right, here none of you consider anyone else above you."

"Not so. There are plenty of people above me, and plenty below. Problem is you lot think above means better and below means lesser. The truth is you can tell how low or high someone is by how many people they have to answer to. The more a person has to answer to another, the lower they are in things."

I smiled at her. "So a slave is the lowest person then, since they answer to everybody."

She choked on the smoke as it escaped her mouth and nose with her laughter. At least she was trying to cover her mouth as she did. I bet it was more for the cough than to cover her mirth at me. "A slave answers to no one but their owner. Doesn't matter who thinks they are or are not doing it right. That is between an owner and their slave. A slave might be the owner's most important person, but that is because they are directly answerable to the slave."

I took a puff of my own pipe. "So a slave isn't important?"

"Oh, they are very important to a person, and that is how it should be, but to society? Not at all. They may be a work force, but only a personal one. A slave should have the most freedom and power of any person ever. A slave is the highest of ranks, all privilege, answerable only to few...more often one."

Confused, I asked, "Alright, what is the lowest position?"

"Ruler, King or Queen, Lord, Lady, and Empress, I am sure you get the idea."

"Bullshit. They get to order everyone around."

"People think that, but no, they have to answer to everyone. It is their job to make sure everyone has a place to be safe. It may not be their job to put food on a table, but it is their job to make sure food is available. They may not pay everyone, but it is their job to make sure everyone gets fair pay."

"Yeah, and if you complain, off you go to the deepest part of the dungeon."

"Only because you've been convinced of it. If people significantly rose up, the jails and work gangs wouldn't hold them, nor would the dungeons. There are simply more of us than there are of them. But that's not what we were talking about. What were we talking about?" She looked at her pipe. "You sure this is just towbaka?"

I shook my head once. "Ain't the weed dear, you can't handle your liquor." I bent down and pulled up the bottle, took a swig and passed it back to her. "And we were talking about how a woman alone is simply a target, whether we like it or not."

"It's not true." With an emphatic set of gestures, bottle in one hand and pipe in the other, she began speaking. He word were slurred, and her demeanor was that of any tavern drunk. "What you got here is a nation of fear. Guys get jumped as much as girls, but people don't look at it the same way. See, guy gets jumped, no one talks about it. Not unless he was doin' one of the things your people don't like, like drinkin', or liking guys. Then he gets in trouble because of that. All the men that wake every morn in the gutter? Na, ya not hear about them. Same with women. You only hear so much about it, so they can keep you scared. Say some woman kicks and breaks or even kills a guy; never here about that unless it is to make her a villain."

I thought about it; it didn't seem right. Yes, I did see a lot more blokes laid out than girls, but...

I thought about it. Hardly a night went by without some guy getting into a scrape, but that was expected of them. It was like people didn't think they could do any better. Of course, she was right. *Light guys*, a term I never got...some of them were huge strong men, were also told as stories to make you fearful. Like how a guy died in a back room because he asked another guy for a lick of his sword.

"Alright, that may be true, but you got to admit that it is better to keep your head down than to be the proud nail that gets the hammer."

"Who says? Is it better to spend every moment of every day in a place you hate with people that think you hate them and that you know hate you? Or is it better to stand for yourself? You will be hated and talked about no matter what. Why not be talked about for truth rather than lies? Ignore the lies; they do you no harm."

"Maybe not harm to me personally, but harm to my reputation. That can cripple you just as quick as having something crush your legs. I agree with you, but if something's wrong, it is best to keep it hidden."

"Yep. Just like it is best not to talk about the wife getting raped by her husband or beaten for saying she doesn't like it. Just keep your head down and shut up."

"That's disgusting!"

"Yes, it is, but it is what you just said." She looked at me before continuing. "Shame, humiliation, disgrace, these are things used to make sure that 'the people bad things do happen to' shut up about it. Enlightened self-interest tells us to take care of you and yours, and I will take care of me and mine. There is probably not a more devastating thought process in my mind. It makes you not worry about what happens to a stranger because it is not you."

"But don't you LeatherWing practice just that? You let others do as they please. You take care of you and yours."

"That we do. We also take care of people that have nothing to offer us. We have a philosophy. The strong exist to protect the weak and to teach them how to be strong. Might makes right doesn't work. Without the second part, you have the strong preying on the weak. It is our duty and our honor to protect those that cannot protect themselves."

"Didn't do such a good job when your lot left us after you crushed the empire."

"Perhaps, but would it have really been better if we had just forced ourselves on you?"

"We were weak. You didn't teach us how to be strong."

She didn't have an answer for that one.

Chapter 16

Something was bugging me. It had been a few days since I had talked to the Red Priestess, and things were going well enough. Alabaster was actually a very sweet guy, and despite that fact that they were definitely a barbaric race, they were happy. People worked and they looked after each other. The sick weren't't ignored; neither were the poor. Kids did work, but none of them did more than most kids back home did for their folks, and they got paid fairly for it.

Adults took time with them and actually listened to their problems. Children were exposed to other kids, other adults, and learned how to live and interact. Despite the fact that there was definitely a class system, no one class looked down on another. In fact, if you were the master of your trade, you were given the deference of a Lord or Lady.

I watched a garbage picker chew out a high ranking priest about him putting scraps of the bandages in the mulch pile instead of the bandage pile which would have to be burned.

It was actually kind of funny to watch. I was sitting out behind the sick house when the collectors made it there. He and his sons were covered in this strange uniform, part of which went over his head and face; a mesh grill let him see out of the thing. They had three carts; one was covered; one open; and one was just a flat with wheels.

As they loaded up the bins one of the sons stopped; said something to his dad. Dad looked at the bin color, then at its contents. He goes to beating on the back door of the place. The guard I had been chatting with off and on, named K'rra, looked over at the commotion and asks me. "Knowing what is going on there?"

I shrugged. "Guess he found something he didn't like."

An old green with his hair tied back steps out. He had gone soft around the middle. The first guy yells something at the second, the second nods and goes back in closing the door.

I looked at the woman I was with. She was large for a woman. I had gotten use to reds being big, but she was large even for that.

"What's up?"

"Nots sure, could be trouble." She tensed and moved herself between me and the disturbance. Not so much as to interrupt my view or hide it from me, just to protect me if things went bad. Shortly a young man walked out. His robes were mostly clean and his adornment said "I am important". As soon as he was outside, the refuse collector began to berate him, and from his tone it sounded as if he was treating him like a particularly slow pupil. I didn't understand a word of it.

"What's going on?" I figure it didn't hurt to ask.

She gestured to the young man, a Yellow. "He is the man in charge of making sure the sick house runs well. He is healer as well and worked up the ranks very fast. Inside that building, his word is law. Brak is trash collector, has been for years. His family is paid well to keep streets clean. Brak is mad. Seems healing bandages and food rot wound up in same bin. They go to two different places. If healing bandage wind up in food waste, whole fertilize pile has to be destroyed." The two men were yelling at each other furiously. "Yonna says trash not his problem. He doesn't take it out."

With that the garbage man's fist flew straight into the jaw of the chief healer. I expected the guard to go and protect the man, instead she continued on with her interpreting. "He says, 'You are king within those walls, it is your responsibility. It is not my job to chastise your workers. It is not my place to say even one cross thing to them. You are leader, act like it. You serve them, you set this right. Do not say not my problem when it is."

Shocked, I watched this wealthy man, this important man, pull himself off the ground. I didn't need her to tell me that he was apologizing to the garbage man. I saw it and understood. Moreover, the apology was sincere. "Why didn't you interfere? Won't you get in trouble for it?"

"For what? Letting Brak teach Yonna to be more careful? Had the old bandages made it to the mulch pile, sickness would spread."

"But it wasn't the Yellow's fault, it was probably an accident, something some kid or someone else did."

"Does not matter. To be leader is to take responsibility for those you lead. This will probably not happen again."

"What stops Yonna from beating whoever did it, or everyone just out of spite for getting him hit like that?"

"A leader is the lowest servant. Yonna didn't get hit because of the mistake. He got hit because he was trying to say 'not his problem.' He answers to all his charges. It is their job to make his job easier. It is his job to make their jobs work right. It is a balance. If he abuse them, they quit, or they fire him."

I had one of those moments. You know the ones. Confused one second, and in the next you not only understand what was said but oh, so much more. I think it is called a moment of clarity. I understood, and it made me mad. No, not mad, pissed. "Let me get this straight...in the smith's shop everyone answers to the high smith, even if they are, say, the Lord Marshall of the Army?"

"Exactly. The Smith should know what they and their apprentices can do. As such the Lord Marshall to use what you understand would have to take his word for it."

"How can that work? The smith could be lying, an attempt to line his own pockets or some such." My voice was surprisingly even given what I was feeling.

"Trust. We live by trusting our fellows not to screw us over. We trust we will look after each other and help out. We trust; simple as that."

"And what happens when that trust is broken?

"Well then, that person either feels bad when we still treat them well, or they really aren't a good person. It is what the stone circles are for, any and all complaints. It is where all grievances are heard." She shrugged with that.

Yep, I understood all right. I had got it. With that my temper went from hot to ice cold, so cold my skin prickled under my furs. "Excuse me K'rra. I think I need to go talk to your leader. I have a question for her."

She went back to her duties, and I went out to find Vela. I knew where she should be now. I had asked Al where to find her. Her office was her home, and her home was fairly simple. It was in one of the smaller caves. I walked in as if I belong; no one stopped me.

I slammed the door of her office. Finding her hadn't been hard once I got inside. I looked at her and beseeched. I let the pain fill my voice. This was a betrayal and I knew it was. I had to know. "Why?"

She looked up from her scrolls and skins with the sound of the door, my question etched confusion on her face. She tilted her head to one side jutting out her chin. I had seen a lot of them do this by now. The gesture was ubiquitous. "Why what Chloe?"

"Why did you leave us to suffer and to be abused?" I started pacing. "Hundreds of years ago your ancestors, your people swooped down on the Unstoma Empire and slaughtered them, all of them, the ruling families, the armies. You freed the Orcs; you freed us. Then you left and came back here."

"Yes we did. Trust me. Unstoma was not a place you wanted to grow up. If you think it was bad for you now, there you would have been sold off and would not have even been a person in the end, just breeding stock." She was starting to rise from her chair. Her concern was on her face.

"NO. You left us!" I could feel the tears streaming down my face. "I thought it was the gods' fault, or more rightly the people who lied to us about the gods to keep us in line, but it was *your* fault."

"What do you mean child?" She was up now and moving towards me, I jerked away.

"You left us. You left us to clean up your mess. They fought over the land you left unconquered. They raised armies to claim the riches you left behind. When they were done, we had new lords and the same old gods. Your way works. If you had stayed I wouldn't have been thrown out to the wolves. My friends wouldn't have starved in the streets with no one caring because we were someone else's problem, an embarrassment to them. You could have stopped that. You could have stopped it all."

"You don't understand Chloe; we didn't fight for land, or treasure. We fought to stop them from treating your people like cattle. If we took land, we would have been seen as nothing more than any other invading army, seen as bad as Unstoma itself."

"In other words, you stopped because someone might think you were the bad guys. The Empire broke those of us they took over; you broke us when you freed us. You could have given direction to us, led us. I know where we are. We are less than two days travel from South Point. You could have saved us, and you didn't. You didn't because you didn't want to be seen as monsters. Guess what? You're the Demons to the south. You're so blood thirsty you came down and slaughtered hundreds for fun. We still fear you."

Chapter 17

Life can be a funny thing. I would never recommend nearly starving to death and then having a barbarian find you, but here I was. I was happier and healthier than I had been in over a year. I was in a place that had problems just like everywhere else. I had seen fights from too much strong drink; I had seen that there were indeed thieves here, though he and his family were taken as servants of one of the healers. They seemed to have the thought around here that theft only happened from greed or need. If it was greed, things went one way. If need, then the family was taken in, fed and given jobs. I refuse to think of those people or myself as a slave. We aren't slaves. We are more like indentured servants, people with rights and pay. That, as far as I am concerned, is not slavery.

These people shake that notion off. They say it is something called re-branding and won't have anything to do with it. Otherwise, people will have to keep changing the name of something when evil does it wrong. They say with that system soon, you lose what was meant and the word, not the deed, becomes sinister.

Sorry, slavery is sinister. I know of no one who has ever done it like these people do. Convincing them to care what others think of them is not easy, especially after it became widely known that I ripped their leader a new one. They didn't become belligerent or even cold towards me. Most of them seem to like that I stood up for what I believed to be right.

On that front, it seems Vela agrees with me, and so does most of the town. Soon I learned that the Empress let the generals and council make that call for her. It confirmed for me that even she could be swayed into doing something against her so called beliefs. Now, some people think perhaps she would have done it differently if she had known how it would go, or if the generals had been less concerned with appearances. I've got no idea. To be honest, the more I hear of this woman, the more I am convinced she was nuts.

I also think she wasn't the original. She couldn't be. Simply find a violet with the right mind set and boom. You have her all over again, and Alabaster has all but confirmed this.

See, they also believe that a follower can embody their hero god so closely that they actually take the mantle of that god. It keeps them striving for it. Their faith doesn't keep them down; telling them they can't do it. It gives them something they can strive for. Of course, they also say that the faith of my people is the same way, even if the religion no longer is.

It's the start of spring or close to it when the city has a visitor, a woman named Ba'call. She is one of the cat people. Back home, we call them Beast Men. Here, they are called the GrassLords. She has a servant called Sliverleaf; it's an Elf. I would say she is an Elf, but I have heard that Elven males also have breasts.

***

Days later, I looked up from my writing as Alabaster came bursting through the door to the tent we shared. "Chloe, get dressed."

I looked at him and then down at myself. *Let's see, pants, yep, tunic, also good. Shoes?* Even had them on. I looked at him like he'd lost what little good sense he had.

He shook his head. "No, dressed, as in travel clothing. We are going after a beast. Well, a creature at any rate. Something pushed up a few trees near one of Vela's farms. She asked us to go and check it out."

"Why us?"

"Well, not just us. Well, not us, technically. Ba'call is an adventurer. She is looking for a few partners. Vela is paying her to inspect and see what's going on. The cat asked me if I knew of any people that might be interested in joining her. She wants a full crew."

I jumped up from the floor hitting my head on the lamp. "She wants to be a Guild Group? A full Guild Group?"

"Yes; she says she's no leader, but she knows the ways, and turns out her Elf is an arcanist, a mage. She says individuals can make a lot if Guild bounded, but groups have a better chance of survival."

Alabaster was a healer as well as a priest. Depending on the type of mage the Elf was, that was two different groups of spells to enhance healing as well as his knowledge of bones and muscle. I was a decent break, not exactly what I was best at. The lift and lay was my big thing. "Who else is interested?"

His grin was as wide as it was feral. "Rowan, and she is good with a sword."

I nodded. It could work.

***

Today was as wonderful as it was frightening. The creature was a huge bug thing that Ba'call called a Behemoth. Trust me; it was worth the name. She said sometimes they wonder off from The Hive. Away from the bug's queen, these huge monstrosities were little more than cows. They were big, dumb, and mostly docile. We didn't attack it as she said that would be suicide. With the huge blades it had for forearms and the ram like prowl it had on its nose, I could believe it.

The thing was a living siege engine, bladed spikes on its armored back, a long tail with blades on it like some cruel whip, gold for its armor, bone white for the rest of it. It looked filthy and yet strangely smelled kind of like cinnamon, well rotten cinnamon.

First problem we had is it was eating a stand of Black Bloods. Not that there were any of that berry, my favorite by the way, this time of year, but it didn't stop the thing from eating the brambles, thorns and all.

The problem was it had eaten pretty much in a straight line, cut a path deep into the stand as the thorns that were not right in front of it scraped down its golden shell.

Ba'call, A GrassLord Warden, stated, "We need to get it out of there without scaring it or pissing it off."

"Without us scaring it?" I said.

Sliverleaf, the Elven Mage, replied, "It's just a dumb animal."

A dumb animal the size of a couple of full grown oxen. I watched as Alabaster walked up behind it; I have no idea what he thought he was going to do, but when a swing of the things long tail proved those blade looking things at the end were as sharp as they look, cutting thought the briars, he backed off.

The path the thing cut through was wide enough, and the stand had twisting paths through it, but they were close. Not where you wanted to be if the beast decided you looked more appetizing than the thorns it was gorging on.

"I've got an idea." Everyone turned to look at me. "Sliverleaf, can you make something glow, something small?"

The elf raised an eyebrow. "I believe so, if it is small enough, and its stricter can handle the magic."

I looked at the cat, this GrassLord. I never seen one before...not really. Oh, I had heard of them, and a few years ago one came through town. It, no idea if it was a boy or a girl, didn't stay in town long, and the only thing I really got to see of it was the black armor it wore. This one was all excitement and orange and black stripes. Her four bound breasts were probably the most startling thing about her.

"Ba'call. Get me a nice long stick."

I watched in amusement as she got it. Then she confused the hell out of me and fell to her hands and ran off on all fours.

Alabaster and Rowan both looked at me. Rowan said something I didn't understand.

"What do you need us to do?" Alabaster asked.

As I handed the elf the rock crystal I had found and on which I had been working, just a piece of quarts I think. I turned back to them.

"I'm going fishing, and I need you two help me get close enough to that thing to get its attention and get back out of the briars before I get chomped."

I explained it to them; there were plenty of trees around and through the briars. I needed them to go up into the trees and use the ropes we brought to pull the briars away from the path so I could get close enough to get its focus on me. Then once it was for me to have enough room to run the hells away.

I watched as the two of them made their way into the trees and into position on opposite sides of the path. They both took the ropes, running them down the path and then pulled them up and tight, giving me room to maneuver. They were also on the opposite side of the trees from where I would be running, me and the Behemoth.

The cat got back with the fresh cut poll and the Elf came through with the glowing bait. Together, with a bit of twine, we rigged up a crude fishing pole. Then it was just a matter of me getting into position as bait.

The sheer stupidity of this plan didn't hit me until, with branch outreached, I saw the things face. At the end of its up turned neck was a human skull, only twice the size of any I had ever seen; in its eye sockets were three red glowing eyes. Its mouth, still chewing the dried and twisted brambles of the stand, held a row of teeth all in the right places but with each coming to dagger points. A tongue longer than any cows and made of sickly green flesh had been busy pulling more of its meal into its maw. That tongue dripped with a greenish black liquid.

I needed *NO* encouragement. I ran. I could hear the sounds of its four back hooves as it pounded the ground behind me. The ground shook with every one of its lunges.

As soon as I was clear of the thorns, I threw the lure one way and dived the other way, hoping that the glow really was what it was after.

I needn't have worried, it barreled past me until it caught its pray. It stopped when it caught up with the light, then ate it. One bite and it was gone.

And you know what? It worked.

Once it ate the rock, it just started walking again, off into the woods, stopping only long enough to eat a bush that was right in front of it.

We made a great team!

With the beast pointed away from towns and people, we came back and got drink and food. It's official. We have a sponsor, and Vela paid us enough for some travel gear. We headed off to parts unknown to me at the end of the week.

***

"Nervous?" Came a voice with just a hint of gravel.

I looked up from the journal. It was something I had done off and on since I was a kid. I have no idea where most of them are. The GrassLord girl was before me. Her smile seemed almost more human that Alabaster's.

Before me was a huge tabby cat of orange and black fur with a white underbelly, Ba'call, the GrassLord.

I gestured for her to sit. "Somewhat. Actually going out and being one of the great heroes is exciting but scary. There are always more adventures than the heroes you hear about."

"That would be because most of them die. This isn't glamorous work, girl. It's necessary. In all honestly, we aren't heroes, and probably won't be. What we will be are mercenaries taking jobs others won't. And mercenaries rightly have a bad name. Mostly because the bad ones, the ones that don't care, outnumber the good ones. Oh sure, you get a lot that retire, and few ever heard about them. The villains and the heroes get all the fame. Of course, no one mourns the dead. In some cases, no one even knows they are dead."

"Then why do it?"

"It's personal. For me, it is because I have seen the guard ignore the cries of a woman whose husband is missing, dismissing it as he ran off with the bar wench. The guard doesn't have the time or man power to track down or take care of everything. They are usually underpaid, making them prime targets for bribes, and overwhelmed, making it easy for them to miss something. Some jobs pay little in coin, and big in 'did the right thing'. That's for me."

I nodded. "Sounds good to me. But why take us on?"

"One traveling alone is boring. I have Sliv, but we want company. She never been out of the forest before, and I've been nowhere but the plains till I went to the Isle of Cats, and that was a pilgrimage. She fresh out of school, neither of us knows much of cities, and that is where the best work tends to be. Besides, I like Al, and I think I like you Clo."

Chapter 18

"You know what the most exciting type of undead is?" Bec was bouncing on her toes as she asked. I groaned fearing the answer.

"All right cat, what is the most fascinating type of undead?"

"It is an incorporeal form of that most wonderful maker of honey. It is called a *Boo Bee*!"

The collective groan of the group was palatable. Our young warden had been at this for hours. It was my fault really. I had asked why her people were known as nature's court jesters. Ever since that innocent question, she had been educating us on the pun.

"Pick a topic. See, punning isn't just playing on words. You got to practice it. A good pun should be able to be slipped into any conversation. If you can do that, you're good. I'm good, but I am not a master yet."

"All right, what makes a master punster?"

"The ability to have people start punning on themselves. It is when they say something to you, and before they even stop speaking, they are telling you to stop because they realized where you were about to pun. Go on. Pick a topic."

Alright then. I thought something hard. I had heard egg puns, and sword puns, and both seemed simple enough. I wanted to see what she could do with something mundane. "Alright then, walking."

"Too easy. That's got legs I could go on all day with. It's a real traveling pun group. I could kick it around for a bit. I might even put my foot in my mouth, or really step in it and make a soulful pun. It's sometimes hard to nail a pun properly. Sometimes they just claw their way out of your mouth." She took a breath. "Although honestly, it is easy to exhaust yourself like that."

I was laughing so hard, I had an all too familiar pressure in my bladder. "Peace, enough. I got it. So puns should be subtle?"

She grinned enthusiastically. "I've always thought so. A lot of punsters go for the quick one, in and out, the puns that can't be ignored. Yeah I like things like the boo bees, but I also like and prefer the once that slip in unnoticed, then make someone smile even if it is only for a moment."

"All the puns I've dealt with have been eggs-ruciating."

"Those have their place, but again, everyone expects them."

"So you went to the big island in the middle of the fresh water sea for a pilgrimage?"

"Something like that. Our people are all over. Mostly, we are wanderers, nomads, often vagabonds. In short, we travel, but my people are not too big on rules. On that island, we have settled, made cities and permanent homes. I had heard of the place and wanted to see it. To see us not moving."

Smiling, I said, "What did you find?"

"Fat cats. We of the Empire of the Five do not believe there is only one right way. Don't get me wrong. We understand there are plenty of *wrong* ways. The right ways of the world are ear marked by how someone treats another. Come to think of it, so are the bad. I digress. The city cats are simply plumper. They are still cats; they still hunt, fight, make love and pun just as fiercely as those of us on the move. They're just plumper around the middle. I liked it."

"Then why go back?"

"My mother got word to me. My birth was hard on my mom. Not my fault or hers, just chance, but it meant that I was an only child. No other cubs of my blood to gnaw on the ears of growing up. I made up for it gnawing the ears of everyone else." She took a deep breath. "I got a message three moons back. A Bard brought it when she brought the rest of the mail. The message was years old. I don't know how many, but the age showed on the skin. It said my mum had gotten pregnant again and had had another little girl. I have a sister. Her name is Blood Claw." A weak chuckle escaped her. "Or that is her kitten name. We earn our adult names. She will be nearly an adult by the time I get back."

"Is your mom alright?"

"Oh, she was on herbs, and some magics, but they apparently failed. The letter said that they simply didn't work this time. According to the letter the pregnancy was hard on her. Though supposedly, the fur ball and my mother are both okay. In short, I am going home to meet my little sister."

Chapter 19

I sat by the fire, watching the flames dance. To say I was mad was like explaining that the sun was warm, true and yet somehow not doing justice to the situation. Alabaster and I had been having a conversation. At least, I thought we had been. The next thing I know, he is telling me I am being childish and told me to go think about why what I said was not only wrong, but dangerous to myself and everyone around me.

When you are that mad, or at least when I am, you become aware of everything around you. Al and Rowan were talking quietly in that damn growling language of theirs. Sliv, as always, was at her books, keeping well away from most of us. Elves really were as stuck up as I had always been told. Bec, however, was about to die.

"Don't even think about it cat. If you pounce me, I will skin you." I felt her hesitate. Instead, she sat down behind me.

"Sorry, your grump was too hard to ignore. So, what's up Puss?"

I looked back at her, eyebrow arched, "Puss is another word for cat, and that would be you."

She sat back and did the "I'm so regal" thing cats seem to be born with. "Puss, short for Sour Puss, one who is being contrary, difficult or just in a bad mood." Pleased with herself, she laid down as a sphinx, flat on her belly, paws in front with head held high. "So you see, Puss would be you."

I shook my head. "Not what I was taught." I looked at her...really looked. If you have ever tried to read a cat's mind by looking at its face, then you know it just isn't possible if the cat doesn't want it to be. Had she heard the fight, the reason for it? "I don't want to talk about it cat. Go find something else to bother."

"Nope. I don't care if you talk about it or not. That is up to you. But I am going to cheer you up, or you are going to fight me." With that she ran her head into me.

I pushed her away. "Damn it Bec. What is wrong with you?" The force of her love-shove had sent me towards the fire.

"Me? Simple, you." And with that she butted me over again from the side this time, knocking me down. "You sit and stew. Alone are you. Yet, people are here to hear you. So talk, or I sit."

I pushed her again, and with that she sat on my head. To start with, Bec is not a light person. Cats, however, have selective gravity. When they want to, they get heavier. And cat butt in the face is not ever pleasant. I pushed again and tried to speak. I was rewarded with a mouth full of fur.

"What?" She sat up enough to hear me.

"I said, get off me you damn sadist. I'll talk. Shit it's not like it's a big deal anyway." She got off of me and helped me up. Then proceeded to lay the top half of her body in my lap, and looked up at me.

"Alright, go."

I groaned. "People don't talk on command cat."

"Cats don't do anything on command. It doesn't stop humans from commanding cats."

"Fine, whatever." Closing my eyes I started. "Al and I got into a fight. He is being unreasonable."

"About?"

Great...I was going to have to tell her everything. She wouldn't go away; she was snuggling down on my lap as it was. There were even those quick little rumbling sounds coming from her, something I realized were the equivalent of her purring. "What if I don't want to discuss it?"

"Well, I can't make you talk. I can try to, but it won't work. But you can't make me leave. If you get up and walk away, I'll just follow you until I get bored, and if it annoys you, I won't get bored." I was being blackmailed by a feline. "Or you could just distract me by petting me. I am sure that would work." With that she stretched out and snuggled in for the duration of whatever I decided.

I started to pet. This was weird; she was a grown woman. It made me uncomfortable. "You realize this is very odd for me, right? You aren't a pet."

"Does it feel good to do this, to run your hands over my fur?"

She had a point. If she had not been a person, this would actually be quite relaxing. "Well, yes, but it is still weird."

"You like it. I like it. If I didn't like it or you didn't like it, then it would be wrong. Uncomfortable only matters if you hide it, and let it hurt you. Never be afraid to talk, which is actually my whole point by the way."

So I sat and petted her. I found I could not hold on to my temper. "We were talking. I was trying to understand why the penalty for breaking one of the laws was death. I pointed out that by killing that person, you were also breaking one of the laws."

She thought about it for a moment. "So what's the problem?"

"The problem is that I disagreed with him. Now, he is mad at me."

"That does not sound like Alabaster."

"Well, it is what happened."

"Maybe if you explained more?"

"He said that it was different, that the people who were killed deserved it. As if that made it better and explained everything. To me, deciding someone deserves death is interfering with their lives. What if they realized their mistake and wanted to correct it? What if they were innocent? If you kill them, then yes, that is the end of it, for both good and ill. That is when he told me what I said was stupid and dangerous."

"So you feel dismissed. I get that."

"How can he not see the flaw in the logic? I thought this was supposed to be a give and take, and yet when he can't come up with a good counter argument he just leaves."

"Mostly because you two were talking about different things. And he doesn't know how to tell you or make you understand."

"No, we were talking about killing people as punishment."

"Exactly. You were; he wasn't. He was talking about discipline, not punishment."

"That makes no sense. They are the same thing."

"Only in the way that milk and water are both wet. I throw either on you, and you will get drenched. But they are not the same thing."

"So what is the difference between the two?"

"The world you grew up in uses punishment. Punishment is meant to deter behavior. Do this or don't do that, or I will punish you. To punish someone is to force your view on what is right or wrong on someone."

"Right, so how is this different?"

"Discipline is not meant to do that. Discipline is all about self-control and self-responsibility. No one makes you behave; you make yourself do it."

"Okay, that makes no sense."

I watched her take a deep breath. "I am not explaining this well." She cocked her head to the side. "Okay, look." She drew a couple of stick figures on the ground. "This is you and this is a guard. In your way of doing things, this guard is there to protect you from other people as well as to keep you from doing things that they say you shouldn't. Are you with me so far?"

Since what she was describing was how the world worked, I did. "Yes, the guard is there to make sure I don't take something or that someone doesn't go out with a sword and start just hacking people up. It's their job."

"How often has the guard actually prevented you from taking something you really wanted?"

I thought about it. She had a point. All I had to do was wait until there were no guards or distract the person who had what I wanted. "Not very often."

"Exactly. In this system of things, it goes like this. The guards come down, and they talk to people, they try to find you. Now, you lie about doing it; your friends lie about where you are and so on. This forces the guards to assume you are lying. It doesn't stop there. Anyone who backs up your story is lying, and anyone that says they didn't see anything is probably lying as well. The guard have got to assume everyone is lying. This makes them treat the people differently. It isn't their fault people who break the rules don't want to get caught. Now, you got entire sections of your population that can tell the guards that the sky is blue and they have got to check to see. Then, let's say that you are in a more well to do section of town and something gets stolen. You didn't do it, but the guard knows you are from a not so nice part of town. A merchant points the finger at you and says you are the one who stole the item. That item is in his stall, but he is blaming you. Whom does the guard believe?"

I had watched that happen a few times. Not to me. When I went to the better sections of town, I busted my ass to blend in, but I had seen it with others. Mostly to good people that hadn't done anything wrong except be in the wrong part of town. "They believe the Merchant."

"This is because the poor lie to them."

"So it's our fault for being poor?"

"Not at all, it is a self-fulfilling problem. See, this causes the poor not to trust the guard and to look after their own. The guard aren't going to do it. So if the guards are asking questions, you cover the flank of the other poor guy. The Merchants and nobles know this, so they make the poor the scapegoats for what is going on. The Guard believes them because of previous interactions. They have to deal with a lot more poor than others do. They know that if they get called down to the less well to do parts of town it is going to be because there is trouble. And they know they are going to be lied to because they have been lied to before."

The cat took a deep breath. "The poor know to lie to the guards because they aren't going to be believed anyway, so it doesn't matter what you tell them. The person with the most money is going to get believed. This, despite how it looks, has nothing to do with the money but more to do with the fact that the people with more money, when they do deal with them, tend to be more honest."

Bec gave me a weak smile. "Again, this isn't because they are more honest. It is because they are more likely to interact with the people with more money when things aren't so bad." She gestured with a paw. It was hard not to see her as just a big cat when she was laying like this.

She kept going. "You know them, see them on the street and so on. Maybe even buy their wives a new dress from the merchant that is accusing you of stealing something he stole. To that guard, the Merchant is a person. You, on the other hand, are the individual they had to force out of the bar in a drunken brawl."

I nodded. I could feel the frown on my face. "The two of them go to church together. Their wives know each other. I am the outsider. I am the outsider that doesn't belong there."

"Exactly. What you have then and just now fell into is the 'US or THEM' way of looking at the world." She sat back smiling. "And not only is it wrong, that is not how it has to be or is meant to be."

Having grown up in a place that if you didn't look after each other, you got shit on; I wasn't buying it.

"That is just the way the world is, Bec. You look after family." I gestured around to the group. "Be it the family you were born into, or the one you pick; you look after family. The rest of the world be damned. It isn't going to look after you. In fact, it will spend most of its time trying to get one over on you."

"And that is the point. From your view on the world, what Alabaster has said looks like so much nonsense. I am telling you that his way allows for something different to happen as naturally as your way allows for the dehumanization of people."

Now she had my attention. I wanted to know what her point was.

Chapter 20

"Alright, fine. Explain why he isn't an asshole."

"I didn't say that. We can all be assholes, but things are different for him. See, with the way things work for you, people are guilty until proven innocent. And that burden of proof rests firmly on the accused shoulders."

The snort escaped me before I even realized it was coming. "Yeah, and if you can't prove it before they take you off, forget it."

"For the LeatherWings it is different. First off, everyone knows the laws. The laws try to be clear, easy to understand. For them, the accused is innocent until proven guilty. Instead of worrying about telling some official, everyone can make a complaint, and they can do it about anything."

"Right, you turned everyone into snitches and spies on their neighbors." Not how I saw it most of the time, but right now, that sounded exactly like what it was.

"Perhaps that is one way to look at it. But it is not the truth of the matter. Each person is empowered to seek justice for themselves, be it through working things out with their neighbors peacefully or not so peacefully or calling in outside help."

"Yes, I've seen that at work. We have a name for it, mob justice. No, thank you." Images of mobs whipped into a frenzy of something someone was supposed to have done. Taking that person out and beating them to death. I saw it more than once; I had even been in a mob once. When you hear about how some guy rapes a little kid, it is easy to get so mad that killing the bastard sounds like a better idea than letting him weasel out of it before a judge.

Trust me, it's not. The kid *lied*. They had no idea what would happen. They just wanted to get their dad in trouble, retribution for something or the other. "Trust me, it is always better to let the proper authorities work something out than to let the people have free reign of it."

"Yes, people are going to abuse any system. It will happen. That is why the Five Laws are like they are. Preventing someone from going to the stone will result in your death. People know that. You have laws for everything someone thinks is bad, so many laws that people don't know what they are. Think on this. When people are good, law is unnecessary. Evil laws are useless. A law has never stopped an evil person from hurting someone. You've lived it. You tell me. How many laws have stopped people from being hurt?"

"Well, plenty of laws have stopped people from getting hurt. We have a peace-knot law. All blades must be peace-knotted within the city walls. It don't do crap to keep violence down, but it keeps plenty of people from accidentally getting hurt."

"Accidents. You have laws to prevent *accidents*. Meanwhile, people who care about the law tie their weapons while people who don't 'know' that it will slow down the defense of that person. You said yourself that it doesn't keep violence down."

"We would be better off if all blades had to stay outside the city." I shrugged. It was one of those self-evident things that people like to pretend would end the world if done.

"Really? And the good folk down on your end of town, would they do it? Could they afford to? They will break that law to protect themselves from thieves, from the guard. They won't follow the law because they can't. If they did, then the criminals would just over run them and keep them in fear. If you did get rid of all blades, then it would be clubs. After the clubs, then they would find a rock. The Unstoma Empire once made it illegal for Elves to carry weapons. Any Elf with a weapon could be killed on sight. So they started learning to fight with their bare hands."

"But if everyone agreed not to and lived by it, then that wouldn't be a problem."

"The Mennen already do. They are a completely pacifistic culture. The problem is when the outside world ventures in, they get wiped out, or taken over. The Mennen survive these times by enduring, not putting up a fight, and moving on and hiding when they can. They won't fight for themselves, and they don't like you fighting for them. They know anyone who wants to can come in and take what they have. They rely on law to stop this. Yet as soon as it breaks down, they rely on something else."

"What? Their god?"

"No, community. Pulling together, helping each other out. That is also what we do. If you are hungry, you ask your neighbor. Need something? Ask for it. You may not get the best that they have, but they will feed you. They will also help you hunt, find work, and so on. It is encouraged. This means that people know each other even in the large cities. That allows the people to help look after each other, and thoughts of it 'not being your problem' to go to the wayside."

"That still doesn't explain why it is not better to let someone work off their crimes in other ways than death. A death penalty, even in a culture with so few laws, is barbaric. Especially given all I have learned about you."

"But it does. Your culture uses laws as fences to modify how people act, to prevent you from doing things. That only works with people who care about the law. Much like a lock will only keep out an honest man, laws will only keep honest men in check. That version of law doesn't work. In order to actually discourage people from breaking the law, you have to have punishments. Remember; one of the Five Laws says it is against the law to prevent someone from using the stones to ask for a judgment?"

"Yes, it is part of the Law of the Stone."

"Well, let's take the penalty down to say something reasonable. It is only stopping someone from complaining. Surely that shouldn't be that big a deal. So what then? A year in a labor camp? As soon as you do that, then the person who wants to report a different law being broken is at risk. In order to keep a snitch from telling on me, I will do everything I can to stop him from going to the stones. What is the worst that will happen? A year in a labor camp? And then when I get out, I will kill the guy that told on me. I risk nothing by stopping the person going to the stones."

"Exactly my point. If the guy has already broken laws that he knows will get him killed, he will stop at nothing to kill the person who is trying to complain."

"You are right, and it happens with the hardened. Since every person accused knows they will be heard out and that even if they did break a law that they might be able to explain why they did in such a way that will not end in their death, they would rather be accused of one law than two. The hardened are never going to care about the law. They may care about a law but only when it suits them. Most evil people have something they consider too far. Laws need to exist to protect the common man, not keep him in line. If you know that forcing your will upon someone else will result in your death and that if you try to stop them from telling others that too could, and most likely would, also result in your death, then you are less likely to do so. When a law is broken, it will usually either be by someone that had no choice or didn't care. That is also why there are so few laws. All cases must be heard and must be heard by five different people. Those people will listen to any complaint at any time by anyone against anyone. The accused is innocent until proven guilty. The burden of proof is upon the accuser, and the guards have to work for both sides to provide evidence. Two different teams of guard, one to check the stories of the accused one, another to check the story of the accuser."

"Like the guard would take that seriously. You guys let *kids* do this stuff. You honestly expect your guards to do this for a bunch of *kids*?"

"Our leaders are servants that answer to the people. Children or adults, rich or poor, service is what is important. If they do not do it to their best of their ability, someone might die. Accusing someone of breaking one of the Five Laws can be fatal if you are proven to be lying."

I shuddered. This was not making me feel any better. "Great. So how is what I suggested more dangerous than sending an innocent man to his death just because the other guy did a better job of convincing people of his guilt?"

"Because we would rather let ten guilty men go free than let one innocent person die. If we lightened it, reduced it, then one day, we may find that we would not take justice so seriously. We might start not looking so hard."

"Oh, how can you be so sure?"

"It has happened before. It will happen again. It is the Fifth Law; the cycle must go on. Sooner or later, you will be proven right, and sooner or later so will I. Just as nature says that there will always be people who break the law because it suits them, sooner or later all laws fail. Not because the law is wrong, but because the people forget."

Chapter 21

All of that was months ago, but it might as well have been a lifetime. Now, I sit at the dawn of this new day with the promise of another hungry morning. Food was scarce, and the provisions were almost gone, a thin stew was last night's fare. I wouldn't go hungry, but my owner would. He would not eat until I had, and with food running this short, he wouldn't eat at all. I looked over at his sleeping form and recognized the signs of the onset of starvation.

Now that I knew him, it was somewhat of a wonder to me that anyone could ever think of Alabaster as a devil. He was sweet, kind, selfless and self-defacing, and everything I was ever taught a priest should be. I thought about it for a minute. True, the boy had a sense of humor that would send my mother screaming if she had still been alive, and yes he could be violent, but so was most of his race. Through him I finally understood what "*meek*" actually meant.

He would sooner calmly face death than raise a finger or his voice against someone he felt didn't deserve it. Against those that transgressed the Five Laws...them I feel sorry for.

Now, his leathery wings looked slightly skeletal, and I had not seen him try to fly in days. I was worried, but exactly what was normal for him and his people? It was not like I had gotten a talk on proper care and feeding of "the man who saves your life" when I was a kid, let alone what to look for in a sick LeatherWing. I had never even seen one in person before a few months ago.

The inside of our tent held what few possessions we had brought with us. Most of it was furs and changes of clothing, a pair of daggers and thin sword for me, a cudgel for him. Our gear was mostly leathers and hides with a few furs for blankets.

As Sliverleaf's owner Ba'call too was going without, but the cat's body had more fat which to feed off of. Sliverleaf, Rowan, and I were getting most of the food, but I knew Rowan was giving up as much as the others. As for the two of us? We were eating out of respect.

Still, I was getting stronger every day.

I looked around the camp and took stock of the others. Rowan was a female LeatherWing whose skin was as red as the blood she spilled. Her wings were larger than Alabaster's, and she was built to be a creature of muscle and power. She was still feminine and did not have the over-cut look to her muscles that some of the idle Lords like to brag about, and plenty of fat to round out her curves, but she was strong. Turned out she was also who Al had spoken to outside the day I awoke. The two of them were very close.

She kept her long hair pulled back with three ponytails, one at the top of her head, one at the back and one at the nape of her neck, and all three were braided together tightly. At the end of the braid, she had a steel ball woven in, a ball the size of a tight fist. Most of the Reds in her tribe wore their hair like this.

I was still getting used to Ba'call. The great cat was a wonder, sometimes noble, sometimes childish. Her people had four breasts instead of most people's two. She covered them with simple leather, and her lower half had no covering at all. Not that you could see anything anyway. She was a Woods Walker, a Warden, a skilled hunter and tracker. The white tufts on her cheeks were still short, showing her youth, but except for Sliverleaf she was the oldest of us. The black stripes on her face acted as kohl around her eyes, accenting them and making them look an exceptionally beautiful green, flecked with amber. Her ears were tipped in black but with a hint of gold when the light caught the fur just right. Overall, she looked like a dangerous tabby that had learned to walk upright and grew to well over the weight of a man.

She was our hunter and a tracker.

What else do you expect an overgrown barn-cat to be? That thought made me smile.

The woman was just an overly large farm-cat when it came down to it. She had honestly pounced at and caught a falling leaf last night after camp had been set up. Coming up with a triumphant look and it dangling from between her lips, and all with a mad grin. It gave us all a much-needed good laugh, all while she played innocent like she hadn't done anything odd. I knew that was why the fur ball did it, but still, she did manage to lighten the mood.

Finally came Ba'call's slave, Sliverleaf. Now, as an Elf, she was something truly exotic. LeatherWings and GrassLords were stories I had heard most of my life. Elves were always spoken of as if they were wiser than the wise and more graceful than any dancer. The Elf was the "property" of Ba'call much as I was of Alabaster, but as I had learned in the first few weeks, property did not mean the same thing to either the Beastmen or the LeatherWing "devils".

In a way, I could get the other three. Alabaster was kind, but his and Rowan's way of looking at the world was as strange as their appearance. The same with Ba'call. It was just hard to relate to something that looked so fierce one moment and then was pouncing after any random movement the next. Their alien nature and looks made dealing with them easier.

Except for the ears and the fact that her hair and eyes were the same color, Sliverleaf was so very human looking, so very beautiful, and yet utterly unfathomable. Her movements were precise, never more or less than was needed. She was as graceful as all the legends said, but in a way, she was also clumsy. She was forever slipping, or knocking things over, much to her embarrassment. Even then, she seemed off. As she put it she was "...only a child of one hundred and twenty years. Barely over a century. What do I know really?"

That was oddest of all when it came to dealing with her. I had always been raised to respect elders and never to question them. Granted, I did anyway, but the oldest elder I had ever met was only sixty-seven summers old. Surely this Elf had more wisdom than Gran, or even a Duke's or the Count's eldest adviser. Yet, she often acted as a girl just starting her teens with the first few years of womanhood upon her.

Though she spent a lot of time being quiet, I thought to my-self that she was fun to be around. She joked; she snorted when she laughed and was coy much like I often try to be. The two of us were the only ones awake. She sat in her simple dress. It was very basic, loose and gossamer. Its long sleeves flowed down her arms, and when she stood, the skirt cascaded down her legs. It was an un-dyed silver with an odd sheen to it. Though it looked delicate, I had seen it snag on briar thorns and not get a catch or rip. She once told me it was made of spiders silk. I had no reason not to believe her.

Her hair was the blue of sapphires, as were her eyes. Elves always had the same hair and eye color, and those colors were always gem toned.

The Elven girl was studying out of a large book that only had its first few pages brought under the yoke of the pen. She sat humming to herself in a strange rhythm that was like no song or poem I had ever heard, yet it still felt as if one piece fit seamlessly with the next.

As I moved around the camp, I was careful not to wake the others. I stirred the fire by adding wood and brought it back to life. What was left of the meager squirrels the cat had caught yesterday at sunset sat still in the thin soup that had been last night's dinner.

Next, I checked the rations. We only had two wheels of cheese left, and it was easily a week more than that to Cliffport. No, we wouldn't starve before getting there, but it was already getting very uncomfortable.

"Ba'call said she spied a deer trail last night. She hopes to delay us a day by bringing in a buck before we are ready to leave."

I jumped. *Seriously, how does she always know where I am even with her head in that book?*

"She said the scent was good and had hoped to get him last night. But the beast caught her 'aroma' and fled. I think she stumbled upon him and like any cat was of the *'I meant to do that'* mind set."

That annoyed me. Bec really tries. "Do you think so little of her?" The inquiry was genuine. That accusation was to say that Ba'call wasn't a good hunter. Something the GrassLord would probably have her feelings hurt by. Yes, she was silly. She was also turning out to be a good friend.

"Not at all. I think very highly of her. She is like us, a child, a kitten if you will, more at play than at war. My people say that the GrassLords were once just great hunting cats until the ancient magics merged them with men and gave them minds."

"As such they understand the folly of hubris and live their lives as the great jokes they are upon the race of men." All of this Sliverleaf said with the aplomb of someone speaking as a teacher, as if it was a known fact, like water being wet, or sky being up.

To me it just sounded insulting. "Surely the ancients have plan and purpose for them. Why else create them?"

"Because they could." And with that the Elf went back to her book.

Chapter 22

I was still kneeling by the fire as I thought about what Sliverleaf has said. Something was tickling the back of my neck. So, I brushed it off and went back to the conversation. Bugs don't really bother me. As I was about to speak, my new over enthusiastic friend made it to my neck again. It must have been in my hair, so I flipped it away.

"Okay. So, what you are saying is that ultimately the Grass-Lords are a complete waste of time and life? That they are nothing more than a mistake?"

"Not at all. They have made for themselves a destiny, but that destiny is to be the joke on the rest of the races of men and even the gods themselves." She had the most amused and sure of herself look on her face as she explained this rather condescending point of view.

The Elf's cocky attitude was too much. From time to time, she would do or say something like this; something one simply doesn't say about friends, even to other friends. This time she was going too far. I was sure that Ba'call would be heartbroken to hear such things coming from her.

The small hairs on the back of my neck were once again being disturbed and brushed aside by something tiny winding its way upward. I am all for not killing something, even a bug if you don't have to, but this little guy wasn't taking the hint.

I felt first one, then two points of contact. Another two were added slowly and timidly. I could just imagine the unseen adversary to my nerves as it worked its way further along. Images of beetles or spiders creeping ever up, climbing the strange mountain that was me. Its little feet were somehow both soft and hard, bending, yet unyielding, these points crept up my neck going towards my hair.

I had thought it was in what little hair I had, and it may have been. My last attempt must have dislodged it down on to my shirt. I had had quite enough of the little creeper by this point and reached back to slap, grab and throw the thing in one movement and as quickly as possible. If I was lucky, it would not be a stinging insect.

My hand encountered something much larger, harder and bristlier than I had anticipated. Cores and soft bristles of varying lengths yielded only so much under my grasp before I felt muscle and bone. Hot breath hit my neck then. Part of that warm wind went up into my hair; the rest other went down into my shirt.

Years of training and muscle memory flipped from "remove annoyances" to "dangerous animal" more quickly than my mind could keep up with. My body was literally moving while I was still thinking about what this could be.

I had a couple of possibilities. One was that an animal had snuck up behind me. Whatever it was, it was larger than a bug, well, a normal bug at any rate. Granted, somewhere around here was supposed to be a hive of bug monsters that could do everything from read minds and bite through metal to breathe fire. Didn't someone once tell me they were invisible? Or it could be a dog.

Spiders, they could be furry. These little jumping things at the orphanage use to freak me out before I realized they were basically harmless. Spider, yes, now there was a thought. Did spiders breathe?

This is why so much practice is so very important. While I was still trying to digest "bug or not bug" my body was already twisting my feet under me for better leverage. The muscles in my torsos bunched and set ready to unleash all the pent-up tension I could feel there. My fingers hardened and twisted, grabbing fur and flesh indiscriminately. I was already moving that way from the twist to grab the bug, so I carried the momentum onward, not ripping the handful out, but pushing past where it was. Imagine someone grabbing your ear, but instead of snatching, they used it to turn your head. Well, that's what my body was doing at any rate. I was still trying to decide if it was bug, spider, or dog.

I was still at the point on that no way this would work if it was some kind of giant spider. My arm cocked and continued the twist. I uncoiled my legs and torso and drove my elbow in to the head of the motherless son of an Orc.

Two things ruined what should have been an outstanding display of self-defense. The first was the idea that it was indeed some type of invisible spider that was bigger than a dog. As such a high-pitched squealing strangled sound escaped my throat as my body was doing its best to save me wasn't what anyone would call dignified. Invisible spider dog things? Who wouldn't sound like a strangled and dying drowned cat? Second was the pathetic mewing cry from the vocal cords of the once proud Ba'call.

Laughter rang through the morning air. As I looked around I realized Ba'call had snuck up on me and tickled my neck with her whiskers.

There was no way that little scrap of an Elf had not seen her. Outrage momentarily burned through me. A lifetime of cruelty, of mocking, of being the butt of the joke for others rose into my mind unbidden. That lifetime had taught me one very important lesson. If I let this stand they would never take me seriously or treat me as an equal. As such, the harassment would never stop, not until I made it.

I stopped myself and thought about it. I had seen them all pull stunts like this on each other. Never anything harmful, but always crap like this. They played them on each other, at each other, with each other. Last night, the cat had made herself a fool so we would feel better. None of the jokes I had ever seen have been to degrade the person they were pulled on.

No one was getting onto me for trying to tear the cat's lips off. So, I took a deep breath and tried to look at life this new way.

I forced myself to laugh with them, more to see how it played out at first, but then I got a look at Ba'call, and forgot all about being made a fool of. That wasn't what had happened.

The tiger girl was still on her ass, legs splayed, with her front paws between them. She was moving her face as if to make sure each part of it still worked: crinkle nose; lick it with tongue; and scrunch the eyes; cross the eyes then uncross them. It was almost as if she was going down some sort of mental checklist.

I realized the girl was "hamming it up" as mom use to say. I could almost hear my mom's voice from the past, *No ham was ever really hurt if they are hamming it up. They want one thing from you and it is not pity. It is your laughter that they want.* But that was before, before the streets. I shut down the pain before it could cross my face. This didn't need my pain.

Ba'call's first words confirmed the dire diagnosis of ham.

"I think I bit my tongue."

The tiger girls face did not have her wild kin's true long muzzle; it was there, just much shorter. It allowed for something closer to human lips, which gave her the ability for something that sounded close to human speech.

Some of it would always be off. The lips did not have the flexibility to make a "b" sound. GrassLords got around this with a bit of facial gymnastics. They used their tongue in place of their bottom lip. It made almost the exact same sound. It just took some getting used to when you heard it. Their voice was the biggest difference when they spoke. Imagine a normal human voice. Now, just underneath that, put a second voice. It was deeper with a little bit of growl to it, and you had what they sounded like almost all the time. With practice, they could make it so that only one voice, that of the more human of the two, was heard, but why do so?

It was said that there were times when a third voice could be heard in their words. This one was deeper, gravelly, like a cart going down a loose stone road. It had a clicking deep purr to it. They say this only happens to them during two situations. One, in the throes of passion such as when mating, and the other, when they are lost to extreme violence. It was something I had yet to really hear from the girl, but occasionally she did purr just to purr.

This was both high pitched and pitiful. It was also said so I could understand it, not in the cats own tongue. That was something Al had insisted upon until I could learn their different languages. If it was said where I could comprehend it, it was said for my benefit.

Rowan walked over to inspect our mighty hunter, her black hair standing out against her blood red skin. I was the only one of them with short hair, but Rowan's was the longest by far. Her braid went well below the middle of her back and almost reached her tail. For reasons that I simply didn't understand, Rowan preferred to sleep in the nude, abandoning her fur tunic and loin cloth even though it was still cold at night. The scars on her body were quite visible. Most were small affairs from the practice of her chosen profession as a swords-woman. A small one here, a cut there, small shallow sword marks from hundreds of almost blows and not quite near misses. A few were longer and deeper. The one that always interested me, nonetheless, were the three jagged tear marks from something's claws. Not that I had yet worked up the nerve to ask her about them.

"Oh'll quit yer flusterin'. She didn't even draws blooded." Rowan was fast picking up Highland, the language common to the humans where I grew up, but she wasn't there yet. And it made for an interesting accent considering her first tongue was Blood Talon. "That ill teeches ya to be so quiet round our beloved tief! If'n you're huntin' is anything ta go on, she is bein' more dangerous than you, ya silly girl! Now off, find that deer ya braggin' about night of last."

With that Ba'call was simply on her feet as if pulled by marionette strings. She threw her left paw high into to the air, her fingers held straight and said something that sounded to me like *"Eye Ball My Hair!"* Not that that made a lick of sense. She turned and marched out of camp with a stiff legged gait and into the morning mist as if nothing had happened.

Sliverleaf was still having a giggle fit as I pulled myself to my feet. "How long are we giving her?" I asked the Red.

"Al's prayers will keep him lest a while. Sliv's book lest 'slong. Bec is good girl, is she don't find it fast, she'nz be back. Say..." she looked out at the risen sun "...two hands whipth from up?" Rowan looked eagerly at me when she finished.

"Al's prayers will keep him for at least a while yet. Sliv's book will take at least as long. Bec is a good girl. If she doesn't find it fast, she'll be back. Let's say two hand widths from sun up." I spoke slowly and formed each word carefully. I watched as Rowan mimed my facial movement and the way my mouth moved. The Red then repeated it again, slowly and with more success. Soon she would have the words right, if not the order. Alabaster still had trouble with that, especially when he got excited.

"You are at turn." Rowan smiled, and the two of us did what we did every day. We cleaned and policed the camp of refuge and got the basics of the packing done all the while teaching each other our languages respectively. We have become friends doing this, and I understand so much more about her and them as I learned.

I thought about what Ba'call said, those words that sounded familiar yet weren't. Has she just spoken one of the three languages her people learned growing up? I knew her people actually had three native tongues.

One was something akin to baby-talk. It is what their cubs sound like. Bec had told me that herself. Another was for anyone not GrassLord. The way she had said that made me wonder if there were Cats that weren't GrassLords. The last was kind of a formal way of speaking, not meant for the ears of outsiders.

Really, we hadn't been a group for that long. We had been traveling together for two months now without hitting a friendly town; two weeks longer than Al had planned. We had had to change our route because of a litany of things. Heavy rains, a rock slide, and war drums in the distance had somewhat slowed our progress.

As such, it left us leaner, but it also left us with the group having more time to work ourselves into a working team. All in all, a good trade off. LeatherWings firmly believed in the good of every situation. Not that there was good in every situation, but of working to make sure good came from everything that happened to them. Personally, I believe they would have been appalled if they knew how the Lords where I was from would turn tragedy into a way to grab more power.

Chapter 23

The mist had finished burning off long before Al's prayers were done. As Rowan and I worked around the camp, I watched him. Unlike when the monks and priests of back home took Morning Prayer, it always looked to me more as if he was arguing with his god.

He would pace back and forth, look towards the sky and spread his arms and wings, then shout as if in defiance. Then he would walk back and forth some more muttering only to spin on one clawed foot and start all over again.

If a priest from back home had seen it, they would have been telling him how the gods would have sent lightning by now. If you are going to pretend that some imaginary being is giving you the magic to heal someone, you might as well get to yell at them.

A black cook pot of iron hung over the fire on a collapsible iron tripod. The water sacks were, as always, near the rest of the gear we carried. The two of us had everything set up to either go, or stay one more day to butcher the deer. Well, almost everything.

"Wahter, we needs it, I'll be back in a few." Rowan gathered up the skins and collapsible bucket. It was an ingenious design really. It was two wooden rings with a metal handle, and a set of water tight skins stretched over it.

"Rowan, why don't you let me get the water? You get it every day." It obviously wasn't a trust issue. I could run away just as easily while the warrior was gone to get the water, as I could if I were getting it.

"Cuse, you said you grews upt in the cities of mens. Da woods, they can be nots nice playsses. Sumten' hutz you, I would feels bad. I likeze you. Why? You being want to?" She gestured with the ensemble of water carriers.

"Sort of. You guys made a big deal about me being an equal partner in this, though culturally I am a slave. Equal split of the take and all. Sometimes I just feel like I am not doing enough."

I am still finding it hard to understand the concept of owning people, of slavery the way they do it. In a way, their ideas on slavery were almost backwards to everything I had ever learned. Almost all of their culture was backwards from what I had been taught. I had made my peace with that being the norm when dealing with all things LeatherWing long ago...well, months ago anyway.

Rowan grinned "Worry knots little fingers. When yous time is coming, you will do work while our *asses get wide*."

I covered my mouth with both hands and let out a small but polite laugh of appreciation for the Red's attempt to use a human expression. I nodded my head and let the woman be on her way. It was odd. They didn't consider laughter rude, not laughter at mistakes. They always seem to encourage a person to show their feelings with their friends.

I went to the edge of camp and stared into the sun. Its warmth shed the chill of the morning from me. To my right was an old oak. It's sheltering branches, not to mention dead fall, was one of the reasons Bec had picked this spot to camp. I sat in a soft spot and put my back to the trunk. It was nice to sit and relax.

I heard it before I saw it.

A small shuffling sound, dead leaves rustling as something moved through them. Turning my head towards the imperceptible and letting my eyes dart to find the culprit. For a moment, I didn't see anything, and then it moved. It was a small scurrying motion that covered about an arm's length in a few hurried steps. Its small body and brownish red fur, big black eyes, a cute twitching little nose and long bushy tail made me smile. A spider squirrel was foraging for food.

Spider squirrels had little in common with the scuttling nightmares of the bug world. They only had the name because of their most distinctive features. These fuzzy little clowns didn't have the back legs of their normal counter parts; instead, they had a slightly modified version of their front paws, complete with thumbs for grasping. They also had two sets of them, both front legs and back, eight legs in all. When running along the ground or up a tree each twin leg moved as if it was one. It took a quick eye to notice if all you caught was a glance. But if it stood, as normal squirrels do, it had to separate the back legs to stand up right. As for the fore legs, they made for quick climbers even by squirrel standards.

The extra limbs had another advantage that this little one was using as I watched. Under one of its forearms, it already had an acorn, and was examining another while it held that one. All in all it would take three of them up every trip, instead of one. With one under each arm and one in its mouth before it made the trek to its hidey holes.

When I was very small, my mother had told me that seeing one and knowing what it really was brought good luck. Now here I was, not more than two yards from one.

They had one other difference from normal squirrels. They did not have the distinctive teeth, the two rodent like ones. Instead, when it opened its mouth I saw fangs, small ones, but where the two teeth would be were four more fangs longer than the canines, the middle two longest of all and all of these teeth came and grew towards the middle, giving the little guy a literal chisel bite.

"Must make walnuts easier to crack." I muttered to no one.

I watched him make the trip up and down several times before I heard Rowan return. This sent my fuzzy new friend back into his branches.

"Doings much goin' on?" Rowan asked.

"Just watching a spider squirrel." At my words Rowan's face screwed up in confusion, disgust, and then horror.

"These words, together, I no like the thought it is bring to my mind." The red visibly shuddered. "Plez tell me you are have joke on me." She looked so honest and hopeful that it took me a moment to realize what the problem was.

"No, oh gods, no. Not a spider-squirrel cross. A *Spider Squirrel...*" I thought for a moment, obviously they had a different name for the critter. "Um, the eight legged tree living nut eaters, you know, acorns." With that I bent down to pick one of the fallen nuts up and showed it to her. I even did the tooth thing and pretended to eat it; I thought it might help get the point across.

Then from behind us came a small amused chuckle. "Val'tall Sittes." Al's words were as relaxed and calm as always. "I saw you watching it. Others may be confused by 'spider squirrel'." As he came up and explained Rowan definitely relaxed.

"Val'tall Sittes. What does it mean?"

"Val is, Tree, Antall is master, as in an expert, and so Val'tall is tree master. I think a much kinder word for it than simple adding another animal's name to its own."

I felt myself nod, "And Sittes?"

His smile went from small, to all the way to his eyes. "Sister."

Chapter 24

Ba'call's return into camp signaled the end of our food problems, at least as far as meat went. The buck was young, lean, and strong. Its rack of antlers still had some of the velvet on it as it was still early spring. There were wound marks from two arrows in the buck, and Bec had already field dressed it.

She came up with the thing thrown over onto her shoulders with her holding the front legs. She bellowed as she came close to get our attention. "Light the fire and stoke the pyre; we have meat." The cat's choices of wording seemed odd. A pyre, as I understood, was for a funeral. The activities for the rest of the morning consisted of hanging the carcass upside down, cleaning, and butchering it. Everyone was expected to chip in.

I, having the least experience with this, found myself doing whatever I was told. Among these was the gathering of acorns, greens such as dandelions, and other such jobs. Most of my companions may be primary meat eaters, but even they need something besides meat. During this, I made a few discoveries; one required a smoke fire, and it excited Sliverleaf greatly, a hive of honey. Another was of a patch of black berry bramble; none were bearing fruit.

On my trips back and forth, I found myself down by the stream Rowan had used to gather the water. As I walked over to it, I got the first look at myself since before I nearly died. The last time I saw my own refection, I didn't recognize the face staring at me. The skin on it hung loosely, and my eyes were dark and sunken. That face reminded me more of a skull, poorly wrapped in old wet velum.

Now most of that damage had been erased. My green eyes were bright once again. Surprisingly, I seem to have gotten mother's lashes. My face was still round; I guess starvation couldn't change that. As such, I would never be the height of beauty, but my lips were once again full and back to being the same color as a pink pearl necklace I was once fortunate enough to "find" unattended. My nose had not improved. It was almost hawkish before, and a fight at the orphanage had made it more so. The sudden and rapid weight loss had only added to that. Now, with the weight coming back, I was actually happy to see my old beak again. My chin was still my pride and joy; as dainty as ever, it was the only thing to stop my face from being a perfect circle.

My red rat's nest of a mop was getting far longer than I liked. The ends were dry and brittle. Starvation is not good for hair. I took my time, and with my dagger, I worked on it until I was shorn almost to my scalp.

Trust me; it was a good thing. My mom was the only one who could ever get anything done with these curls. All in all, the last few months had been very good to me, if a little strange. They were hard too, but a hard life and I were old rivals, with it trying to keep me crushed under its weight, and me finding escapes through other people's pockets.

Next I went on walking through the woods seeing almost no animal life, but hearing the various song birds who were glad winter had released its grip upon our throats. I enjoy it the most when spring is like this; still cool enough to be cold, but not cold enough to hurt, with the promise of nice warmth later in the day if it didn't rain. There were almost no patches of snow left and definitely no ice in the stream. That stream was fat with the run off from the nearby mountains. They were still mostly white, but that too soon would change.

The sun was high above me now, almost noon. And the slow wind did carry with it the scent of warmer air to come. My body was getting back to normal. I was still too thin and had ribs showing, but it was better. My strength was almost completely back as well. Personally, I believe that the real reason Rowan didn't let me go get the water was not because she thought of me as weak, but because she knew I wasn't there yet.

Yeah, that fit what I knew of the girl.

It was warmer than it was this time last year. That was apparently a sign for new life to aggressively reclaim territory that had been taken from them thanks to winter's cold grasp. Though I couldn't see the animals, that didn't mean I couldn't see signs of their passing; fresh trails for the deer the cat had hunted. This time of year, Bec would only take buck for some reason. I even saw signs of dragonets. They were smaller, less intelligent breeds of the dragon species though it was probably still too cold for their reptilian cousins to be out other than to sun themselves.

Everywhere I looked, I could see one flowering plant or another blooming, some with just buds, some in full blossom.

This is going to be a good year, a warm spring leading into a hot summer maybe, but still good. Hopefully it leads to a better harvest than last year. That thought made me stop for a moment. With the war still officially going on planting and harvest were going to be less than they should.

I stopped myself. That was on the other side of the mountain range from me, and it wasn't my problem anymore. I felt bad for the people back home, but it was not my problem anymore. All in all, I found myself enjoying the day.

We were headed up to Cliffport to hopefully get a delivery job headed into the plains and down towards Five Rivers. I had often heard of both places from traders.

Cliffport was built into the cliffs above the great freshwater sea and, according to the merchants, was easily larger than my home city by more than twice.

Five Rivers sat in the middle of the convergence of four of the largest rivers of this land to make the truly impressive and legendary river The Mistress of the Land. Often called "Ol' Miss" for short, it divided the land in half and was completely uncrossable without a boat. Some say she's a mile wide; others that at her widest she was as many as five. She's supposed to be deep enough to sail a sea vessel up it all the way to Five Rivers.

A tension was creeping up my neck, making it feel stiff. I shook my head. This only served to make the leaves dance.

I found some place to sit before I fell over, headache and light headed. I must have come further than I thought.

A gnawing pain started in my stomach, down low like I had had bad food last night. Maybe the stew didn't agree with me.

No, I had eaten far worse than that before. Besides it wasn't like I was hurting badly; it was just cramps.

***

Twenty minutes later I quickly made my way into camp, as dignified as I could with wet thighs. I tried not to think about it. I was so glad I had supplies just in case. Of course, everyone was watching me.

How nice. I headed back into the woods faster than I had come out of them.

There was only Alabaster who might not understand what was happening. Although given everything else that was screwed up with his people, he probably knew all about it. Nothing was safe, no bastion of womanhood sacred. No secrets. In a perverted world like theirs, they probably even had men who got off on it.

It seems I was healthy enough for the "gods" to hate me again for not being a good wife.

Great! Lovely! Wonderful! And I bet it has even soaked through my small clothes.

Chapter 25

The rest of the journey to Cliffport was unremarkable. Walking through woods still gray from winter with only the barest hint of spring green starting to show showed we were headed further north. Every once in a while, a rebellious cacophony of early flowers would assert their dominance over the landscape, each hoping for the first rays of the renewed sun.

Even with this, the days flowed by, one into the next. The gray monotony was only broken by those riots of color. With each passing sunset, we were closer to our destination. With every morning's sunrise, I could not help but hope that this was to be the day.

Ba'call had rigged up some sort of mobile smoker for the meat and hide of the deer she had brought down. Hunger was no longer the issue it had been. We had enough meat to stretch out our supplies and foraging for nuts and dandelion roots, which were already springing up, gave us something to enjoy besides venison. She and the others tanned the hide but kept the bone, sinew, even the offal. They used it all or planned on selling it, Ba'call said, bone for tools and jewelry, sinew for wrappings to make arrows and other things like that. I found out how sausage casings were made. Needless to say, I was a little put off.

The smoker itself was an interesting contraption to look at to say the least. We had made its wheels out of a cross cut log and its floor out of green wood which we kept wet by soaking it with water from our skins so that the heat wouldn't make it catch. The low fire was kept going on an old rusted round steel shield; it was more coals than flame. Ba'call had walked into camp triumphantly bearing the old shield before her as if it was the "find of a lifetime". Her tail was lashing side to side, and a grin was plastered across her face. Where she had uncovered it, no one knew, and no one wanted to ask.

The ungainly mess made a copious amount of smoke with an almost foul smell, but I guess that was the point. Ba'call assured me it was necessary to properly cure the meat and hide, and the others didn't seem to mind. She took up position at the back of the line so that we weren't walking in the miasma of the stuff.

Much to Rowan's disdain, it slowed us down, making us days later coming into town than we had wanted. All told, we were late getting to Cliffport by almost a full month.

***

The first thing I saw was the water through the trees. If you have never seen a fresh water sea, it is hard to imagine.

Think of it this way; picture in your mind the largest lake you can think of. Now, envision that water being deep enough to have a sailing ship upon it. You can still see the bottom when you are close to shore. As you go out deeper, the water begins to turn into a rich emerald green. It was like that, not the blue of the ocean I have visited many times before.

That green was the color all the way out to the horizon, and it stretched to the left and the right of where I was standing. We were coming out of the mountain pass with its line of sight, being only a few hundred paces ahead of us turned into a vista of land and water that was breath taking.

I had grown up a few days travel from the ocean and loved to go there when I could, though it wasn't often. We were at one of the narrowest parts of this mammoth lake. Yet even with the noon day sun giving its light, I could not see the other side. I once heard it was two days travel by ship to the nearest shore from Cliffport.

The city itself came into view just beyond. It didn't look that different from where I grew up. Granted, the area around it had far more farms than I was used to. If they counted as part of the city, then it truly was huge. Other than that, it was a town with no real wonders. It had walls, parapets, and a large castle gate up next to the drop off. The town I could see was about the same size with which I grew up too. But I knew that the bulk of it was down by the waters. Indeed, it might be as big as I was promised; it just looked so...normal.

I guess I was expecting grandeur and not just a larger version of what I knew. My disappointment must have shown because it got Ba'call's attention.

"Something wrong?" Her voice was strained with the dragging of her make shift cart, but there was still humor in it. She came closer to me, "Not what you were hoping for?"

"Not really," I tried not to sound disappointed. "I had just always heard it was somewhat..."

I tried to think of a way to explain the grand images that the trader's stories had crafted inside my head. "I don't know, more? Bigger?" And now I sounded like every other country bumpkin. *Way to go me.*

As we came around the bend, we arrived at the actual road instead of the trail that we had been forging through the mountains pass. I was happy to keep cutting through, but Rowan turned to go down the road.

"Why not keep going straight?" I hadn't been in a real bed in nearly a year. Well, over six months. At this point, an actual chair would have been nice, and a bed, heaven. Cutting through on the straight path sounded better to me.

"Being because we is coming up onna' the farms soons. Onna' top of that we needs to go in the gates, as well as this will making that contraption easys to drag."

It was hard to argue with logic like that.

***

Our time improved enough that what I thought would be another day at least turned into a few extra candle marks. The road offered one more advantage; it let me see off and down the cliff face to the town proper.

Yes, the town I had seen was not impressive, but it was barely a scratch on the surface of the place, more of a strip of the actual town than the actual city. Down three hundred feet of cliff to the water below was a bustling harbor. It had five large docks and several more small ones.

Massive masted vessels showed the size of the docks as the largest one looked like it could have handled ten of them if the shore men did their jobs well. On the shore of the natural harbor was a sprawling town twice the size of what showed on the top, with warehouses for anything that could be shipped. The two most intriguing features were part of the cliff face itself.

An entire town was carved into the cliff. Not unlike the LeatherWing encampment, they had turned caves into homes. These buildings were literally cut out of the rock. Others were built and anchored to the cliff face. Buildings, catwalks, roadways, carts, and people, all of it slowly descending down the cliff on boardwalk platforms cut into the wall then expanded with wood, masonry and flying buttresses.

The second was what I had taken for an out of place castle. This magnificent edifice started on the top of the cliff, and from the outside looked like a massive gate with two towers reaching up into the air. On the other, you saw the towers had arms that reached out into the air arched down and connected with two towers coming up from below.

It sort of looked like an illumination of a bridge I once saw in a fairy book. This was much like that, but where bridges cover length, this one covered height. Part of it was a road that wound back and forth making it easy for wagons to go up and down. It also allowed access at every street that was built into the cliff. Amazingly, there were platforms being raised and lowered, carrying people on them. I was in awe by the sizes, scale and scope of the place.

Never before had I even dreamed of such a thing. If this was Cliffport, what must Five Rivers be like?

Five Rivers, after all, was supposed to dwarf Cliffport.

Chapter 26

One thing I sort of missed about being in a city was the smell. Like all cities larger than a few homes, this one had its own unique and slightly foul smell. An undercurrent that was ubiquitous. I could identify a tannery somewhere around here, could smell the fish from down below when the wind shifted, but ever present was the smell of dung from animals and faint hints at urine from alleyways. Somehow it was comforting to be surrounded by such familiarity now. Especially now, considering all that had happened.

As we were moving along Ba'call called out, "Sliv, go with Rowan and Al, find us a place to stay to your liking. Al, with your permission I am going to take Chloe and sell the extra meat, bone and hide."

Alabaster looked back at me, asking if I was okay with this. I shrugged and he nodded. With that, the three of them were off. Once they were out of sight, I turned to Ba'call, "What was that about?"

The great cat actually managed to look embarrassed and sheepish as she hung her head and laid her ears back. "I grew up on the plains; I was a traveler. My tribe went from place to place but...we didn't use money. Last time I was here, I think I got taken advantage of." She said the last part very quietly, as if she had just revealed a great secret. I could understand at what she was getting. She had just probably grown up with barter; money would be more than a little confusing. How was she supposed to know how to count it or what it was worth?

"Of course. You want me to do the dealing?"

Bec flinched backward as if slapped. "Gods no, I want you to teach me coin." So we went over the basics of money. What to look for and what things were worth.

"A Farthings or a tin piece..." I held one up "...one of these would usually get you something like a bone sewing needle, something quick to make and cheap, or for food. Something like a single egg."

She nodded, so I went on. "Now ten of those make a Pence. They are made of nickel metal; one of those will get you a copper needle. Again, not too expensive, all things told. Ten Pence is a penny."

I had been holding up the coins to the cat and was pleased to see her avidly listening. "Now, a penny is worth about a burlap sack. The kind used for most hauling of base goods like feed for animals and such."

Ba'call turned and pointing to a woman emptying out a bag of turnips to be sold at her stall. She had several bags. "Like those?"

"Yep." I smiled, the cat was quick. "It is still cheap enough to lose but still good enough to use again and again. A bone needle probably won't last very long, and as such, it's cheap. The copper last much longer, but it's small, easy to lose, so still not that expensive. Now, ten Pennies make a Bill or Bill'a'buck." I was holding one up when Bec interrupted me.

"Why is it called that? That seems like a funny name."

Considering some of the things I had heard the cat call common items, it seemed a more than a little strange. She just wasn't used to what I thought of as normal. "Because that is what it is made of. Sort of. Pennies are copper, see?" I held one up again. "And Shillings are Silver; well, the Bill is between them and has both silver and copper in them. This is known as Billon, hence Billon buck, or Bill'a'buck. Or simply Bill for short."

"Ah! *Favfava*! So that means there are ten Bills in a Shilling." She seemed quite proud of herself. "So what is about their worth?"

I thought about it. "Well, for a Bill, you can get about a pint of oil, or lots of thread, or a good beeswax candle. Two bills if you want the colored ones. As for a Shilling, it is about what you or I could make in a day working on the docks just starting out."

"*Favfava, favfava*, so what is ten Shilling?"

"That would be a Small Crown. It is made of Electrum, which is a mix of gold and silver. See, it is about one part gold to nine parts silver, and to answer you before you start, it will buy you a rich meal with coin left over. I am talking beef, good cuts like you find at a minor lords table." I had been lucky enough to have gotten a few Small Crown from time to time, most of which I saved up. Some of it had gotten me such dinners. Granted, in Shillings I had much more than a single Small Crown, but the coins were still nice to hold.

"Next comes real gold, right?" The cat was getting excited.

"Yep. A Gold Crown is next. Just like before, ten Small to a Gold Crown. If a man worked for one hundred days and saved all his earnings, that is what a Gold Crown is worth. Now, what you can buy with it? Think a good draft horse; one of those big things they have to pull the huge wagons loaded down with stuff."

Once, just once, I had gotten one of these. I put it in the poor box at one of the other temples. No way was I going to get rid of the thing without questions, and even I liked to believe it helped out. The rich were oft in that temple. Surely mine wasn't the first the box had seen.

"Then you have the Full Crown, and I have never even seen one to be honest with you. It is part gold and part platinum. I think mostly it is used by Lords and Ladies to buy and sell kingdoms. Well, large sections of land anyway. At any rate, nothing you or I need to worry about." I smiled, walked a step or two away, turned and winked at her. "Yet."

Together we unloaded the last twenty pounds of meat and the hide, as well as some of the bones that Ba'call had made into crude jewelry. The cat seemed to have a knack for hamming it up to get a better price on things. All in all, we walked away with five shilling. We also had tried to sell the make shift smoker, but the guard ran us off before we could. Something about it being a menace or some such.

Together, with some food we kept from the cart, we waited at the top of the sky bridge for our companions. As we waited, I watched the people passing by. I noticed something I felt was strange. Almost every single person was human. No, not *almost*.

Everyone I saw and had seen was human. Even back home, we had a few Orcs or even some Dwarves on occasions.

"I thought this was a LeatherWing city?"

"It is, sort of. This city doesn't fall into any human kingdom; it falls within what the LeatherWing considers to be part of their lands. As such, the Empire gives it protection as well as helping out with laws and aid when needed. The Empire believes in letting a city or a territory be more or less self-governed. Cliffport wasn't started by the Empire. It was started by a bunch of traders and fishermen, a bunch of merchants who thought it was a good place to load and unload goods. The cliffs offer protection, and long before the sky bridge was built, there was a sort of natural switch back that made getting things down to the water easy but made invading the town very hard."

I had forgotten Ba'call was a bit of a historian, and having already been in the city probably took the time to learn all she could about the place. A history lesson was as good a thing to do as anything else. It definitely beat waiting in silence.

"Cliffport is older than Unstoma actually. The city itself is about nine hundred years old and has been growing this whole time. When the Empire of the Five Races came into contact with this place shortly after it was founded, the locals resented it. The founding families of the town thought they were going to impose their will on them and kept running them off."

She smiled at me then, and after traveling with LeatherWings, I understood why. Running them off wouldn't work.

"The patrols kept returning year after year and even set up trade with the people here. Still, the people wanted nothing to do with the 'heathen beasts' other than their money. One spring when the patrols got here, they found Unstoma waiting."

Now the story was getting interesting. Unstoma had met the LeatherWing before the war.

"The LeatherWing freed the town, helped protect it, and even set up trade between them and the Northern Empire as the LeatherWing thought of Unstoma at the time."

"Wait, the Empire had contact with the LeatherWing before the war?" I wanted this confirmed. The LeatherWing could have killed everyone there and let the humans of the Empire of Five Races do all of the talking after that.

"Some, but they consider them nothing more than barbarians. The LeatherWing didn't think much of Unstoma either, but how they lived wasn't any of their business. Remember, at this time, Unstoma was still ruled by a council who answered to elected representatives. Those people were elected by the people who did the work, everyday people. The LeatherWing did not believe they had the right to tell others how to live, so they left the Empire alone."

"Right, the Fourth Law: the Law of Self." I nodded. "So what changed?"

"That I don't know." She sighed. "Something happened to make not just the LeatherWing, but all of us in the Empire of the Five see the Unstoma as evil and needing to be stopped. Not being a tale singer, I don't know the particulars that started it, but the Unstoma that we toppled was not the one we defended this town from. By that time Unstoma had a God King, an Emperor who could not be questioned."

I nodded. People still talked about the God King. Some felt he was a villain; others thought of him as a hero. Given what I knew now, I was more inclined to vote for villain.

"After the LeatherWing protected the town, the council that ruled here at the time chose to join the Empire in full. They expected a lot of changes. When it didn't happen, they relaxed. Now ships from here go to Cat Island and all over the Empire. Meanwhile, wagons from here go all the way down to Five Rivers. As such, this is a very rich trade city, and they probably have thousands of those Full Crown coins." At that, the cat giggled and let out a purring sound. She obviously thought it was funny.

Chapter 27

A runner, a child of about seven summers, came to get us and told us to go to the Red Eyed Boar. I asked him if he had any troubles finding us, and he said he hadn't.

"A human and an Orange Cat woman is hard to miss, miss." I gave him a Bill for his troubles and sent him on his way.

The ride down the lift platform was a joy. I could see the whole of the town from this remarkable feat of simplistic design. Yes, I know, but I felt like a kid again. I kept my hands on my coin purse. See, not a rube.

The lift was little more than a block and tackle system used for heavy loads. The runners that keep the lifts in line had a toothed grove that matched wheels at the top, and I hoped the bottom. The runners were a guard rail system that kept the platform steady on its journey. It wasn't the first time I had seen their like. They were Gnome made. If they went too fast, a spring would open up and slow down the descent. If it couldn't, it would break and bind the gear. The weight was counterbalanced so that two donkeys at the top could do the work without straining themselves too hard as long as the load wasn't overly heavy.

That is where the built in road ramp came in. Heavy wagons literally cork screwed inside the protected structure of this behemoth. The road was made to handle a standard width wagon. If your wagon was too large, then it would have to be unloaded and repacked into smaller wagons for the trip.

There were actually two roads, one for up traffic, and one for down. The up road had a different set of pulleys. This one was done with chains so that the wagons could be hitched to that to save the draft animals from having to do all the work on the trip up.

The roads cost a lot of money to use as maintenance and upkeep of such a marvel could not have been cheap. I had counted at least thirty people working the various ropes, chains, wheels, and pulleys keeping things moving smoothly.

The lifts were cheap to use at only a penny a trip. With as many people that went on one trip, no more than twenty five per platform and eight platforms, they were making some good money. I hoped they had good guards to go with that good money. I may have never stolen from hard working people, but that didn't mean others wouldn't.

As we walked from the lifts to the Inn, I used the time to keep myself in practice. I had collected a handful of small round pebbles and would slip them into the pockets and pouches of passersby. The goal was the same as if I was working the crowds; don't be seen, don't be suspected, and don't get caught. In this case, the penalty if I messed it up would be much less.

We were almost to the inn when I got made. As I was laying one of my last stones in the crease of a man's belt, a good place to stash coins if you were worried about cut purses, I felt his hand brush mine.

Quickly, I glanced up to read the situation. Not at him, but more around him. Focusing on someone is a good way to draw their attention. The man was not tall but not short, golden haired, and well-manicured beard. He had the look of a minor noble or some well-to-do merchant. I saw the recognition in his eyes and fear creeped into me. Though I knew I could not get into real trouble for this, old habits die hard.

He winked at me, turned, and went...that and nothing more. My face burned crimson. I had taken a fellow thief for a mark. The fact that I made such a stupid mistake said to how skilled the man was, but still, it was embarrassing.

Rowan chuckled. "Hands caught in cook's biscuits?"

Ye gods, even Rowan had known what I was up to. I'm a disgrace to the profession.

"Worrse don't, is okay. You recoverings from sick."

Wonderful, two more things to be ashamed of myself; pity from Rowan and I hadn't realized someone as big and intimidating as the Red had joined back up with us. Not my day.

"Months, not been in crowded city. Me? I walks beside you every day!" Her mirth was palatable. "Insult I would be if cringe from me you still did."

"True, but still, I should be better aware of my surroundings." I straightened and forced myself back to being tougher than nails. "Besides, I wasn't doing anything wrong. I was simply handing out pebbles to people."

Rowan chuckled and good-naturedly patted me on the back. "Here's we are staying." She gestured up at a sign. It was a black boar's head with a red eye. Under it written in trade was the words "Red Eyed Boar".

"It's being one place in few that takes adventures, and one of only set up for long to short stays." Her highlander was getting better even if her words' order was off. I nodded my head and smiled at the obvious effort made by Rowan.

Walking into the place was leaving the smells of a city and coming home to the smells of a good inn. The place was rich with the aromas of food and drink. Round tables were spread out throughout the place, at most with only four chairs but some with five or six. One table was large enough for the fourteen chairs that were around it. The lighting was done by several clean lanterns hung on all sides of the seven pillars that broke up the room. A large bar sectioned off a corner area with a small window for food to pass back and forth. Behind it was a woman I took an immediate likening to.

This woman, who was in her thirties perhaps, with a single streak of gray in her otherwise bright copper hair, oversaw the place. Her eyes held laughter and wisdom that said they knew every inch, notch, knot-hole, and crack in this room and every thieves worth as well. I would not bet a fathering on the chances of any rook's success within these walls.

She seemed to employ girls to check the tables and bus the orders. None were older than myself; some were as young as nine. Any customers with amorous intent and wandering hands who found these girls to their liking would probably be rushed out by other customers, saving the staff extra work.

By the bar was also a mountain of a man, an Orc who was as large as his true blood relatives, yet his one remaining eye shone with an understanding of his surroundings they often lacked. His features also showed he was not of full Orc ancestry; blond hair hung down to his waist even though it was tied high with a top knot.

His job seemed to be the fetching and carrying of any item too large or heavy for the girls to manage easily, and his eye was ever about them but watching the customers, not the girls. The small cudgel at his side told his true job, keeping the peace.

Sliverleaf was over in a corner table reading her ever present book. Ba'call wandered to the bar to see what culinary mischief she could cause. Rowan and I sat at a table furthest from anyone.

I took the opportunity rarely presented; the opportunity to get to know the group's strong arm. Of course, the reason for the opportunity was not lost on me.

"Al put you up to this didn't he? What excuse did he give?"

"Ee' is looking for the jobs, the opportunity to getting us close to Five Rivers and being paid for it is good."

"All right," I gathered my thoughts. Alabaster always wanted me to get other perspectives on things. As such, he gave me ample opportunity to explore and talk to the others, even if he had to make up reasons to get me alone with people. "The scars on your stomach are claw marks. How did you get them?"

"Al actually." She said to my surprise. "We were children, and playing. I was not kind. His tail and my foot had a meeting at my insistence. He lashed out without thinking. It was my first lesson in my own stupidity and he in his. Our mother was very scared for both of us. Al did not talk for a month."

I winched, but it explained something about the both of them like why they were so close. Time to change the subject. I could ask about Rowan anytime, for this I didn't want Alabaster here. "Your culture, it is female dominated, right?"

"Yes, this is so."

"And you have no problem with nudity, or sex, or even gender roles, so long as the person is responsible for what they do, right?"

"True also..." A look started passing across Rowan's face as she said this. I had better get to the point.

"Al is a priest, a female role, with a female color, and to some extent a female body, yet he hides it. Why?"

Rowan thought about it for a moment as if considering if it was hers to tell or not. "When we are born, our parents name us, then at reason we name ourselves. I became Rowan. I was also called Blood. Alabaster picked his name due to the stone that was like his skin; however, he was named Cyn. Cyn, in my culture, is a girl's birth name. I got a warriors name, but Al got a girl's because white he was born. All of his life, special treatment he got because he has been blessed-born. Cyn hated it."

Rowan had her eyes closed and spoke slowly. Obviously, she did not want to be misunderstood. "One day, a boy wanted to court him, and a big deal he made of this. Al, even as Cyn was...different, maybe because god touched he was, maybe because he was just Al. Boy would not take no for answer. As of yet, Al had not chosen. All children get to choose who they are, but are treated like what they acting like." As she was getting more into this, she was losing her careful grasp of the way words go.

"Being woman born male body, should not matter, but to some it did. Our parents tried to do right, but everyone expected things of greatness from Cyn, from Al. Meant to, I am sure, was not the point. However, this was still done. And this boy who would not take no-" She paused thinking of how to put it. "...pushed Cyn too much, too far. He screamed at him '*I am not a girl, I am Alabaster, I will do my duty as a priest for it is what I wants, not what they wants.*" She smiled broadly remembering this. I could picture it too. A small little white, all bowed up at some jerk, telling him off.

"Never have I been so proud of my brothers as that day." Her face then turned a little sour. "That was his day of reason; he was just six summers old, too young perhaps. When nature stretched her hand to make him full, it also gave him a woman's hips and top."

She looked down, sadness filled her eyes. "When he was twelves, I showed him how to tie them down like a warrior not used to them yet. He has done it ever since. A good thing, I am not sure I did." She looked out and far away, as if seeing the past. "My culture, I think is best, knows we are not supposed to putting it that way, but still. Even best is not always good. Hurt Al is. Bad I think. Some fault lies with our family, some with the boy, some with the pressure Al put on himself, the pressure he thought others were putting upon him. Our failure was not in seeing this; he was doings to himself."

"That is why you are still here traveling with him. Does he know?" I had started to love Rowan like a sister, and this just confirmed she was worthy of that love.

"One good thing about us and how we do things. He *knows*. He also knows his attitude towards himself, off by a bit it is. But our teaching say, always to question. For him, childhood prepared him to answer quest deeper than if he had simply realized that our parents and the town would have been happy for him either way. So long as it was truly him that did it."

I nodded my head. I had never seen Al without his chest wrapped. I had seen every other part of him, but not this.

"Um, you are obviously the older sibling; how old are you and how old is Al?" I had to know.

She smiled at me. I think she was getting at what I was suddenly worried about. "I am twenty-two winters, Al is twenty.

Twenty years old, he been wrapping himself up for years. I had seen LeatherWing Women in fullness of blossom. They could get very ripe. Alabaster showed despite the wrapping, if you knew what to look at.

"How old are you when a woman will ripen no more?"

Rowan cocked her head and looked at me strangely; confusion played out on her face much as it did her brothers so many months ago. Then she started laughing. It was a deep rich sound, like a fine drum being hit by expert hands. "Breast dear, they are called breasts, and we are in our late twenties before our hopes are dashed of them getting bigger. At least until be milk."

Chapter 28

Alabaster was back an hour later and after Ba'call had gotten us all a nice dinner. Seems she knew the cook from her previous trip through here. "So, what is the job?"

He smiled. "A delivery, basic guard duty stuff. Us not being in the guild isn't a problem."

"All the way to Five Rivers?" Bec asked looking hopeful.

Al's face fell. "No, it is a few days ride out and back, deliver a strongbox with payment, and pick up the merchandise and return. Here's the thing; it pays a Small Crown each." He was grinning again.

Sliverleaf whistled, and I couldn't blame her. That was a lot of money to be offered to a bunch of non-guild members. It set off my paranoia. "Why so much?"

Alabaster grinned. "Relax. His name is Corbin Shale. He is the descendant of one of the founding families of Cliffport. Seems his grandfather lost most of their holdings long ago, and he is just now getting his feet back underneath him. He has a gem mine, but no one knows where it is, and he wants to keep it that way. He doesn't trust the guild but is willing to pay well for our silence in the matter. I did some checking around; he does this about once maybe twice a month. No one has had any problems."

Still, it didn't sound right. "Why doesn't he trust the guild?"

"His grandfather hired some guild's men to take a large sum to Five Rivers; they never returned. That was what lost them everything, or so the story goes." Al spread his hand. I could tell how much stock he put in that.

It happened from time to time. Hiring guild adventurers was one of the safest ways to get something done, but things still happened. Lost caravans, raids, anything could happen, and it was said about the guild and those that hired them, "big money came with big risks".

Then it hit me. "When do we leave?"

"Relax, not until day after tomorrow. We have time to enjoy a roof over our head for a while. But with this payday, we can get our papers, and as such, when we hit towns below here, we won't be run out." All in all, Al had done a good job.

The Adventurer's Guild was a lose affiliation of mercenaries. Guild members paid dues to ensure fair treatment no matter where they went. Those dues made sure that members stuck to contracts and didn't just run off with a client's money. It also encouraged members not to make trouble. As such, even a band of Orcs could expect good treatment in a town, so long as they behaved themselves. Much further north than this and no one was going to know what a LeatherWing was outside of three-hundred-year-old legends. Joining the guild was a damn good idea.

I enjoyed the fact that tonight and tomorrow night's food was something I didn't have to cook. That and the fact that the bed had fresh straw in it. It was nice not to be traveling. All too soon it was time to meet this Lord Shale.

Chapter 29

Dawn broke, and with it, the noise from the common room increased. As I went down, I could see that the kitchen was indeed in full swing. The smell of bacon and ham, as well as the roast cooking for later filled the air, permeating every inch of the place. The girls were busy taking the mornings offerings from table to table. I sat and had breakfast while I waited for my companions to finish their morning routines.

Once they arrived, we went down to the beach and dock area at the bottom of the cliff. The smell of stale urine was overwhelmed by the catch of the day. The sounds down here were definitely the sounds of an open and hardworking port. Anyone that could do the work was being hired as quickly as they came.

True, the fishing ships had already left for the day, but a stevedore's work is never done, well, at least around here. Everywhere I looked there were jobs to be had unlike back home.

As we walked, both Alabaster's and Rowan's heads snapped around at almost the same time; they were looking out over the water. I turned and for a moment my mind would not make sense of what I was seeing.

Out in the water, still a good ways off from any of the docks, a boat was on fire, and what's more, it was moving rapidly towards here. Black smoke billowed up from the deck, and I tried to see where the fire was.

I couldn't find it.

What I did see was glimpses of shining red as if sunlight was glinting off of copper. The ship had two things sticking off the sides that were moving so fast that they were spraying water into the air. The sails were gone. As I could see, there was neither mast nor place for one. The ship itself was long and wide and the people sitting at the front of it seemed calm.

"Magic! It has to be." Though Sliverleaf was a mage, I had yet to see her do anything as big and certainly nothing as impressive as a magic boat.

"Better." Rowan grinned. "Gnomes."

A Gnomish boat. I had seen Gnome gears most of my life. In some places, they were common, but Gnomes had figured out that if you boiled water hot enough, it could move things. They enthusiastically tried to show everyone who would listen, but so far, only the Gnomes had managed this "steam power" without blowing things up.

It was closer now, and I could hear what had gotten the attention of the two of them. A god awful cacophony of hissing and noise, everything from what sounded like someone swinging a blade fast enough to cut air; only continuous, to rhythmic hiss that sent the hairs on my neck to full attention. As it got closer, I could see the gleaming copper of what I could only guess was the water tank. All around it was toothed wheels and interlocking gears; some spinning furiously, some in short fits before stopping. They were of what I think was brass.

Either way I could see those teeth eating lose clothing or careless fingers, and I understood why only Gnomes had mastered this art.

Gnomes, I had heard, were part rock; it was in their bones, as well as showing on their skin. Now that I was seeing these people for the first time I could see why people thought this. They were gray, a deep color like rich soil.

These short Dwarven cousins moved around quickly, maintaining the machine that kept the bladed wheels on either side going at speed and pushing the water out behind them. They were shorter than human average but still well within the height range of a short person at about four to five feet tall. These swamp dwelling folk were said to be able to eat anything, including rock. I had something else confirmed as they came into dock. The women were indeed taller than the men. Most of them were at least a head height above their male counter parts on the boat.

I turned away before my staring would be considered rude only to find all of my compatriots were still gazing out at the boat. Rowan had a look of admiration on her face; her smile was plain to see. Alabaster was looking at it and the Gnomes with a quiet, knowing grin playing across his lips. Ba'call seemed to be contemplating the sight with quiet amusement.

Only Sliverleaf looked my way after a moment. She slid in close to me and quietly said, "For them, not to stare would be impolite. They are big on communication. They openly wear their expressions on their faces for all to see. To hide your notice to them is to show you do not trust the people you are looking at or are with."

"But won't the Gnomes think it is ill-mannered? To be gawked at as if some creature in a cage?" I had always been taught that staring at any one different from you might hurt them in ways that could not be seen or perhaps even understood.

"And ignoring them makes them feel welcomed? By not staring at the little things, they believe it lets us turn a blind eye to the big things like girls starving in alleys."

Her words were sweet. Her meaning was barbed but clear. As I got close to dying and even days before, people would turn away from me. I became not real to them. I was nothing more than a reminder of their own pain and suffering.

How do I know this? When you are sitting there slowly freezing to death, you suddenly remember every face in need from which you turned away. Turned away because you didn't have much, or didn't know what to do, or were scared it was some sort of trap. I watched people that knew me turn away, not because they recognized me, but because they didn't. I turned into nobody. So, I turned back around and made myself stare. I showed on my face the wonder I felt for being able to see such a sight.

I was glad I did. The boat had slowed considerably and was not actually approaching the docks. Instead, it was coming up to a cobbled stone roadway that extended into the water. As it angled in, the prow of the ship rose up out of the water. Shortly, it could be seen that the keel had a wheel jutting out from it much like that of a wheelbarrow. A shield of sorts protected it from unseen dangers in the water but allowed for the wheel itself to spin freely. The big wheels on the side pushed it right up the ramp and on to the street. The paddles on those wheels were end-capped by what looked to be traditional wagon wheels allowing for this boat to move on land. It was steered by one back wheel turning slower than the other. It took forever to turn around, but when it did it let its passengers disembark down an ordinary gang plank. This was more than just a great boat; this was a water going coach.

Of course, once the thing was settled down, it made a loud pop that either sent its crew scurrying for cover or scrambling for the huge copper pot at the back.

We all turned away. Alabaster was shaking his head and Rowan was laughing. Personally, I was hoping everyone was okay. That popping sound was painful to hear, and I can't think of anything that makes a noise like that other than a knot exploding in a fire.

We continued on to what looked like it was a fish warehouse in its last life but had been converted into a kind of storefront. As we walked in, it became quickly apparent that this place was a jewelers. No sign outside gave it away, and from the look at some of the stones and the creations of said jeweler, I could see why.

Lord Shale may not believe in the adventurer's guild, but if there is a thief's guild in this city, then he had better be paid up on his insurance. A city this size either needs a guard that was always on their toes, or a guild to shut down freelancers; otherwise, crime would be a major problem. Seeing what I had seen in this city, I would bet both, probably with an uneasy alliance between the two. The piece in front of me was a solid carved piece of tiger's eye agate, probably weighing forty pounds easily.

It was a statue of a Champion of Luth'hart. And the way the light sifted the bands in the stone, made it the perfect gem to use for the God of Change. Its layered strata also showed the order Luth'hart still taught that laws were there to protect man, not bind him. The detail-work on the holy symbol was simply breathtaking, especially to be so small.

I had often wondered when I was younger and dumber if life for me would have been better if my mother had followed Luth'hart. They saw charity as a joy, unlike followers of Ca'talls who saw it is a duty to be performed for those lesser than themselves.

Habit shook me from my thoughts. No windows, three doors, one to the outside where I would be easily seen. One further back to a work area given the size of the building from the outside, and the slight dust tracks coming from it, and one to what was undoubtedly some sort of office. No windows going into this room or skylight either. The antechamber acted as a foyer; it was set up as a welcome office and storefront. In short, a nightmare to get into during the day. At night, there would be no guarantee where the piece would be. Not that I could fence such a piece without help anyway.

I shook my head. Old habits die hard. I looked around and my mind jumped to numerous other pieces that would be easier to take but also noticed the large guardsmen hiding in the corner.

He hadn't noticed me. I stopped scoping the place before he did. Our employer owned this; no need getting his attention. Not this way at least.

I had completely missed something Al had said to the man behind the counter. I had heard him speak but could not tell what was said. The shopkeeper directed us back to what I took to be the office.

I love it when I am right. We were escorted back and let into an opulent room with a large desk and the assorted trophies of a sports hunter. Some of them were what you expect: bear, dear, ram, but some were exotic. One was a small dragon kin, all gray scales but having two wings and two legs, but no front arms. A huge glass jar with what looked like small golden grubs packed into it filled to the brim. And finally, there was a kind of winged horse like thing with a beak, rampant with its hooves, frozen, lashing out at its attacker.

I heard Rowan suppress a growl. I agreed with her; hunting for sport is a waste. There are plenty of people that could use the meat.

The man behind that desk of black wood sat in a chair made of bone and hide. He was a good-looking man, somewhere in his late twenties, possibly early thirties. He had a clean-shaven face. His smile was welcoming but his blue eyes were cautious. He was gauging us as I was gauging him.

His demeanor was calm, but he was aware of all of us. The two LeatherWings made him nervous but also excited him. The GrassLord he dismissed as well as the Elf. Me he spared only a glance, but I was willing to bet he pegged me.

For his part, he was fit and healthy. A scar on his left cheek came from a knife, but it was older, at least ten years. He sat ready for trouble but giving an air of complete trust as if he knew we wouldn't start something. His clothing was very nicely made and down played the plated leather vestment he was wearing. In short, a man that was used to double dealing, to cheating; a man used to dealing with freelancers like us.

He stood to welcome us. His armor may have been hidden, but his sword was not. "Welcome to my humble establishment. Compared to my ego, the art outside is humble." He chuckled at his own joke; at least he was honest.

"I am Alabaster, and this is my partner Rowan, our security specialist Chloe, as well as our tracker and mage Ba'call and Sliverleaf." He gestured to each of us in turn. "As your ad said, we are not guild, and we are very discreet."

You can tell a lot about a person by their first words to you. "All female, good. It seems the sharpest minds in the Empire are going to be working for me on this. Sadly, I do not think this first job is up to your obvious qualifications. Having a company on retainer would not be a bad thing."

Okay, so he got it wrong, but hey, Alabaster is a white. Listening to him speak was actually kind of soothing. That set me on edge. Any time a man worked that hard to soothe a woman he was usually trying to get into her pants.

With him working his charms on five of us, honestly I wasn't sure what to think. Maybe he was just a nice and sweet guy, maybe I had not met the right type of men yet.

New lease on life, new outlook. I was supposed to be a changed woman.

"Now, as to why you are here. It is a simple courier job, not too much danger, payment to my partners." As he was speaking, two men brought a small chest in, small for a chest at any rate. It was about two foot high by two foot wide and three long. "You will take this a week north of here." He reached onto his desk and took a piece of parchment. "The location is marked on this map." He handed it to Rowan. "There you will meet my contact, and he will give you my merchandise which, of course, you will bring back to me. Now, I am sure you have questions."

Rowan looked at the map, then at him. I could feel her thinking. The fact that he was inviting question actually did make me feel better. Con men and smugglers do not like questions.

"Why all this for shipment of gems?" She spoke slowly, as always did when faced with something unknown. Rowan was a cautious woman.

"The town that has the mine is small and not well defended. On top of that, they wish to stay small. I think for religious reasons. However, they do want to sell their wares. A few years ago..." he started moving about the room, much more relaxed than he had been. "They found gems in what they had thought were worthless tin mines. Now as far as everyone is concerned, it still is. I was approached by them, they knew my family as the mine was originally owned by my grandfather, and one of many he sold to the towns they were in to keep our family afloat. I had the resources to pay them for that first shipment, and as they say, it has been very good for both of us."

Rowan nodded. "What is pay?"

"What you have there..." he sat down on his desk as he gestured to the chest. "...is a substantial amount of gold. As such, it entails some risk. I hire new adventures like yourself, looking to make a name because you are less likely to be noticed. To ensure that it is worth your time, I am going to pay you a Small Crown each." He had just offered us more money than we could make on the docks in three months.

He had my undivided attention.

"If you take the job, I do expect you to keep the details private. And if you make it back within two weeks, one for getting there. One for getting back, then I may, may…" he stressed "…have further job opportunities for you."

Five Small Crown for two weeks work. I was in.

Rowan nodded. "What will we be, should we be, bringing backs with us?"

"Two huge steel chests filled with what I hope is the next month of work for my artisans. I am not actually sure. It is the gems they have mined over the last two months, and it may be more." He was all smiles at this point, and with a mine paying out that, well he deserved to be.

Needless to say, we took the job. The rest of the day was spent getting what we needed together, among other things armor for both Rowan and Alabaster. Both of them got fitted for plate, a medium armor made for LeatherWings that was easily adjusted. The smith seemed happy to see us. I guess he gets just enough business from their race to justify making the base, but not enough to do it regularly as he only had three bases ready for fitting, two female and one male.

We also picked up a real cart. It would make hauling our load much easier. Ba'call wasn't happy until we agreed to buy a mule. I guess she was tired of dragging things.

Chapter 30

Alright, let me explain a few things. Everyone in a group like this has a *job*. Every job is the most important job in the group when that job is needed. No one had all the skills needed to do every job. It just isn't feasible, but trust me, it is a good idea for everyone to pick up a bit of everyone else's job when you do something like this.

Sliverleaf was in charge of things we needed to know before we needed to know them. At least that is how she puts it. She is also our toolbox. You know, the person that has the odds and ends we didn't know we needed? So, I guess she's right; it's her job to know things before we know we need to know them.

Ba'call is our scout, always on the lookout for the next problem, and always working on how to avoid it. Rule number one in adventuring life, avoid the trouble if you want to live. Of course, rule number two is the trouble *will* find you anyway. There is a reason why most adventurers die while still so young and pretty.

Alabaster is in charge of day-to-day health. In other words, making sure we don't get sick, or if we do, we get better. So basically he's a mother hen. Considering snakes and plagues roam the world, you will always need a good healer. Besides, it is nice to have someone that can stitch up a wound or set a bone.

Rowan is our cover. If things go badly, she covers us and tries to persuade the people or things trying to hurt us it is not a good idea. See, the way my mother used to put it, adventurers weren't heroes so much as small armies. A friend later told me they were something called a small tactical squad.

I am the person who tries to keep others from noticing us. No really, that is most of my job. In this case, we had a big heavy chest filled with gold, a wagon and a mule. I need to make it look like this was a perfectly ordinary wagon that would still have five adventurers going with it. If others got an idea that we had a chest with gold in it, they may decide they wanted it.

So I took and bought a bunch of furs, as well as feed for the mule. I kept it in the large sack it came in rather than buying a barrel or something for it. Not the best nor smartest move as wet feed can be very bad for an animal. So I bought a lot of it. Way more fodder than we would need for this trip, but it also meant we would always have good food for the animal. When it came time for packing up, the chest went in first, and then the feed went in, then all of our travel gear. I even bought us some new pots and pans.

By the time I was done, that cart looked like we were ready for anything we would encounter from here to Five Rivers. With us and this cart, two of us with new armor and all of us with new weapons, no one batted an eye when we left. We looked like a bunch of complete amateurs and fools that did not know how to pack.

In other words, we looked perfect.

As soon as we were out of the city, and past the farms that fed it, we used one of our greatest advantages. You see, GrassLords can't run, not on two legs anyway. But, when Ba'call hit all fours, she could more than keep up with the mule's trot. With Sliverleaf riding in the back with the equipment watching our rear and me driving the cart, it left Rowan and Alabaster to take to the skies.

Now rather than traveling at a walking pace as we had to before, we could travel at a trot. If it was a week to get there, we should make it with two days to spare.

Sliverleaf and I named the mule David. It seemed to fit him.

As the day turned into night, it found us setting up camp a little late. We could all tell that Alabaster had pushed himself hard to keep up with Rowan. The armor was obviously giving him problems. I took out some oils to help ease the pain. It was a mixture of pressed nut oil and a mint infusion. He came over to the fire, and I helped him strip out of steel and leather. As I peeled off his shirt I noticed the smell, a sickening aroma that he had not had to him just three days ago.

I bent my nose in close. Piper had once found an old pair of boots that actually fit her. She was so proud of them that she wore them every single day. About a week afterward, I took her swimming. She took off the boots.

This smelled like that.

"Alabaster, when was the last time you took a bath?"

He stopped for a moment and thought, not the best of signs. "It was that river we passed, shortly after the deer." He winced as he turned towards me. "No, just before we got into the city."

Rowan had taken note of things and was sliding over. "*Dinla, Das It'tu Nell Lon?*" I had picked up enough to understand what she was asking. *When was the last time he took the thing off?* At the question Alabaster looked away, avoiding her gaze.

Together we took it off of him going as slowly and gingerly as we could.

A pressure wound can be nasty. You get them when something is pressed into you for far too long. I had seen most of them with begging carts. That was the nice name for what those who were so lame they had no use of legs sat upon. A small plank of wood built up to a box with wheels so they could get around. The worst I had ever seen were the bed sores I had been shown when I had asked for room at the temple of Ba'teece when I was trying to find shelter from the cold. One look at what the healers there had to wade through was enough for me to think myself "quite good thank you". The sickness those healers helped people through was remarkable, but not all would recover.

Alabaster's ribs and breasts were not as bad as those bed sores thankfully. With the amount of filth on the wrap, he was lucky he wasn't sick. The worry on Rowan's face spoke more to him than any yelling I could do. So, I slapped him in the back of his head. It was something I had seen the cat do time and again and therefore knew it would get my point across.

"Al, some of these are bleeding. Not badly, but still." I was caught between anger that he had done this to himself, rage that he thought he needed to and pity that he felt he could not tell us. I also feared what drove him to do this.

Sliverleaf simply walked up and slapped him across the face. "Elven men all have breasts. It does not make them less of a man. Perhaps you have Elf blood in your veins. Your personal issues with your body are not my concern. You and we are at an agreement, we look out for each other, and our health is part of that. You told me this when you said you need to know if Elves were any different from the rest of humans. Now you have done this, even bought armor that will make it worse, and stand beside good Rowan to protect us. All the while this," She jabbed two stiff fingers into the tender flesh of his breast, something that would hurt normally, but was obviously agony for Alabaster at the moment.

"This you hid, even though it will slow you? This could kill us all." She turned on her heels, snatching up his breast plate. "This I will fix by morning. Your magics alone will only ease what you have done to yourself."

It was the most anything I had ever seen out of the elf at once. The three were so caught off guard by it Rowan had yet to react. Alabaster's pained expression also showed sorrow and a deep shame within it.

Ba'call slowly raised her gaze our way and locked eyes with him. "She's right healer, and the Empress would not be pleased." She then turned her head over towards where Sliv was setting up by the fire. The Elf was already casting magics to alter the metal to allow for the gifts of nature bestowed upon our dear Alabaster.

I slid over to Sliverleaf's side of the fire, giving Rowan and her brother time to talk as a family. As I sat down, she was working on the front plate of the armor. All this time, she had spent muttering and mumbling her little tunes, and now, I was getting to see her doing something.

As she spoke under her breath, she was tracing her finger back and forth on the inside of the plate. Each pass of her delicate finger left a faint blue trail that was only visible in the shadows cast by the fire light. As she worked, slowly the metal bowed outward stretching to make room for the comfort of its owner. She was not doing cups as I had seen the highborn lady of the town I grew up in do but instead bowing both sides out to make what I could only describe as a shelf. Between them in the middle of the plate she started forcing a ridge to grow outward. In other words, it was becoming functional armor for a woman's comfort, or in this case, our dear priest.

I settled in to watch her. It was fascinating to see something this powerful for the first time. I had seen her light the evening fire and had watched as she lit candles but this was literally re-molding metal. "How do you know how big to make them?"

She glanced my way and smiled. "I don't. He wore it all day. He may have been bound, but he was also in pain. As such he has imprinted himself on it. It knows how big; it will not let me make it wrong for him."

I frowned in confusion. "He had them tied down all day; won't that mess it up?"

She thought for a moment. I hope about the point I made, not how to explain things to a simpleton. "No, not really. His pain and what he is told the armor how big it needed to be." With that she bent her head back to work.

Rowan walked over to us. Her face showed the concern I felt. "His chest is bruised, as is the muscle underneath. Some of the spots are leaking blood." She stopped and took a deep breath. "This is not the first time." Sorrow filled her, "There are scars, some old. At least the cage of ribs is not misshapen." She glanced back at her sibling. "It should be okay, but it needs to air out. He will not be flyings for a whiles."

***

The next morning saw a slight rearranging of the cart. Sliver-leaf was still working on the plate while she was riding in back. It seemed by morning was too much of a promise as the girl had exhausted herself the night before. Now, after a good night sleep, she was back at it working diligently.

I took to riding on David so Alabaster could be seated on the cart. He was completely topless, and as such, the days light showed the old scarring, the fresh bruising and wounds in all of their gore. He assured me they were not as bad as they looked, and that he had already used some of his priestly magics to, as he put it "*...ensure no infection or scarring.*" He said it should work. It made me wonder how bad the last time was if he could keep the scarring down.

This was my first time seeing this side of him, seeing him naked from the waist up.

I had seen Rowan naked every morning since I had known her, and this morning I realized this was as bare as I had ever seen the man holding my collar. I felt a stab of inadequacy when I realized his were better than mine. It didn't seem fair that. Here I had what I was supposed to have, and he hated and covered his, and mine were the lesser of the two?

You ever get jealous of something someone else has, then realize it was a burden to them? Alabaster had hurt himself over this. I felt guilt wash within me and pool at the pit of my stomach. Watching him that day, I realized he was body shy, something I had never seen in his people. For his part, he looked miserable. His morning prayers had consisted of what looked like one huge rambling apology.

I looked back at him several times as we rode. As noon approached I finally worked up the nerve. "So, why...I mean, what is wrong with-" I stopped. I was stammering.

A dull chuckle came from deep within him. "I guess that is something." He shook his head. I don't think he was talking to me. "At least I can call them by name." He turned towards me fully. "Breasts, they are called breasts. They are given to all of us for the care and feeding of our young, and yes, mine will probably work just fine for that. Yes, they can also be quite nice at other times, or so I am told."

He sagged as if the sarcasm took the last of his will, if not his energy. He looked off into the distance as if seeking answers. "And to answer your question, nothing is wrong with them." He turned his head back, looked at the ground that past beneath his feat as the cart rolled on its way. "But I think something is wrong with me." The softness of his words broke my heart. It's not comfortable to watch someone else's heart bleed.

***

Night came and with it, camp. The night was alive with a thousand sounds; bird, bug, bat, lizard, and frog all seemed to finally believe spring had come. It was nice to sit by the fire and just listen to them, all of nature's creatures enjoying their new lease on life. Rowan and Bec were swapping sword blows using sticks as swords. Sliv had finally finished the armor and dived back in her book while Alabaster and I sat and talked.

"It is not a matter of me hating myself, though I can tell that is exactly what *Sittes* is worried about. They just get in the way of everything. At least down I don't feel like I have something pulling at me with every step or bump." He looked at me as if he was trying to convince me of how annoying that would be. I simply looked down at my own then back to him. "Right, sorry, but you do know what I mean then."

"Yes I do. I have had them for a while now. Trust me; you get used to it. Just like you got used to the pain of tying them down." His face flamed crimson as if I had struck a brand to oil.

"Al, Master..." being formal might help to make the point. "You wounded yourself for shame of having them. Even I can see that is not right. Your culture is not perfect; your friend Shatel is proof of that. Your culture sees nothing wrong with..."

I hesitated. His culture may not, but in a way I understood his pain. Every young man where I was from would have done the exact same thing he did. Considering that that was part of the problem. "You have breasts. Back home, if you were a young man of my town, hells, I would have agreed with you. None of the men I knew growing up would have done a thing differently. But as you have pointed out, that kind of thinking leads to people harming themselves and others very badly."

I watched the bitterness of my words turn his sweet face into a mask of internal pain. He could not even look at me. "Alabaster, you are you, and you can be no one else. You are kind and sweet. You are not-" I couldn't say it again, so I gestured "...those. You are your heart. Isn't that what you told me was most important, to be who you were in your heart?" Look, I have no problem cussing. I have no idea why I couldn't say *breast*. I could think the term, and others: tits, tatas, melons, but someone saying breast just felt wrong.

He sighed, and quietly, a voice not yet loud enough to be a whisper escaped his lips. "What does that mean? I am me, yes, but am I man? Am I woman? Both or neither?" His voice was rising with each word. "I am Empress Touched; I get to choose. But what do I choose?" As he spoke, he rose and started pacing, the quicker he moved and fidgeted, the louder his voice became. With the last few words he was shouting, at me. His breathing had become labored. Rowan rushed over and caught him as he collapsed. To be fair I was in shock; he had never yelled at me, not like that.

"His skin burns; we need water." I nodded and fled into the night to fetch it. Really.

It hiding my tears was a happy bonus.

Chapter 31

The water was a clear stream. A good half mile away, so it took time to take the bucket and go fetch it. While I was out it also gave me time to think.

When I had had met Alabaster, I was terrified. His gentle nature was punctuated by savagery. Over time, I realized that as a culture, they were more honest but less civilized. As I grew to know the culture, I realized that we, not they, had given up something very real and necessary for our "civilized" life. On this journey and seeing a different world, one where I fit, I had forgotten that it wasn't without flaws. In a culture that encourages you to be yourself, Alabaster had succumbed to the expectation he thought others had of him. True, he had done it on his terms, but he had hurt himself with his own childhood assumptions.

I myself had not been much different. I hated the world for hating me. I was poor, homeless, without parents, and helpless. For that, they laughed at me, ran me off, and ignored me. A few moments out of their day would have made my life so much better, and yet they did nothing. So, I started stealing. First, only what I needed to live. Then, anything I could get, so long as it was from the rich bastards who ignored me.

They didn't see me. They saw a pickpocket before I was one. They saw a waif who was a sign of where their way had failed. I made them uncomfortable. They didn't hate me; they didn't care enough to hate me.

I wasn't making them pay. I was just giving them the excuse to do what they did. I have come to understand that the Fifth Law covered every aspect of life. That everything was that type of cycle, and that even the LeatherWings and their Empire would become sick and die.

Their only advantage was the fact that they expected it, welcomed it, and welcomed the renewal of it. Their empire wasn't an empire. It was a series of city states, baronies and duchies, as well as small kingdoms and fiefdoms, all under the same Five Laws. They constantly attack and raided each other, not for territory, but to keep each other in check. It was a war of ideals on who could help out all of people of the lands better. Each kingdom would start growing, gaining dominance, becoming corrupt, and fall to the next idea. Each and every generation was taking from the past to build the future, as well as coming up with new uses for old ideas.

Alabaster was an example of how bad things still happened to good people. This time last year, I would have called him a fool for believing in a god that did this to him.

Now? I had come to understand that whether a god existed or not, whether they did this to him or not, that wasn't important. What was important is how I helped him. How he helped himself, and what we as family, all of us took from this.

Blaming a god was childish. If gods did actually exist, they had to have a better understanding of the world than I because they could see more of the world than I did. If they didn't exist, which I think is much more likely, then you are blaming thin air. Either way, who to blame for stuff like this isn't important. It *happens*. Always has and always will. I used to hate it. I used to think it was so unfair. Now I understand that if this stuff, this bad stuff did not happen, no one would ever do anything. I may not be grateful for this, but I wasn't going to waste my time being mad about or blaming something that no one could prove was even real.

I suddenly stopped moving. I had learned long ago that meant something. I turned my head and listened. Growing up in the city with all its noises I, like most people, thought of the countryside as quiet. No hustle, no bustle. My first night on the road, I learned that the forests and other wilds of the world were a city, several of them in fact. A city for insects, birds, and all other animals and they all had something to say. The wilds were as noisy as any city.

Only this one no longer was: no chirps, no whistles, no crunches. Most creatures moved at night to prevent other creatures from eating them, at least that was according to Ba'call. Now none of them were moving.

Predators could cause this. I had watched it happen from time to time, but the thing is some creatures don't recognize others as a predator. A cricket might shut up if the lynx was on top of him, but as soon as it moved away he would keep going. The chipmunk and spider squirrel would remain still for longer so as not to attract its attention. This forest just went dead quiet. As I stood there, it didn't start back up.

First I checked the skies. A few birds flew silently by. Good, not a drake or worse to deal with. I quickly crouched down. Quick movements attract the eye, but slow movement will leave you exposed to casual glance. A natural creature would take my quick movement as a sign to move. A sign that the prey was spooked. By moving quickly and holding still, most natural predators, the mindless ones, would move and look for the movement or perhaps try to chase it hoping for noise. Intelligent predators often doubted themselves. Thus the movement might register, but they would wait.

Nothing moved, no sound, no stirring.

Shit. That meant intelligent. So around here somewhere was a thinking enemy that I hadn't heard come up, that meant they were good at what they do.

Still, they didn't have me yet.

I started slowly circling around, moving more and more towards camp, towards backup and help. I got my bearings. I had been so lost in thought that I had almost made it all the way back to camp without noticing.

The quiet was all encompassing. No animal made a move or noise. It was so still I could make out the sounds of the fire before I got close enough to see its light through the brush. As I peered through the tangle of branches and leaves to get a look, I realized I would find no rescue from my friends. They had problems of their own.

Camp had been overrun by Orcs.

Chapter 32

I saw fifteen Orcs, all true bloods, silently moving through camp, going back and forth, checking things. They had not got to the cart yet. But they were methodically checking everything; sooner or later, they would. Alabaster was lying in the clearing by the fire, hands tied in front of him. The fever was doing more to incapacitate than the bindings. Rowan was kneeling, tied the same way, hands in front of her with an Orc on either side pointing spears at her. Sliverleaf had her hands wrapped in bandages holding onto sticks.

Not good. They had made her out as a caster. Ba'call looked as if someone had stolen her puppy as she lay hogtied not far from the rest. I couldn't blame her to be honest. The only wounds I was seeing on the Orcs were claw wounds and a single knife cut, nothing major. So they had to have taken the group completely by surprise.

Understandable considering I was watching them from less than twenty yards away, and they still weren't making enough sound for me to tell the difference from background forest noise.

They had been here long enough to secure the group but not long enough to finish the check for others. A full Orc raiding party was little better than scavengers; this methodical and non-lethal approach suggested somewhere there were half-bloods and that they were in charge. That didn't make them less dangerous. In fact, it made them more so, but it also made them more reasonable. So far, I had only seen full bloods.

As I watched, more came in, so it became a matter of the odds. Right now, I may be able to make enough of a distraction to get all of the Orcs here to chase me, as well as probably most of the ones coming. This as well as the way Orcs feel about LeatherWings would give Rowan enough time to use her claws on the rope and maybe get out. Neither she nor Alabaster were as well secured as the other two.

Two problems with that. One, the longer I waited the more there would be. Two, it meant running blindly through wood that the Orcs could see just fine through but that I couldn't and hoping for the best.

If the half-bloods could be dealt with, I might get us out of this without risking life and limb.

Do I risk killing us all for something that may not work and relies on the enemy being dumb? Or do I do something stupid that will probably not kill us and just get us taken prisoner?

"*Slacix*!" I screamed. Since most of us were prisoners anyway, what could be the harm?

"*Grilnix aH! Grilnix aH!*"

Okay, stepping out of cover into the waiting arms of Orcs isn't the scariest thing I have ever done, and if I could keep telling myself that I might get through this.

Knowing the Orc language also helped. "< *You are better/you are stronger/you are clever, I am yours.*>" Repeating my surrender as I walked up on them with my arms crossed across my chest felt so very wrong. I was hidden; they hadn't known I was there. I could have slipped off. I may have a few months ago, but these people had been more my family than anyone ever had been. Now for the opening move to this mental match. "*<Why have you taken my tribe; what have we done to come to your notice?>*"

The sounds I make as I speak are guttural. In some cases they sound almost familiar, and I couldn't help but spit when I spoke. This often lead people to believe Orcs were dumb. Don't get me wrong; they are. A smart Orc is about as mentally capable as a dumb human. However, they are something most humans aren't, cunning. The Orc language may not have as many words as others, but it is more how you say a word, and what words you pair it with. It is difficult to learn, or it was for me at any rate.

One of the brutes, a woman of about six and a half foot tall, who probably weighed close to three hundred pounds, looked at me with surprise. Good, I had found the leader of at least this party, and I had surprised her. I had once been told that surprising an Orc can be very good. Not jumping out and scaring them, that is a quick way to a grave. No, by doing something un-expected you can buy yourself some time while they try to figure out what is going on. I hoped Piper was right about her cousins.

She came forward, her brow was furrowed. Her chin came to rest upon her upper chest, thus protecting her neck. It sat lightly there. Then she spoke. "*<Clever girl chick speak to us, surrender to us. This her clan, her people. Devil Bats, here.>*" She gestured towards Rowan and Al, "*<They be yours or you be theirs?>*"

I lifted my neck and showed off my collar. For the token of my servitude, it was just that a token. Plain and simple, mostly leather with some silver wire weaved through it. The dagger he gave to me my first night could cut through it. She merely grunted. "*<Good owner or bad?>*"

In response, I pulled the dagger off my belt and showed her its edge. The fact that I had it was a sign that he trusted me with it, a sign that he didn't abuse me. She relaxed when she saw it was well taken care off.

"*<Which one is yours?>*" I pointed at Alabaster.

All of this was done slowly. Though I knew she would not react to the bare blade as a threat, fast movement could still get us into trouble. It helped that I could answer all of her questions without words. Too much talking would mean I was trying to fool her. "*<She sick. What were you doing while she sick?>*"

Alright, here it was going to get tricky. She understood I belonged to Alabaster but thought he was a she. Correcting her would mean she would prove me wrong, which meant she would strip him. Also with the fact that most Orc tribes viewed LeatherWings as liberators with one hurt, there was no guarantee how she would take things or what she thought was going on. After all, she had captured them.

"*<Water for the fever.>*" I held up the bucket skin from my side. It was filled with the cold run off of the melting snow.

"*<Why priest breasts cut up?>*" Her tone left nothing to imagine. She was not happy. I looked around. Most of the Orcs were in a protective posture around the two siblings. They had come up on the camp and took the two of them prisoners to protect them since they could not communicate. Rowan had probably made this very necessary, followed by Ba'call. The Orcs thought they were saving Alabaster.

"*< Priest was wearing battle bindings too long.>*" Sounded lame even to me. I just hoped if it couldn't run, it could at least hobble me across this finish line. "*< It cut into Priest, made sick. Priest did not tell us was hurt. Was worried about it hurting us.>*"

When in doubt, go with the truth. If they do not believe you, then you move to the lie. If they later find out you were telling the truth and they didn't believe it, you can turn it on them. If they believe the lie after the truth, they can rest easy seeing through your crap and accepting the truth.

"*<That hurt tribe, not help.>*" Her scowl was deep, and she was trying to understand how a priest, someone who should know better, could let this happen.

I shrugged, "*<Young.>*"

Chapter 33

As the rest of the band moved out of the woods, I finally got to catch a glimpse at their chief. He was large in a way only full-blood ever seem to be, but he was flanked on either side with what looked to be half-blood as his advisers. I found out they were the Blood Rock clan and had been in the slave pits for generations before they were freed. As such, they still very much felt indebted to the "Demon Bats".

A good portion of the tribe was half Orc, but only six of them spoke trade and that was only so they could work with the one or two merchants that didn't run when they saw them.

One of the Orc scouts had been out looking for a small band of adventures when he came across our camp. He was apparently ecstatic when he saw Rowan there. When he realized that one of the two was hurt, he went back to the scout group, a small party that goes ahead of the tribe to make sure they don't run across anyone and stay out of the way, for help.

They decided to rescue the two of them from the very "mad" Elf and cat. It appears Rowan and Ba'call had gotten into an argument after I left. They went in hard and took them all prisoners until it could be determined by the Shaman and Chief what exactly was going on.

In short, the Orcs meant well.

I learned all of this as the scout was explaining things to his Chief. Rowan was quite vocal for me to have them untied as soon as possible, so I missed why they were looking for people like us in the first place. I walked over to her once everything was okay.

After talking with them and explaining in more detail what had happen, their shaman looked Alabaster over himself. When he was satisfied that indeed things were as I had said, the others were released.

"Sorry about that. If I had said anything to you, they would have assumed we were plotting, or you were telling me what to say."

She glared at an Orc walking past us. "I didn't hears anything, neither did Bec. How can we have missed people this large being going about?"

I smiled. "From an early age, clans like this are taught to hide, to move without making a sound. They don't want to be captured again. The full bloods are always waiting on it, and the half-bloods know that in some places, people actually still want them locked up or worse just for being Orcs."

"I have seen Orc tribes move, they are normally loud." She shook her head as she looked around her; even now, they were a quiet people.

"That was either a war band or raiders. Full Orc tribes still live like they did beforehand. They raid and are noisy because...who is going to stop them? The half-bloods work very hard to keep them quiet like this. Otherwise, they would want to go to war with any people that treated them badly for fear of it happening again."

Ba'call bounced up with her normal cheer, despite having ripped one of her claws out in the fight. "So, what's going on? Why they attack us?"

"First, are you okay?" I gestured at her hand.

"This? No problem; the bud still in tack so it will grow back, but our claws really are too soft for serious use like that. I'll heal. Besides, their medicine woman is awesome! Now, wa' da' flock?"

"They were looking for help for something, and came in to rescue Al from you and Sliv, something about you fighting."

Rowan winced. "Al. Bec came over and tried to make Al feel better, tried talking to him. Al snapped and hit Bec. Sliv got between them, and we got Al to lie back down, but it was a near thing. He almost fainted."

I nodded. "The Shaman and Medicine Woman are working on it. We should know something soon."

In all honesty, we got off lucky. They caught on to Sliverleaf but bound her instead of breaking her fingers. Had Rowan and Alabaster not been with them, it could have gone a lot worse than it did. So we waited. We weren't prisoners anymore, but we were also surrounded by people whose leader wanted to ask us something. Sitting pretty was about the only option.

The Orcs went about what was apparently normal for them and set up camp; they just set it up around ours. Considering dawn was hours away, they were giving up travel time. This must be important.

Once everything was settled down, the Chief's main adviser walked up and addressed us in trade. He was a big man, mostly greenish brown, with greasy hair. "You, we need, we have problem." He stopped and considered what he had said. "We have unwanted guest. You take."

Rowan looked at him closely. "What kind of unwanted guest?" The caution was plain in her voice. I was proud at how much better her trade had gotten in the last few weeks.

"Holy man, tall, black hair." He was gesturing at just below his hair line. On the rest of us, that would have been over our heads. "He is good guy, but no can talk to him. He stumbled on us while at camp. Chief not want him talking and tracking us. But we talked Chief out of killing him. He do nothing wrong." The large half-breed actually looked uncomfortable, even embarrassed that he had to be asking this. Embarrassment is hard to read on an Orc, but I knew it when I saw it.

Ba'call cocked her head to the side. Her ears crept forward a little further, the slight hint of pink flashed from between her lips in the fire light. "What did he do?"

The Orc smiled. "Called chief's daughter ugly. Seems it is only Orc word he knows. Don't know if he knows what means." The big guy just shook his head. "But he knows it has effect; for first two days we had him he said to everyone that passed by…that be until he make little girl cry. Now he no talk. No eat. I not have any idea how long a he can live like that, but he not speak trade nor Orc, and we not have anyone who speak his tongue. After makin' Slow Cut cry, he just sits there." He sighed, and I could see he actually had a genuine worry for the man. I did the only thing I could.

"Bring him to us. If nothing else, we will talk to him." With Alabaster down sick, it looked like I had become the leader of the group. Rowan had made it clear from get go that she wasn't interested in it.

Ba'call was technically second, but that was because, as she put it, she wasn't a leader. She was the person making sure that the leader wasn't dumb. In that she hadn't done too well so far. I had a decent chance of speaking with him, at least a little bit. That is, if he was from around here somewhere. Being a thief has its advantages. I got to talk to a lot of different people.

Chapter 34

A tall well-built human man was brought before us. He was easily a head and shoulders taller than me. His black hair was well past his shoulders and down to mid back even with it being mostly knottcd. His eyes were the green of fresh chipped emeralds, and his features were those of someone with what the high born of my village called "good breeding". He and his hair were dirty. His britches were torn, and his white tunic was loose and not tied. From the look of him, I knew we had a slight problem.

A white shirt, one that had stayed that white even when dirty, meant wealth. Not being able to speak trade meant he was probably not high enough in the birth ranking to have to worry about him taking over the house yet too high for him to have to seek a second vocation. This was a man that should be on someone else's estate getting ready to be married off to some woman so he could get old and fat, not someone that should be anywhere near where he could wander into an Orc's camp.

He was not fat, not by a long shot. He had one of those bodies cut from doing too much exercise and not enough work. His shirt also bared a familiar crest, one that was a rampant deer on a blue shield, the house of Glon'glas.

As a House, the Glon'glas family wasn't what I would call the worst family in town. They were on the outs with most of the town due to their allegiance not to Ca'talls but to Pentagla, Goddess of dance and song.

Basically, for our dour little town, they raised a few too many eyebrows. They fell on hard times at the start of the war; all of their sons had been shipped off to the front. Apparently, they broke themselves ransoming some of their sons back.

I skipped trade and went straight to Highland. "Well, you look good for someone set for ransom."

His head snapped up, and he looked at me. A smile like a cool wind on a day too still, too hot, spread across his dirty face. It made his eyes dance as if flickering flame had been caught in them. "A lady if I ever heard one, and my savior to boot. If you would be taking me from these good people, much would I be in your debt." His voice was not what I would call smooth; there was a gravel in it not meant for one so young. It was a voice used to growling.

"Your family sold off all their lands to pay ransom for you and your brothers; you have nothing left but what is on your back. If you will answer me about why you called the child such a thing, I will see to your release." It might be minor, but I wanted to know why he had upset the girl, if he even knew what he called her.

"My father said it meant Orc in their own tongue. After I called the girl and ask for water...well, water she gave me, but not the kind I had asked for." His face fell; as I watched sorrow etch lines into it, it made me think a little better of him. "Obviously, my father was misinformed and as such misinformed me. I had no wish to make her or others cry again, so I did the only thing my lady could expect me to do. I shut my mouth." His voice lost some of its high-born grace as he spoke, and his contrition seem real.

"We'll take him." I said to the orcs that had brought him to us. With that our party grew.

Chapter 35

The Orcs were gone by the following morning, moving on in the night as quietly as they had come. They left us with a tended to but still somewhat sick and sore Alabaster and our new charge. Turns out Mister Blueblood had not only a horse but a full suit of steel armor. His weapons were left in our care. Those included both a true long bow as well as a sword that was the largest I had ever seen.

Its cross guard was six hand widths wide. From rain guard to pommel it could be gripped easily by two different people. The blade of the thing went from ground to his shoulders. Rowan was trying to explain to him both what we were doing, as well as what it meant or rather could mean that we had saved his life. Collaring was an offer, not something that was mandatory.

We found out his name was Arwen, and yes, his house was noble. According to him, that never meant much when it came to him. As the third born boy and having two sisters ahead of him, he talked of his life as if he had been mostly ignored. He was aware his family land was seized for back taxes and that the war had wiped his family out, but as he put it, "Pentagla always provides."

After he cleaned up, I was somewhat at a loss for words. His black hair shined and his eyes were too green to be real. He was tall and broad with arms that could most certainly swing that ridiculous sword of his with little trouble.

Last night, I had taken him for an idol Lord "Pretty Boy" due to his size, but those muscles gleamed under the sun and showed signs of real work not just the lifting of heavy weights again and again. The day brought an unfortunate golden glow to him making him almost look tan. It made looking at him difficult. Still, he was a Lord and would probably act so. He also did have a rather unfortunate amount of not so useful supplies, like separate soap for hair and body as well as creams for his skin.

We rearranged our cart for his Lordships extra baggage as well as to give Alabaster a good place to rest up. At least his fever had broken. I think it is good that Rowan is practicing her Highland by talking to the guy. It sounds like she is even trying to teach the fop Trade.

I personally believe it to be a waste of time. No way he was going to be staying with us. A man like him would be on his way as soon as we got to the next town.

As we got moving, Sliverleaf took to the driving of the cart, and I was stuck in the back with our healing priest. Looking after the bone head isn't an onerous task, not when he was awake, but the herbs the shaman gave us to give to him knocked him as cold as a sap to the back of his skull.

I wish I could say it was curiosity that got me started, or even greed, perhaps one day I could convince myself it was me wanting to keep my skill sharp. The truth of the matter is I was *bored*.

So I, my picks, and the lock on the chest started having a chat. It took me over an hour to pop it the first time, after that it became easier and easier.

When I got it down to being able to beat the lock in a few moments, I took to using different picks. I took my time and listened on and off to what Rowan and Sir Useless were talking about.

"So we aren't talking chains and whips, base labor and dehumanizing the person you own?" Arwen rode on his horse while Rowan walked beside him. If you read his face, it actually seemed like he was listening and open to the discussion.

"That all dependings on the Slave, not the Master. If you be one of the ones wanting such treatment and it can be done without breaking your spirit, yet to fulfills it, then yes, that can be done." Rowan was speaking to him very matter of fact. I knew how much trouble I had had with this concept to start with.

"Who would want that?" Arwen had a look of horror on his face. "That would break any spirit, let alone someone damaged enough in the mind to want such a thing."

"The leader of our clan for one. She spent seven years as such herself. Reveling in the freedom of having nothing to worry about and trusting her owner to do her no wrong. She did this from the ages of nineteen winters till she was twenty-six winters. She once told me that had her mother not died in battle, she would have done it for seven more." Her words held no anger, only instruction. With the pulling out of Vela was to show that strength was needed for such endeavors, at least to me.

"Your clan leader did this and now rules? I find it hard to believe such a person could endure treatment of that nature and not be changed by it. As for the trust needed in such thing? How could you be sure that her mind was not broken?"

Rowan laughed, "You have never met Vela. The only thing broken on her during that time was her maiden hood. As for trust, yes, it takes a lot of trust for such things, but also all slaves keep weapons. A slave without a visible weapon or for who is not seen often enough warrants investigation by the tribe."

The knight frowned, "She was high born and meant to rule. I am assuming you watched her closer than normal. I know her family had to." To be fair, I had assumed the same things when I was introduced to this.

"She is of the blood of the Empress, yes. Her blood means little. More disposed in mind to rule perhaps, but ability is not guaranteed with blood. As to watching her any more or less closely...why would we? The lowest of slaves' blood is still a person who may one day be better than your equal in something's. They may one day hold your collar. To turn a blind eye to mistreatment or improper training may well have your neck in a noose rather than a collar."

"Ah, enlightened self-interest, the hallmark of the selfish." He said this with an air of self-righteousness that was about to get my blade in his throat.

I can make the shot from here. Really, I could.

"When teaching the basics of morality to those who believe differently from you, always approach it from this avenue first. To do otherwise is to have those who do not understand morality argue with you over the finer details and reach the self-interest conclusion and assume you were hiding it from them." Rowan said this with a smile as she watched him struggle with the idea.

"That doesn't seem right, good and just. Altruism often has no self-interest reward. If you sell your morality based on self-interest, you will only get those that use your ways to further selfish ends." He was explaining this as if to a small child. To his credit, he wasn't doing the whole "I'm right and your wrong" thing yet.

Give it time.

"To those with a good heart, you need not explain a morality system's higher calling; to those with a selfish heart, they must come to it themselves. Now, you have seen the selfish; look at how we look after people to ensure they are not harmed. What is the unselfish reason?"

"I can think of none. The treatment of any being as less than a person is wrong. Slavery is outlawed in civilized lands because the potential for abuse is inherent in the system. You merely get around this by putting everyone's head on the block and blunting the ax. But a blunt ax will still sever heads. A truly good man will help end suffering; your system seems to create it, to make suffering a virtue." His face said he was serious, and I have to say, I could not disagree with him, but suffering was a part of life. Only fools thought that was ever going to change.

"Do not your gods deem suffering is from mankind's sins?"

"Ca'talls says so, but All Father to my knowledge does not. My Goddess says that suffering is a stain upon the soul that is erased by forgiveness and learning. Suffering one day will be gone out of the hearts of men as men make each other suffer no more." He told the empty promises of his goddess with the same reverence it was probably told to him.

That he could believe such things, him, an adult that had been to war, someone that has seen the sick houses, that was what was truly dangerous. Not the LeatherWing way of looking at things. Their "way" just used the system already in place to try to do some good, with all the crap stripped off.

"A noble pursuit, to be sure, and an interesting goal if achieved. Suffering does not just come from the hands of man. Bad weather, sickness and other such things, how does that fit with your ideas?"

"Storms are part of nature, and if man's heart was clear, he would help his fellow man when it came. As for sickness? Acimdesy and her followers spend a great deal of time and have stained many hearts wreaking havoc on their fellow man."

"All the answers you have. And a heart that has made up its mind, that knows the truth, can never be wrong. What have I to teach you then?" Rowan looked out over the landscape of trees and grass and closed her eyes. She breathed deep the smells of the world around her. "One day, if your world is reached, then no fox will hunt a rabbit; no ox will have to till a field. What think you of what will happen to those rabbits?"

"They will be fat and happy living once again as intended." He was so smug and happy with this. I had to fight not to choke on my own laughter.

"Have you ever been seeing a rabbit population that did not have predators enough? Not ones in hutches, but ones in wilds?" She asked it gently. I knew the teeth of this trap, and I waited for the click of the spring.

"Well no, but I imagine their lives all the better for it." Doubt crept into his words.

Rowan turned to him and smiled. "You would be wrong. First they eat, then they breed, then they eat some more. Soon, they are too many rabbits and not enough food. Did you know a hungry rabbit will eat its own? Their screams are most disturbing as they hunt their own kind for food."

He slouched in his saddle. "Rabbits aren't men. We can and should do better. That is the way of good. Good does better."

"How many good men have you found in your life? You say men are better than rabbits, but ask yourself this. You had food aplenty, as did others of your rank. And yet in a place where you threw food away for it had gone uneaten and spoiled, that woman starved to death or nearly so in your own streets." She took a breath and as she did, he interrupted.

"We always took our extras to the houses of those with less. I was raised to do this, and will raise my children to do such. Wealth and power means a burden for you to help those that have it not."

"True, and before me, I see a good if naive man. But how many others of your fat, fed, and breeding rabbits did this? How many will do it now that you have fallen on hard times for going against the will of Ca'talls? Chloe has taught me that Ca'talls says feed the poor, but also says that the poor did something to deserve their fate."

"That is not within his holy writ. It may be a common teaching where she and I are from, but no writ I have read on Ca'talls has that the poor are poor due to 'place'. Ca'talls calls each man to elevate the man below him." His tone was somber and surprised me. My entire life, I had been taught that being poor *was* my place. Now here a follower of the goddess of wine and drinking was saying it wasn't. More importantly, he *read* the holy writ.

Looking at him, I would not have guessed it. I sat up with the lock still in my hand and bumped the lid open when I did.

"You're a priest."

Of course that revelation paled in comparison to sand leaking out of the chest I had just bumped partially open. A chest filled, we were told with gold.

Chapter 36

Sand, the box was full of sand. Well, at least that is what leaked out. I looked down at it, and I wasn't the only one. Alabaster's eyes were opened. He too was looking at it. He had probably been watching me tinker with the lock for some time. Some of the sand had leaked down onto the floor.

Arwen continued not realizing the implications. "Champion actually. A full knight of my Lady." He rode over to look at the box as well. "You seem to be losing some of your cargo."

"*Gold*. The box is supposed to have gold in it. We were paid to transport gold." Shock rocked through me. This was bad. Really bad. I opened the lid, and sure enough, it was full of more loose sand and a single leather folio.

"If it contained gold, why did you open it? It was locked last I saw." Despite his admonishment, he too was running a mailed hand through the sand.

"I was practicing. I bumped it open."

"I am glad you did," Alabaster said as he sat up. "I think we've been had.

"How much were you paid for this job?" Arwen looked at Alabaster to be sure he was okay; at least, I hope that was the concern on his face.

"A small crown each." He reached in and took the only thing that might be of value in the dirt. He sat up and brought the ledger to himself and opened it. He leafed through the papers, one at a time. His face grew confused at first, then grim, finally angry.

"Slaves. It is vouchers for slaves." He was quiet as he leafed through the documents. "Two hundred of them." His voice rose with the number. He was getting close to the creature that I saw the night I told him about my past. He rose up, putting his free hand on the wagons rail to steady himself.

Arwen reach out a hand and steadied him.

"Easy girl; you're not yet well." His concern was evident on his face. For all that he was a high born, I could see why he chose champion. "Besides, doesn't your ilk keep slaves?" A fair question, but he would have had it safer sticking his hand into a fire.

Alabaster turned a gaze on him that I knew too well. A gaze filled with total savagery, yet a savage that had complete control and reason. The words from his throat were low, barely a whisper. He delivered his words with a slow procession of one sound to the next. Somehow that made it far worse than a yell.

"We don't sell them. They are people, and they are our most prized possession. They are how we learn, grow, and become more than we were before, more than before we owned them. It is a sacred bond and duty, one that allows us to grow, and help others to do so. If the slave wishes it may be rented, they may even be traded back and forth only to come home again. And maybe, maybe if they really wish it and you trust the new owner, you give them away. But you *never sell them.*"

The last words were spoken through bared teeth. Saliva slowly dripped out from between the gaps in his fangs. His beastly grin bared for the entire world as if he was a skull with no lips. His head tilted down much like a bull challenging a new arrival in his kingdom. His voice dropped a notch to deepen into a growl. "They are not cattle."

Arwen had pulled back, his face calm. A single eyebrow raised. "You," he paused looking over Alabaster from his face down. His eyes settled upon the Priest's chest. "Are not a woman."

The white, my owner, stopped moving for a second and blinked. Then his face relaxed. Slowly humor returned to it. Finally he let loose a small chuckle. Shaking his head he turned fully to look at our newest party member.

"No, I am not." He sat down on the chest itself. "I am Alabaster, Priest of The Empress, and Empress touched." He looked at the guy. "That means I was born with a females color and some of the attributes a woman has."

Arwen seem to take it and nodded his head. "It means you have tits." I nearly choked. I had never heard a high born speak so crassly. "Do you have a hole as well? I had a cousin like that, had all the tackle of both."

The White blinked. He had been set to take offense to the question; I think the cousin threw him off course. "No, the blessing is not that complete." He cocked his head to the side as he often did when confused. "What happened to your cousin?"

"She was a wonderful girl, but was a bit of an embarrassment to my Aunt. Aunt Nadia was at her wits end. Gave the child a girl's name and raised her as a proper lady in hopes that she could be handmaiden to some Lady and remain a maid her whole life. Kath had other plans apparently. She showed everyone in the family as well as the servants how different she was once she figured it out. My first look at what made a woman different from a man came from Kath."

"So as soon as she was old enough, Aunt Nadia sent her off to one of the temples. She would not tell us which one. She said, 'the gods made it so that she could not be a man, despite giving her a man's septet to rule, and could not be a woman despite giving her the well of life. Since the god messed up her body, and I can do nothing with her mind, let the gods have her back.'" His eyes took on a faraway look of pain. "It was a shame really." He looked at Alabaster. "That child was the sweetest person I ever knew: kind, loving, open, and honest. Beaten almost daily, and never once did it dull her spirit."

"How long ago was this?" My curiosity was piqued.

"Oh? Nine years ago, she was older than me by a year or two. Sent off when she was nine. She would be seventeen now. So I guess eight years." He turned and looked at Alabaster. "Had she been born into your ways, what would have happened to her? Gone to your Empress, I would guess? A life of serving the gods?"

Alabaster pursed his lips. "First off, they would have been raised with the ability to pick for themselves whether to live as a boy, girl or both. Second, they could have become anything they wanted. I chose to be male, and I chose to be a priest."

"Personally," he cocked his head looking into Alabaster's eyes, "I think the Priesthood is right for you, but I think perhaps you are more a girl than you pretend to be." He nodded as if this was a great wisdom.

Confused by his statement, I chimed in for clarification. "You noticed he wasn't a woman just a few moments ago."

He looked at me and smiled "I said he wasn't a woman. And I just said he was more girl than he currently claims." He turned and looked at Rowan "On behalf of my cousin, I accept your offer. Teach me a better way to handle those different, those touched by the gods. Show me a new way to see the problem. And I will see if we can find a better word than slave for what you do, for what you do is not slavery."

Chapter 37

I searched the rest of the chest; I found there were three more folios like the first in it buried deeper in the sand. Slavery was illegal in most places of which I had heard. Slave documents were also recognized in a lot of cities including the one in which I grew up. You couldn't buy them, or sell them, but if you owned one and bought it in a place it was legal then the slave was still yours. Between the four sets of documents, we held the lives of nearly one thousand people. We rode on continuing to our destination with no idea what to do.

Alabaster had me going over things, and I believed I had come up with something. "These are pick-up papers. Yes, they are letters of ownership, but they are also what you need to pick them up from the slavers. Look here," I got up in the seat beside Sliverleaf. Arwen rode over and Alabaster looked over my shoulder. "Here, that is the symbol for lake, and that for west. Anyone know a lake to the west of us? The fresh sea is a completely different symbol. Besides, the Sea is to the north, and this is to the south and west."

Ba'call called back to us. "Dragon Breath Lake, it is a bit of a well-known place."

Well known places make good meeting spots, but they made poor ones for this kind of stuff. "No good; too many people. A thousand slaves would be noticed."

"Not at Dragon Breath. It is known, but the fumes from the lake can be deadly, and it occasionally catches on fire."

Sounded like one of the places where the ground gas leaks up. Maybe even black tar. "Yeah, that would work. How far is it?"

Arwen spoke up. "Excuse me, why does it matter? Are you not under contract?"

Rowan's voice came out more than a little gruff. "Law is to protect the good, not for the wicked to stay behind. It should offer no protection to those that grind others into the dirt." She had not really had a chance to bring him completely up on the Five Laws. While she was annoyed by what he said, I was confused. Pentagla wasn't exactly known for being that big on the law of the land. She was big on doing the right thing even if it meant going to jail. Then it hit me. He was a champion, a Paladin. I felt myself smile. He was testing his new group.

Boy was he in for a shock.

"So what then do you think we should do about this?" His question may have been a test, but it was also a good one. Hells, I was about to ask it.

Alabaster's answer made me want to hug him. "Deliver the documents and see who they are going to. See what we can find out about them, where and who they are. Then we take them into custody. Once that is done, we go free the slaves, taking them back with us to the nearest city, and some of them back to Cliffport. Once the slavers are in custody, we bring down the man that gave us this job." He was matter of fact and calm, but his voice was the same whisper he used when he didn't trust himself not to scream.

"What good is that going to do? The papers are from Galvestone. Slavery is very legal in Galvestone."

"Cliffport is ours and governed in base by the Laws of the Empire of the Five. This is wrong. The man who is behind this must answer for his part in it." The glare he was giving Arwen said that his patience with the man was running out.

"Most kingdoms are smart enough to know alienating such a large trade partner as Galvestone is not a good idea." Arwen kept riding his horse, seemingly oblivious to Alabaster's scowl.

"The Five do not care about such things. Wrong is wrong. We will bleed, and we will die to the last to stop those that hide behind the ways of terror." The growl at the back of his throat told me he was thinking Unstoma.

Arwen simply bowed his head. "Then the Lady of Joy and Dance has put my feet where I am to walk. I was wondering if this was my path or merely the gateway to it." He smiled back at the priest. "I had to be sure. I needed to know which of the rumors of your people was to be believed."

***

As we road on, I repacked the trunk with its documents secured elsewhere. Rowan started telling Arwen about the Five Laws. I have to say once he got it, he seemed happy despite the severity of the punishment. From what I heard, he asked decent questions.

I made sure Alabaster as well as everyone else ate as we kept moving. The rolling landscape was a wash of greens and browns that slowly dulled to the gray of sameness in my mind. Each tree may have been its own work of art, but to me, it all became a blur. Breaking out of the wood didn't really help as it gave way to shrub and grasslands we had so recently left.

I am not sure which I prefer for traveling to be honest. Yes, traveling in the wood meant shade was to be found unless it was dead noon. You also had only one real way to take a wagon. The wind was both blessing and curse on the grass plains. A blessing because it could and often did cool you off. Curse because it also blew seed, dust and other light things at you. As day rolled into night, the cloying warmth of the day would not abate and seemed to even become worse as it seeps its way into every crack and fold of my body.

That night's watch was for me a draining experience. My armor kept the heat close to me, and the wind was not strong enough to even stir the green shoots of this year's grass. My own sweat sat upon my skin, acting as yet one more thing to trap the heat. Don't get me wrong. It wasn't hot, not like height of summer heat. No, this was due to the still. If you've never been this kind of hot, I hope you never are. Moving does nothing nor does sitting still. The only cure I have ever found is to strip or find water to sit in. To think, just a few days ago and not that much further south there had still been some snow on the ground.

I was sitting there and wishing for water so hard I imagined I could actually hear it. Those trickles of sound, the gurgle, and cool *tinkle* of it running over the rocks. That heavenly sound of cool water, that sound just below a noise. Wistfully I inhaled deeply.

I could smell it. I blinked. I could smell water. I never realized water had a smell but it does. You can't describe it. It is just something deep in your mind, perhaps your very spirit that recognizes it. It was close. There was not a stream or river near here. We had checked. Water supplies weren't getting low, but with a horse added, water became even more important. If you are ever traveling, water is better to find than gold.

I got up and started searching around for it. The sound wasn't my imagination, I could hear it more clearly now. And it was definitely moving water. How could we miss a stream? If I could smell it surely Ba'call could as well.

As I searched, I looked at it logically. It was late; it was hot, and I was hyper focused on water. It must have triggered something in me to become more sensitive to it. Also, thaw was still happening in the mountains; it could be a seasonal stream, and its water was just now getting to us, to here.

Thing about logic? Sometimes all it is good for is being wrong with authority. I hope that I can describe the next series of events in something that might make sense. Had I not been there, I would never believe something like this could happen.

At the edge of camp, I spotted it. A small wave, a wave of water on dry land. It glistened in the fire light as it came towards us. It was about a foot, maybe a foot and a half high, and about six times as wide. It was also headed straight towards our supplies. It moved as fast as any other wave, moved just like any other wave; it just had no business being on dry land. Something about it offended me in ways I can't describe, and it moved like an animal going for food.

I yelled out and jumped in front of it.

Its crest rose as it gathered itself together coming up to meet me face to face. It had a face. Its "mouth" opened to reveal fangs glistering in the moon and fire light. The water that made this thing was clear; I could only really see it by the refractions of the light as they passed through it. That was the last thing I really got to understand as it slammed into me.

Go up somewhere high, jump off and do a belly flop into a deep enough pool. Go on, I will wait. That crap hurts, doesn't it? It took my breath away, then it filled that empty space with itself.

The ache and burn of your lungs wanting air is nothing to the scalding pain of having them filled with fluid. Having it forced into my mouth, down my throat and into my windpipe is a violation beyond pain. It filled my lungs, pushing against them, forcing them past my deepest breath. Then just as suddenly, I felt it pulling itself back out of me. Slithering out of my nose and mouth. Air rushed in as my body fought to undo the damage.

Upon the exhale of that sweet breath, I screamed. My sword, all two foot of blade, had found its way into my hand as if conjured there. I lashed out blindly at the creature in front of me. My blade bit into it and passed through it, sweeping the surface of the thing as if I had just thrust it into any pool. As I adjusted the grip and sliced, I removed some of its mass, flinging some of it off my blade as if it was blood being flicked off the steel.

It answered my scream of terror with a scream of rage and pain. I had hurt it.

Blue balls of light, no bigger than pebbles flashed out of the darkness and hit the thing at its center; a hiss of steam the only sound to be heard. The thing twisted in place without moving and looked over to the source of the magic.

Sliverleaf, naked, one hand still glowing blue stood at the other end of camp. Her voice roared with the sing song words, *"Cav'la*

Die hidra. Yon Thelnla. Ioll wantata. Tonight, you go back to the energy that spawned you, thing against nature's order."

It charged for her, flowing over obstacles as if they weren't there. Suddenly, Arwen, clothed in only trousers, swung his sword with its blade turned sideways at the creature. Water was slapped out from it once again. Yet still, it hit the elf like the crest of a flood, knocking her flat against the dry ground. Dust rose up and settled on the intruder.

It had left some of itself on me after its attack. That water cooled me as I rushed for it. The dust made it easier to see. I stabbed at it, pulling my dagger as I ran I plunged it and my short sword into the thing as quickly as I could. I may not have been doing much, but I was someone else for it to attack. Working as a team might not save us, but then again, Sliverleaf was doing something again, and that caught the things attention.

I needed it to focus on anyone but her, "Hey drip! I make most guys at least buy me dinner before I let them force themselves on me. We ain't done dancing."

I got a mouth. It tends to say stupid things when I am scared. It must have understood me; it turned away from Sliverleaf and went after me again.

Ba'call helped the elf up and saw to her while I kept it focused on me. Rowan had grabbed a flaming stick from the fire; she shoved the brand into it. We were rewarded with another hiss of steam.

Alabaster brought his sword to bear. The fire showed a fierce joy painted on his features. The flickering making him look feral as well as enraptured by this. The three of us kept the thing busy while Arwen and Ba'call got Sliverleaf back to her feet.

As soon as this was done, Arwen helped us corral the thing and started trying to steer it into the fire. Don't get me wrong, this much water would put the fire out completely, but it might hurt the thing more.

Alabaster yelled across the thing to me. "Cutting of water seems to hurt it. Is that right?"

I dodged out of the things grasp but felt what seemed like claws on my arm tearing at me. "Seems so, but it leaves me wet every time it touches me, so not sure how much we are actual accomplishing."

"I bladed it, but it didn't seem to notice any more than many of my other strikes. We hurt it; it bleeds water, but it does seem to bleed." Arwen was trying to flank it, but with every move, the things face simply shifted from one of us to the other by flowing through its own body. It could keep up with all of us at once.

Rowan's stick had gone out after the first hit, but her sword was still by her bed. She grabbed the brand as if it was a club, lashing out at it whenever it made a swipe at her. "It looked like it tried to drown you to start with."

"It did, but it didn't stay in me long. I don't think it can. And I don't think it can do that unless it gets a hold of you." I was panting, still not yet recovered from that first attack, and now it had me bleeding.

A ball of flame hit it from outside our circle; we were rewarded with a roar. This was the most magic I had seen our Mage throw around, and it was taking its toll on her. That or she was more badly hurt than I thought. Ba'call was standing between her and the water beast in case it broke our line. She called out to us. "Sliv says all we have to do is wear out its magics, most of which it is using to keep itself together. Keep hitting it, and it will keep using its magics to keep itself whole."

Keeping itself *whole*.

I got an idea. I stopped trying to damage it and just started hitting it as many times as I could. I wasn't going for vitals; it had none, but you can sacrifice precision for speed. Against a live foe, what I was doing would hardly hurt at all. Against this thing, it seemed to hurt a lot. It ignored the rest of them and started focusing solely on me.

Finally Sliverleaf screamed "*MOVE!*" at the top of her lungs. I rolled left and ran as soon as my feet hit the ground. I didn't look back. The sound behind me was a crackling as if the fire had been stoked to unbelievable levels; its heat reached my back and drove me forward. A sound, part the hiss of steam, part the scream of the things pain assaulted my ears at the same time. It stopped before my body hit the dirt.

I looked back, a blackened circle had scorched the ground, and the blast wave for the spell had blown all of us off our feet. I had been the only one in the radius of the spell with the thing; it had been following me. Looking over I asked, "What was that?"

Panting Sliverleaf looked over and said, "Burst. It is a fire spell that causes a small exploding ring of fire to be conjured into being. It is very hot and very short lived. It displaces a lot of air. It is only a few feet in height, but it is very wide."

Great, I nearly got drowned and blown up in less than ten minutes. Funnily though, I wasn't as hot anymore.

Chapter 38

The morning sun found my skull easy to beat upon. It felt like the worst morning after a night of too much drink I had ever had. I didn't remember going to sleep last night. I certainly didn't remember getting out of my armor.

Looking around, I was in my tent in my bed roll. I looked under the blanket...yep not a stitch.

Alabaster.

I tried to remember what happened last night. It hit me, so did the cold sweat. I had been in fights before. If you have you know, "*don't freeze*" isn't just a saying; it keeps you alive. I didn't freeze last night. I was still alive. Now that I'm safe and secure with people I trust at my back, I could allow myself to feel it. The terror I had felt as the water pushed itself into my lungs. They still burned. The coughing that was wracking my body didn't help. I could still feel the wet feeling slithering against my skin. My body wracked with a shudder.

I must have cried out. Alabaster was suddenly at the open flap, blocking the morning sun from my face. He came over to me and simply wrapped himself around me.

I cried.

I have no idea how long he held and rocked me like that. I do know that when I finally came out of the tent dressed for the day, everyone else had already broken their nightly fast. Thankfully, the stew wasn't cold, and the broth felt good on my tongue and throat. Looking around the camp, I wasn't the only one shaken by the fight with the creature last night. Sliverleaf too was huddled up, still wrapped in a blanket despite the realness of the day's heat that had already started its arduous climb.

I nodded at her, and she at me. The creature had violated us both with its full embrace. We knew each other's pain and as such knew we could not truly speak of it, even to each other. Not yet. That knowing...it freed us to share the knowledge of that pain in a glance. A conversation of understanding that had no words and never would.

We broke eye contact, and found something else, anything else on which our eyes to focus. That contact was both blessing and curse. It would help us heal, but was salt into wounds bleeding still.

Arwen walked up beside me as I ate, kneeling down and staring at the dying embers of the watch fire he let out a long sigh. "These people seem like a good lot one moment and the next..." He shook his head.

I knew what he meant. So much of my life before was so very out of focus now. Like some dream, no, a nightmare I had woken up from. I realize it now, that dream was the daily shuffle, the never ending sleep of daily life, of doing as you should, instead of living.

"Then they say something like 'cracking the skulls of my enemy between my bare hands' or they do something and starkly remind you that they aren't human. Like an odd gesture or some such. Sometimes I swear that when I am talking to Alabaster, that he has the same mannerisms as a hunting dog."

He thought about it for a moment, "Rowan is like a great hunting cat."

"The way she tilts her head, pulls her lips away from her teeth when… she does it when she is happy I think, but I would not call that a smile. Smile is far too polite and not nearly so primal."

"We were told they were monsters, that they weren't civilized," he sighed as he watched the last of the coals grow cold. "I was always told that they were devils."

I looked over to where Alabaster was feeding David. So very gentle, and the animal didn't shy away at all. "So what this time?" I turned back and looked him in those incredible eyes of his.

"Not much, just they seem to have a philosophy of life that plays to all of the worst of instinct. They don't bother to control their tempers or lusts. At best, they are mercurial, and at worst they are monstrously violent." He eyed the two of them as they packed up camp.

I looked up at the sky, then at him. How did I explain what I had seen, what he would see eventually? Did I have the right? Considering the trouncing I gave Vela on something similar, I didn't feel I had a choice.

"Tell me about it. Their way of doing things is good, but they need a little civilizing." I let out a small chuckle. I had never used this type of argument. I hope it worked. "Teach them how and when to say their piece, when it's better to just roll over and take the insult. That community and the 'proper way' to behave is more important. Teach them how to act to be taken seriously when needed. At best, right now, they come off as children, at worst they are ignorant of any true civilization."

The man's face blossomed with excitement. "Exactly. Think about it. Their way of doing things is to learn from us as much as we learn from them." He looked giddy as he tried to keep his voice low and his excitement controlled. "We might have a real cultural revolution on our hands. They put the welfare of others above their own. They don't judge. Almost everything I was ever taught that my Lady wanted us to do they do as a matter of course as a people."

"Yes, they don't care who you are or what you have done as long as what you are doing is trying to help someone else. It is as if they found a wounded man on the road, they would stop to help him and never think of their own safety, or what someone else would think of them." I waited. He would either get it, or not. If he got it, then good for him. If not, then a lesson I learned from that Red Priest would come in handy.

His grin told me he had completely missed it. "Precisely." He slumped down and smiled to the heavens. It was if he had finally found something he had looked for all his life.

"Too bad you want to get them to care." I sipped my water. It is interesting watching someone's mind try to catch up with basic logic. "You want to get them to care what others think. As soon as you do that, well then, I guess they will stop helping people on the side of the road just because it is the right thing to do. They will be too busy being worried about what people will think of them as is proper. Fitting into civilized society is one of the most important things in life."

He jumped up and looked at me; his expression was the same as that of a landed fish. "Now, that is not what I said. I was talking about how they are promiscuous. If there is a child, how do they even know whose it is?" His words carried. Everyone was looking.

"They don't care. It is a child; they love it. They don't put conditions on that love. Not for the child, not for me, not for you, not for a stranger they have never met." My voice was soft.

"What about lines, lineages?"

"Counted through the mother, but again it doesn't matter. If the child is good at and shows an interest in something, they are allowed and encouraged to pursue it."

"But, what about marriage, and the sanctity of it? The union ordained by the gods, blessed by them."

I let out a long sigh. I had seen this. I had asked this. I didn't have the patience that the people that had taken me in did. Not yet anyway.

"You mean with them being woman centric? How do you tell who the father is? So that the father can be useful, needed? Because we were always taught that the man wasn't wanted, he was needed. The simple truth is they don't need men. They *want* them. They enjoy them as friends, lovers, brothers, husbands, and so much more. You don't need to be needed. You are loved here. They simply love. You don't have to pretend to be important, and they certainly won't pretend to be. They will live, love and grow." I got up and stormed off. I don't know why but he got to me.

I looked back over my shoulder. Don't ask why. I'm not even sure. It was just a glance, a moment. Was I still in need of approval? I may have started to come to realize that if you spend your life looking for it from others, you will never know yourself.

First, we seek approval from our parents. They, Mom, and Dad were the true gods of a child's early life and as such we crave their blessing. Then we look for it from friends, and finally from society.

Was I still seeking approval?

Yes, I was, but I was starting to choose whose approval I sought. Now I looked for it from people that actually mattered to me.

Rowan was looking at Arwen with a slight smile and a shaking of her head. Alabaster seemed confused. Sliverleaf was disgusted but not with me. Ba'call was looking dead at me; she smiled and nodded. I felt better. I may have lost my temper, but I felt better. I was starting to let go of the expectations of people I had never met.

Chapter 39

David plodded steady and true towards our date with the person who was to give us uncut gems in return for slave labor. It was no wonder that Shale was able to make so much money so fast. He was buying all of his material with slaves; the same slaves that were undoubtedly cutting the gems from the rock of the world for him. He had a work force that had slipped below the notice of others in a mine no one knew about.

Now though, we knew about it. We knew about the slaves, the mines, and the whole thing. If we just went back to Cliffport with what evidence we had, we might never find out where they were. There was a chance that no one would. So, we deliver the chest and make the person picking it up tell us where it was. Then we were going to the pickup point for the slaves and free them. Once that was done, we would free the ones already toiling away in that dreadful place. If we were lucky, we would not only shut down the mines and Corbin Shale's dirty little business but also a slave ring.

Arwen asked if there was a reward for doing this. When Rowan said yes, that doing it was the reward, he actually seemed to be a little happier. They hadn't really spoken since his little talk with me this morning.

Granted, I agreed with them. If no one ever knows who we are, if they never knew we did this, that I'm fine with. Alabaster would prefer it that way.

But if there *is* a reward? I intended to make sure it isn't turned down. I would want some of it to go to the freed people, but we too have to eat, equip ourselves, and have enough to make sure we can do things like this again. A real rescue mission? Not a bad start for a bunch of kids just starting out together.

Arwen rode up beside me on the cart. His smile was weak. It made him look like the boy he had proven himself to be. "About this morn...I was wrong. I sounded like-" He trailed off, so I finished for him.

"You sounded like a champion of Ca'talls. I am sure your Lady would be so proud of you." Ba'call jumped up onto the back of the cart and dusted the road grit off of her hands. Seemed we were going to have a spectator for round two of this.

Arwen had the mind to take the sting I had given him. For the followers of Ca'talls, appearance was everything. His church worked hard to loosen some of the more stupid restrictions placed on the town.

"I deserved that. I've spent my life learning how to fight the lies coming out of the clergy of that temple, and now have I wound up sounding like one of them. Forgive me."

A dry chuckle escaped my throat before I could stop it. "I'm not the one you need forgiveness from."

"True, I will have to atone. My Lady is undoubtedly quite vexed with me."

The groan, I didn't try to stop. "Not her you git. Your god probably didn't even notice, seeing as how she isn't real." I thrust my finger at Rowan. "*Her.* That is who you owe an apology to."

"Actually, she has already forgiven me. I didn't even get a chance to ask. She said '*How can I expect you to understand what you have been taught to misunderstand?*' she was smiling with her eyes when she said it. I think the fact that I was about to apologize meant something to her." He nodded to himself. "But that's right, you are an unbeliever."

"Yep, I'm a heretic."

"No, a heretic is one who claims to follow one of the gods but perverts that god's message."

I raised an eyebrow. "Heathen?"

He shook his head again. "That would be the proper name for the raiders, the ones who Vike. It is not meant to blemish, it is simply what they are called. The ignorant use it as a slur."

I blinked at him. I thought they were called Vikings. "So what is your special name for me and my kind?"

We both jumped when Ba'call answered. "*Atheist.* Although technically, it simply means against theology, and while theology is always about a god, not all followers of the gods use theology."

I had never heard the word, and from Arwen face neither had he. "What is your faith, cat?"

"Me? I follow the Southerner of Southerners, The Tiger who chased the wind; I am an adherent to the one that pulls the Empress's tail and wings, and the one that performs rectal-craniotomy upon the Dark One. She who cuts Conqueror and Paladin alike. All to ensure they did not follow pain, but hope."

"Ah, the Southern cat." Arwen smiled as he said it.

I was a little shocked. "You know of one of the Gods of the Empire? I didn't think learning of other faiths was something that was done."

"Back home? No, I suppose not, but Pentagla actually encourages it, both to learn your enemy and to know your allies." He turned on his horse to look fully at our young Warden. "So, it is said that your people have one of the most complete histories of our world. That you even remember from before Elei's birth."

She looked up at him with one of her eyes squinted as if to block the light. She growled her voice with her words. "Aye, tis said this. But no cat who has made it out of their first fur has ever or will ever give a straight answer to a question. If'n we do, it be best if you be afraid of that answer." Then in her normal voice, she continued. "We teach our young things that are meaningless, and with age meaning becomes apparent."

He chuckled. "You also trick and pull pranks. Steal into cities who think their defenses above reproach, all to paint the town the color of a barn." He turned and looked at me. "Probably because red paint is so easy and cheap to make."

The grin and look on Bec's face said there was more to it than that. "Perhaps, young paladin. Or perhaps we just think all towns should be painted red. At any rate, when it comes to seeing things, my people often look where others will not." She turned to look at me. "We are the jesters and punsters of a world that is too serious to laugh at its own folly."

I myself had watch Bec perform this duty with our group, lighting dark moods and pointing out the obvious that none of us saw.

Arwen looked at us both and continued. "Hers is one god that doesn't really have a theology. They don't study their god, and what one generation uses to praise and placate her, the next doesn't. From one wandering tribe of them to the next, it still will be different. They simply don't do dogma."

Ba'call's ears when back flat against her head as did her whiskers. She pulled her head back and ducked her chin as if to protect her throat then said with a hiss. "*Praise her?*" She sounded offended by the idea. "Even my own people are fond of the curse *'damn the cat'*. You don't praise the claws; you just try to stay ahead of her paws. Or so the old saying goes." She relaxed her posture and continued as if speaking of the blowing of winds. "We are just aware that life needs laughter, and the best joke is the one that makes you think."

"Then why do you follow her?" I could feel my smile and my laughter was music to my own ears.

"Someone has to make you do that." The only warning I got was the sound of claws digging into the wood. With a flexing of her legs, she sailed over my head and hit the road on all fours then proceeded to run literal circles around the wagon. After a few rounds she took the lead. The size of her head, her weapons, and the clothing she wore were the only things distinguishing her from a plains cat.

"So what now, oh great lady of the shadows?" I think this was him joking with me, but it was a little stiff for my liking.

"Now we ride on. In a few more days we will meet the other villain of this tale."

"You speak as if this is a story."

"Isn't it? We have heroes, villains, and life lessons. It could be one of your morality plays."

"Not unless we start including naked demons that happen to have a better understanding of father's message than some of the brethren. I just wish they were a little more...I don't know. I don't think I have words for it."

I snorted, "You mean you don't have words that aren't insulting."

He nodded, "Something like that. It's just, you spend your life being told not to do something. She said not only are they free with intercourse, they also enjoy those like themselves." He sighed. "That act is a joy, but it is also what we have for the making of a child."

"Animals mate for procreation. Only in season, only for offspring. I always wondered why we are taught it is animal like to enjoy sex. Animals don't. Cats are barbed, dogs swell. Nothing to me about animal breeding seems like fun. Yet you lot expect me to believe that the gods made it fun for us and then told us not to enjoy it? What sense in that is there?"

"Not the gods. *Lunavner*. She was jealous of men, so made it so men could not resist woman's wiles. Made the flesh pleasant so we could and would sin more. Hers is the base nature that drives men from father and his children."

"So the All Father, maker of all, most powerful of all, all knowing, all seeing, all present, he that rules the skies and he who defeats Lunavner at the last, after the testing of his children, let Lunavner change us?"

"We were given a choice; we chose this."

Alabaster spoke up. "That story has always bugged me. Always seemed like just one more way to convince you that you were not worth it. That you were a flawed, pitiful creature." His voice sounded better than it had in days. With Arwen here, it now sounds more like a woman's than ever before. Or maybe it was just that I was more aware of it.

"How so, priest?" Arwen's question struck me funny. Not that he would ask it, but something about his voice when he did.

"Answer me a few questions first, and I will show you. Do you find that to be fair and just, good Sir?"

"Speak priest, I will answer as truly as I can."

I was missing something; I had never heard Alabaster speak so formally. Out of a high born like Arwen, sure, but Al?

"Is not your All Father all knowing?"

"It is so."

"Is he not all powerful?"

"Aye..." Arwen's answer was a bit slower this time.

"And is it not also true that he is all present, at once everywhere, ubiquitous?"

"This is what we are taught, and I believe to be true."

"Then the way you teach, your fall of humanity makes of him a liar."

I watched the armored man bristle. "Choose carefully your next words priest. I will defend his honor."

"Then crusade against your own church. I do not besmirch his name, but they do. I merely point it out." Alabaster cocked his head as he turned his gaze on the horsed knight.

"I will listen." Arwen's words were low, a judge waiting for the case to be made.

"They say All Father is all wise, all loving and he puts no conditions on that love. Yet I say to you the way it is taught, your all father is a villain who uses his power to torture those that know no better."

"How so?"

"First off, all knowing; if he is indeed all knowing, then as soon as he set the test upon the stone he knew man would fail."

"Ah, but it was man's choie."

"It was no choice, man did not know evil, and man had no concept of evil. So to go against Father's words bore no weight."

"Man was told he would die if he did such as he did."

"What is death? Again, man had no knowledge of death. Besides, man did not die when he failed, so the way it is taught also makes your All Father a *liar*."

Arwen's face showed his mind working furiously.

Alabaster continued. "Also, Lunavner was one of the host. Man may have free will, but your work says the host does not. As such, she was doing as All Father made her to do."

"An interesting thought. I would say nothing but a thought. For one, do you have anything to back this thought up? Also, if you think you truly understand this story better than I and those that taught it to me, what pray tell, is its point?"

"It is in how it is told, not how it is taught. I doubt the people in the story ever actually existed, but whether they did or not is not the point. The point is how the story is told." He spread his hands and begun. "After the failing of this test, they cowered and hid, knowing first that they were shamed, and second that they were evil." He took a deep breath and paused for effect. "And as such were at once cast down from their heaven." He thought about it for a moment. "No, wait. That isn't right. They *weren't*."

"'Tis true, All Father came down and caught them."

"Yes, the god that is everywhere all at once came down. This is where you shall see the point. Like a parent coming home to find the children in the sweets with jelly upon their faces, he asked them if they had been where they should not be. Obviously, if he is all knowing, he already knows the answer."

"True enough, and fair when put that way."

"And the first thing said was by man, not woman. *'It is not my fault but hers.'* The woman was asked, and she said it was not her fault but the tempters. That is the failed test? For now they knew evil, and knew what they were doing was wrong."

I had never heard it put that way before in my life. I always thought the story was told to point out that this was one more way that man was superior to woman. She was responsible for the fall of man. It was her fault. That all of the suffering originated with her, but this way man, not woman, fell first.

I took a chance and joined the conversation. "All right, if I remember what was taught to me well enough, that was when the father figure kicked the kids out, and it was because they lied to him. Is that correct?"

Arwen looked at me. "Yes, I suppose so. It was when they were expelled from heaven. And lying would be the reason if you look at it that way."

But the white shook his head. "No, and I have the proof of it if you believe. All of the children of The All Father offer one thing in common; forgiveness for your sins if you ask. Or to put another way, forgiveness if you admit *you did wrong*. The failure wasn't in lying; it was in blaming others for your mistakes. After all, she did partake first. Even though at the time man didn't understand, he did when asked. As such he knew blaming others to be wrong."

I looked at Alabaster. "All right, then why? Why do any of this? Again, he would have known they would not take responsibility. At that point, he is back to being a villain."

"Well, with innocents and ignorance you know without a doubt that a creature not knowing will behave in a certain way. Small children inevitably reach for fire even if you tell them not to do that, that it will hurt. For the answer of why, look at the host themselves. They are perfect, unflawed and always obedient. As it is said the race of man was in the start. Perfect has a problem. It will only do what it is designed to do, no more and no less. It can't do more. A perfect ball will only roll; a perfect cube will only be a cube."

"That is the point." Arwen said. "Perfect servants. We weren't supposed to mess up."

"Really? There are two things are wrong with that. One, he already had perfect servants, and servants of spirit who could touch the physical at that. He didn't need us. If he did, then he had us, we were perfect. So, then, why the test? Why free will?"

"He is an asshole." I couldn't help it. It is how I honestly felt about it. The discussion so far only proved it.

"No, he wanted something that could learn, that could grow into more than it was with its making. The only way to do that is to let them make mistakes. In short, to sin."

"But man isn't better for sinning. We became monsters, rebelling against the gods on all fronts!" Arwen's voice was full of scorn.

"Did we? Oh, to be sure some have. Evil exists, but so does kindness, love, fellowship, and healing. Some do evil; it is true, and all do small evils. We also do good, great goods; sacrificing ourselves for others, giving of ourselves freely. What is more, we learn. We learn new ways to help each other, to alleviate suffering, and we stand by our brothers even when we have nothing to gain and everything to lose. No religious order, no sect, and no set of beliefs have a monopoly on that."

"So more than those in service of the Father serve the Father whether they believe in him or not?" Arwen shook his head. "No, some worship great evil, and some do harm out of spite. I can't believe that all serve the Father."

"They do not. That is not what free will is about. Some do, some don't, but belief in your god doesn't mean you get it right, and lack of belief in your god doesn't mean we get it wrong."

Chapter 40

We arrived a little early to our rendezvous. We stopped about a ten-minute walk from where the map said we were to meet our contact and sent Ba'call to scout ahead. She came back quickly.

"One guy, sitting, hooded and robed. Looks like some kind of monk. Basic chair with a table beside him, four chests, no guard."

Arwen raised an eyebrow. "No guards on a jewel run? That doesn't seem right."

Alabaster spoke up. "He said he'd done this run several times. Pays us well up front with the rest to be paid with delivery. Not to mention he has our descriptions. No doubt when we are late. The guard will be looking for us. I don't think they were expecting trouble."

Our Priest's assurances aside, Ba'call hissed. "Something else. I smelled grave spice. Frankincense, myrrh, cinnamon, strong smells meant to cover other scents, foul odors."

Sliverleaf groaned. "Great. An undead maybe? If it is, it's an intelligent one." She left the rest hanging. Intelligent corpses meant trouble.

"No clue." I said. "But we don't have much choice. We aren't late. Stick with the plan. If it doesn't talk, we know it's not intelligent. Maybe it has instructions with what to do with the chest, and we can follow it. If it is intelligent, we will burn that bridge when we come to it."

The approach was clear, and the guy was sitting there just like Ba'call had said. Our brown robed monk nodded as we came up. His voiced rasped out like that of an old man, somehow dry and papery. "Ah. Right on time and good too. You have the payment?"

So much for unintelligent.

As odd as the sound of his voice was, his words were also somehow hollow as if there was nothing inside them. My skin crept up my back with it.

I put on the low street drawl I hadn't used for years. "It's here. Them's the gems?" The problem with sounding like you're from the streets when you're a thief is people tend to peg you as dumb at best and as a thief at worst. Here, I was hoping for dumb.

He gestured, the hand hidden by the robe. We took the box of writs off the cart and started loading up the cart. All the while, Ba'call kept staring, not at the man, but his feet. "You've dirt on your robes, monk."

He looked down then back up. "And you've sand falling out of your wagon."

He moved fast, and I was closest to him.

Whatever Ba'call saw by his feet already had her pushing me out of the way. Even with that, the old monk should have had me, and would have, had he moved his feet.

A sword like none I had ever seen sliced through where I had been moments before, the space Ba'call now occupied. That sword gleaned white and looked like it had broken glass along its edge; its blood red eye blinked at me.

The sword had an eye.

It bit through where I had stood and into Ba'call as she fell. Her face showed no pain as she landed with a thump upon the ground. Then and only then did her blood start to flow. Her teeth bared in a grimace that showed all of her formidable teeth, both the delicate canines, and the great fangs behind them.

As he stood up fully, he stepped out of the hole he'd use to hide his height. It was a monster, easily thirteen feet or more, taller than any Orc I had ever met. We may have been better off if he had been undead.

The robe that had veiled his visage tore as his crest came up and what was left was thrown aside when he drew his other three swords. Four arms, two legs bent and shaped like that of a locust. Its gaping maw was filled with crystalline teeth. The armor on its back was that of burnished gold; its front looked like the white bone of its ribs. I had seen this coloration on the behemoth we had led away from Alabaster's home. What stood before us was no mindless monster this time, but a Warrior, a Child of Am'met.

In a way, it made sense. We were only a couple of days south of the hive. A hive that hadn't grown or been aggressive in years according to Ba'call. Now we knew one reason why. They were buying slaves. How many slaves had been used to feed the hive?

Rowan charged in; she voice raised in a wordless and bestial battle cry. It was a reckless move, and the bug was ready for her.

It swung one of those swords at her. She rolled and threw herself sideways at the last moment.

Her attack was never meant to connect. It was meant to get her close to Bec. With the swing already committed, it left the monster opened for a brief moment; that was all Sliverleaf needed. Her arrow went into the monster's side, biting deep, as it was one of the few places not covered with the armor of its shell.

I moved. We had an advantage, even if it wasn't a good one.

The creature had moved back when the arrow hit. Not by much, but it was still very close to the hole it had its legs in to hid its height. I struck low, hitting its body just at the knees. I hoped that would knock it off balance and either send it back into the hole hobbling its movement or knock it on its ass.

I got lucky. Hitting with my body felt like I had rammed a tree, but it moved again, one of its feet sliding into the pit. Had it not been so close, that would not have worked. Now it was completely off balance and trying to recover. What I can only assume to be anger played across its face. I hit its armored hide, but part of it was a soft skin and under that skin I could feel the muscle underneath, muscle and bone. Everything about this bug was just...wrong.

The sound of hooves pounding sent a trill of dread down my spine. Behemoths have hooves and two arms shaped like bladed picks. A mauling by one would be a quick but bloody death. Images of me being trampled and dismembered danced in my head, bringing a pain with it not yet inflicted. I flinched hard when something shot past me and into the thing's armored chest. It took me a moment to understand that something was a fallen limb and that I wasn't its target.

The branch that hit the thing knocked it the rest of the way down. Arwen had gone for reach and had mounted and charged on his horse. Limbs do not make the best lances or spears. The thing shattered in a rain of splinters. It probably didn't do much in the way of damage, but I for one wouldn't want to be on the receiving end of such a blow.

Alabaster took the chance to slide in beside Ba'call. He and Rowan grabbed her under the shoulders and quickly moved her away from the fight.

The thing rose to its feet far more quickly than I had thought possible for anything that size. I was the only thing within its reach. Its slashes were precise. I was only one step ahead of each of its swings. It didn't seem to have a dumb hand.

How is that fair? I busted my butt to learn to use both hands in a fight, and I still feel slower with my left. This thing? No, it moves as if each of its four hands had its own mind and knew exactly where I was to be with each swing.

If there are gods, they fucking hate us. How else do you explain a world where the Children exist? On the plus side, the improvised lance had sheared off, leaving part of itself inside the thing.

"A little help?" I called out.

I like to think I said that last part calmly, but I swear somewhere on this field there had to be some scared to death six-year-old also screaming the same thing. I hope someone gets to her...

Rowan answered my call by bringing her sword down onto its back. Its golden carapace turned the blade aside with little effort. The shell itself flexed slightly, taking away the bite of the edge and allowing it to skitter off and down. Little balls of light that

I remember from the fight with the water thing darted past me. They found their mark, and bit into the thing causing blackened dots to appear upon its burnished hide.

"Surrender now, meat. The hive is generous. We may not eat you." Its voice had taken on a clicking rattle now. Its head had raised three pieces of bone; the loose leathery flesh of webbing between them looked wet. It made the thing look like it was wearing a slime covered golden crown. "Who knows; she may make you into a Child."

My blood ran cold. It chose that time to strike. The thing had been trying to shake us up. It used its two arms against me, two against Rowan. One of its attacks cut into my arm. I had been cut before. It is like feeling something slide into you, a pain, a bite if you will, that your mind tries to make sense of.

But this? Now I understood why Ba'call didn't cry out at first. There was no pain. Those swords were so sharp that at first the cut neither hurt nor bled. Seconds later, only as I started to move did I feel it. It was deep, into the muscle deep, but my arm was still responding. Rowan's armor saved her from a similar fate to Ba'call. The hit was straight across the chest. As it was it left a score in the steel. This was not going well, and we were too close for Sliverleaf to cast burst. Somehow, I doubt this thing would let us back off so that she could.

Arwen had wheeled his steed back around again. His sword was out, but the bug was ready for him. It dropped all four swords at once and grabbed him as he came in, lifting him off the horse.

"And who is this little knight?" He said as he held the weight of a fully armored man several feet off the ground with no problems. "Your scent is up, boy. Is one of these females your mate? Do you wish to breed?"

The swords never hit the ground. I looked. Each one was still dangling from its arms by a fleshy tether. The swords had what looked like a tail, and the end of each was embedded into the arms of the beast before us.

Couple of quick words of advice. One, never think you are winning the fight. As soon as you do, you will do something stupid like unhorse a knight by picking him up off his mount instead of just cutting him down or slapping him aside. Two, don't drop your weapons. You never know who will pick them up. Three, don't ever take your eyes off an opportunist.

I dropped both my weapons and went in for a shoulder roll under Arwen's feet. It brought me right up beside the Child. I grabbed at the dangling weapons. If they could score metal they had to be sharp enough to hurt him. I took two, one in each hand and ripped them from the thing's arms. I then drove both into its sides between the hard white bone of its ribs.

Pain lanced through both of my arms. The damn swords had stung me. Then they started pumping fluid out of the brute's chest and into me.

I screamed. My arms were on fire. My mind heard a thousand voices buzzing around inside, Compelling me to obey, obey, *OBEY*. My throat quickly became raw with pain, and I could not tell why.

My only consolation was that the thing went down twitching. I watched it collapse. Arwen caught me as I fell. He landed on his feet; apparently, he's part cat. I felt relief as his hands clasped around the tails and ripped the stingers from my body.

Black fluid began leaking down my arms, scorching my skin. I moved like it was molten and burned just as badly. The need to obey, and that ever present voice, receded from my mind. The sudden reduction in pain made me lightheaded.

Blue sky was the last thing I saw.

Chapter 41

I awoke in pain. My blood was boiling. Arwen stood over me, cutting my arms and letting them bleed.

"Lady, guide my hands." He looked down at me. "It's in your blood girl. I'm working as fast as I can." I couldn't see Alabaster. Arwen's hands glowed, at least I thought they did, the burning intensified. I screamed. With the last of my scream, I realized the world was no longer golden around the edges.

"How's Bec?"

"That damned thing cut through her armor and into one of her breasts all the way through the bones of her ribs, but thankfully no organs. The wound doesn't seem to be poisoned." He looked me over. "And I've cleaned the creature's blood out of your body. Damn quick thinking grabbing its swords. Next time, don't let them bond with you."

I agreed. I don't know what he did, but it helped. I rolled over to look and see if I could find her. My heart broke. Ba'call lay on her back with her eyes shut tight, mouth opened, and she was panting slightly. Above her, working on the wounds was Alabaster. His normally pale face having taken on an insipid blue sheen. Rowan was trying to help, holding one of the blankets over the wound, one hand on one side of it, one on the other trying to force it back together.

A moan, a scream, cursing even. I could have handled any one of those.

Instead Bec was mewing.

A soft, sad sound. She looked over at me. "Do me a favor," she said. "Find my sister and pounce her for me please." With that, her eyes lost something, a shine that had been there a few moments before.

Bec was gone.

I could see the two of them realize it too. Rowan seemed to deflate as she leaned down and closed the cat's eyes. Alabaster went rigid and just stared at her for a moment.

I lost it.

"Why didn't you use those healing spells I keep hearing the gods give you? I've seen them work."

Alabaster's face showed a pain likened to my own. "Magic doesn't fix everything. It would make the muscles knit, and the bones right where they were. It won't realign them. We were trying to get her ribs back into place. She was even holding still for it though I think that was more the shock than courage."

"It was courage. I could see it on her face." I stood and looked at him. "I thought the organs were missed by the cut."

"Your insides can be untouched, but if there is no blood to fuel them..."

She bled out. My friend died while I screamed.

She pushed me out of the way, and then I may have distracted them when she needed it. It was my fault.

"Bring her back." My voice was low and cold.

Arwen looked at me. "What?"

I turned my face to him. He stepped back a pace from me. "Bring her back! Your precious gods do that, yes? The priests sometimes do it. I heard the tales. *Bring her back!*"

"I can't." Arwen's head hung low.

"None of us can." Alabaster stood up, his front covered by his sin of failure. "None of us understand enough to do so. If we tried, we might trade our life for hers, and she, nor you, would want that. Besides, she is not of the faith."

"Then what good are gods? If one won't help another, if they all are such jealous children as to not help just because you don't cower to them."

Alabaster was suddenly there. He cradled me in his arms, bloody as they were, and wrapped his wings around me, holding me tight. I struggled against him, but heard his words. "It's not like that. Think of it as several homes, several families. Right now, Bec is in the hands of her ancestors. The Southern Cat watches over them. If the Empress, or Ca'talls or anyone else went in it would be a grave insult."

"Bullshit." It was all that I could say as I collapsed against him and cried.

"We'll take her home. Talk with her shamans. If Bec has a reason to come back, they may be able to help. But the dead never come back without a toll upon them, and that is only if she has something to come back for."

"She does. She has to pounce her sister."

Chapter 42

Whether we were to take her back for her shamans to raise her, or to bury her, Alabaster spent the rest of the night preparing her for the journey. I busied myself with the new chest. Our gold chest was full of papers and sand. I wanted, no, *needed*, to know for what my friend had died, for what she had died protecting me.

Each was indeed full of gems, raw and uncut. Problem was none of these gems had ever seen a miner's pick. It looked as if the rock has simply been removed from around the stones; it gave them an odd, eerie quality. One stone looked a strange, twisted cylinder of glass with tendrils reaching out from it. It was if it was some great worm reaching out to grab food to shove inside of its hollow mouth.

We had decided to stick to the basics of the plan. There was no longer any reason to find the mine as the mine was obviously part of the hive. Any slaves already delivered were long since dead or worse.

We knew where the slavers were delivering the people they held. So, we were going to head there and stop them, freeing all the slaves we found there. Then, with some or all the slaves in tow, we were going to head back to Cliffport with the gems, papers, and slaves to make sure that bastard paid. Paid for what he had done to people for who knows how long. We only had to make one stop first.

***

It took two days to make it to a small-town called Snake's Turn. According to legend, a demon of all things, once saved the town. A snake woman with her band of heroes fought alongside of the paladin who redeemed her. Yeah, I don't buy it either, but people have the most interesting stories of how their nowhere towns got their name.

Ba'call once told me of a town called Dragon's Rest, where a dragon once slept for a fortnight. She said they had something there called ice cream. It was made with milk, cream and honey as well as whatever fruit you cared to put in it. We were going to have some. Frankly, iced milk with honey sounded too sweet for me.

Snake's Turn was a nothing town in a nothing place. It had a well, an inn with two rooms for rent, and a blacksmith shop. It also had what we needed, a coffin and the herbs to turn the smell. Alabaster had done his best, but poor Bec was already starting to ripen. I had expected Arwen to argue, but he was actually supportive of getting Ba'call home.

I had to go. I had to find this kitten. By Ba'call's reckoning, she could be as old as eight, maybe more. I had asked Alabaster how long it had taken Bec to get here. He said she told him that it had been twelve years since she set out, but he also said that young cats were known wander in circles, not out of ignorance, but out of some need to see everything. It shouldn't take us more than four months to get to where her tribe lived. The problem was they were nomads. We would not be sure of where they would be until mid-winter when they would be outside of Five Rivers. So, we would definitely see them inside of seven months.

Some would say a body is a heavy burden. It's not. Causing that body's death is. I had a job to do; I had to. I had someone to hug who I had never met.

A casket for a friend is not a big thing. This one was a foot and a half deep, slightly over five feet long, and three wide. Its wood was hawthorn, something usually seen in doors. It's normally tan grain was polished a somber black. It had an unusual oddness to it's grain, one that made it look as if it were hand carved and sculpted in parts.

It should have been bigger, there should have been more to say on it. This simple box was important, damn it. Only it wasn't. It was a foot note, something forgotten or only mentioned again when absolutely necessary. Otherwise, I don't think any of us could have gone on.

I was broken out of my mourning when I overheard some of the town's people gossiping.

"Look at them things. Barely dressed and not covered. The one's got no shame, showing her breasts. Bet that's way that cat woman died. They were too busy messing around with the one boy. Ta' think five women travel with one man. It's not seemly and just asking for trouble."

There is a time to stand and a time to let such talk wash away. In a town full of strangers was not the time. We were very outnumbered. Hells, this time last year I might have said something similar about people I didn't know. I didn't know any better then.

That was then. Now I did. I also knew if you didn't stand up to this crap, no one would. We were outsiders, but how long 'til some woman or worse a girl was blamed for something that befell her just because of something she wore. How long before they thought of one of their own what they said within ear shot of five heavily armed people.

I had been raised to believe people like that were right. That a woman got what she deserved if she didn't dress a certain way or acted in other ways. It was one of the hardest things I had had to overcome when I started living with the LeatherWings. Yet in the LeatherWing town, I had seen no woman born there degrade herself when she took her lovers. I had seen no LeatherWing woman who let others degrade her no matter how she dressed. How someone dresses is not an excuse for bad things to happen to them. The fact that we were mostly women didn't mean we were lesser, or that Arwen and Alabaster were lesser.

I spun around. Everyone else was shocked by what happened next. Besides me and Alabaster, only Arwen spoke highlander. "How dare you? You pass judgment on us. You don't know us or what happened."

A man who had been standing near us, leaning against a wall, disengaged himself from the rest. He spoke in trade, so everyone could understand his words. "You and your crew travel together, with only one man? Everyone here knows his bed's not cold at night. No man is going to be around that much tail and not be distracted. Even if you weren't warming the pervert's bed when it happened, his arm was slow when protecting his women, wasn't he? Not much of a man are you lad? Can't even protect all your slits."

I was completely aghast by this man's words. So taken aback that I didn't realize I had movement behind me until Arwen's sword and Alabaster's claws were both at his throat.

As Alabaster pressed him back into the wall, growling, with that maniacal grin of his showing off his fangs nicely, Arwen held him at sword point and challenged him.

"I am Arwen Glon'glas, Paladin of the Light and Champion of Pentagla." The hot-headed champion began. "This young man is Alabaster, a LeatherWing Priest of their Empress. Under his customs you have just insulted him, his sister, his property, and my master; under my and your own customs you have just besmirched my friends and a Lady. I pray you have proof to back up your boast."

He struggled against Alabaster's grasp. A slow trickle of blood was starting to run down his neck, another at his throat where the paladin's blade was. "I don't be seein' no Lady."

"Rowan." he nodded over towards her, "...that would be the red one. Her mother is leader of three counties, boasting three days walk in any direction from her lands. She has nine villages under her name. The largest has over a thousand strong soldiers. She is the Queen of the Kingdom of Bone. A nasty sounding title to be sure, but that is the LeatherWing for you. That makes her a Lady, and as so with more power than probably any one you will meet in your pathetic life."

The guard had shown up by this point, having talked to them and warned them about the hive creature this far out earlier, they knew what and who Arwen was. The guy looked at Rowan, and then looked at Alabaster. My owner was at this point barely restraining his rage. "This one is a boy?"

"That one, my fine fellow, is a man."

"He's got…" The man seemed to be at a loss for words. Funny how a paladin in front of him made him think better of his language. "Those things on 'im."

"Aye and his people are ruled by the female. His god personally touched him to give him a quintessence. A something extra to set him apart."

Not quite right, and I doubt that the guy knew the word at any rate. I am not sure I did either. He apparently got the gist.

"That's disgusting. How could you be with such twisted creatures and call yourself a man of God?" The crowd was over their shock and was beginning to rally behind him again. The guards seemed less inclined.

"Break it up and go home folks. Like it or not, this man is a Champion of the Church, and he's the papers to prove it."

From somewhere in the crowd, a lone voice spoke, but echoes soon followed it. "Some'n should be seen 'bout that." Another piped up with, "Make formal complaint, sidin' with demon folk over his own kin."

All I could think was that someone should know their own town's history.

The guard were having none of it, instead intent on keeping the peace. "Maybe so, but not today. Take it up with the deacon when he gets into town on service day." The lead guard turned towards us. "So besmirching a Lady, huh? No offense, but she don't look like one. Can't blame the man for not realizing. She should have been dressed in something to show her rank."

I ground my teeth and Alabaster hissed through his.

Arwen smiled as he looked over at the guard. "I'm sorry. I didn't realize that royalty was required to wear a uniform. I'm sorrier that you think it's okay for this man and presumably others to talk that way about any woman, say a mother, a sister, a daughter."

"My kin know better than to dress as sluts." The man continued, despite the predicament in which he found himself.

"That, good sir is indubitably because your kin knows you only love them so long as they do as they are told. You, I have no doubt, do a great many things that shame them every day, like *speak*."

The man growled at Arwen. Funny, now that I had them side by side, the look on the man's face at this moment matched Alabaster's. Maybe they weren't that much more feral. Maybe they were just more honest.

The guard turned to Arwen. "Be that as it may, the man has the right to speak his mind."

An audible pop sounded as Alabaster opened his mouth. I think it was his jaw, but I'm not sure. "Yes, his mind he can speak and should feel free to do but accountable for harm done with his tongue he also should be."

"Maybe, but not by you, and not today. This is not how things are done down here. You can't go beating and killing people just because you disagree with what they say. He had no way of knowing that the Lady was noble, and it isn't a crime to object to the way someone is dressed."

Both boys backed off. The guy was grinning. "Now ya see how things are done right." His smug face begged for a fist, but the guard was not done with him yet.

"No, they won't. If they wanted to make a case of this, you'd be in so deep you'd never get out. By the same token, if I wanted to make a case of them attacking an unarmed man in the middle of the street I could hold them up for days or weeks. I think we are all just better off if they move on about their business, and you go on about yours keeping your fat mouth shut." He turned towards us then. "I think that is fair, don't you?"

Alabaster was staring at the ground, shaking all over. Arwen was meeting the guard's eyes straight on. Rowan had enough of it. She walked up and slapped both of them across the back of the head with open palms, one with each hand. Instinctively they both flinched and ducked their head slightly.

"We'll be off." Then she turned and looked at the man who was still there and glaring. "I know your type. Follow us at your own peril. I will take you and all you bring with you as my personal servants if you come after us. I will teach you how to treat a woman. Trust me, your wives, daughters, and own mothers will thank me for it." With that, we gathered what we had and left. Can't say that I was sad to see the place behind me.

Once we had crested a hill, Rowan started in on the boys. "Arwen, I expected posturing from. He knows no better yet, but you Alabaster, you jumping to a woman's defense as if she was helpless. Chloe could have handled that brute. I understand wanting to help, but you all but confirmed that you think women need men to protect them."

"Slandering a Lady's honor is a killing offense." Arwen stated.

"Dear gods, and we are the ones labeled as barbarians. Killing a detractor only makes what he has to say more significant. If his words have no sting, why pay them any heed? You got it so backward that if not denied, it must be true. The way you have it set up in your culture if I call you a *godder stalker* and you don't deny then it must be true."

"What's a *godder*?"

"Nothing, as far as I know it's a word I just made up. It's meaningless. But the point is valid and proven. You automatically leap to find out what is was in order to know which way to stand on it." She turned towards her brother. "And as for you, what was going on in your head?"

Sliverleaf answered, "Same as through the other males. They were trying to impress the woman they both like, the woman who snapped at the male."

"Well, she is mine." Alabaster began.

"You own her contract, not her mind and heart." Rowan turned to Sliverleaf, "And you damn well know what Bec would say to hear you assume all men must think with their cocks."

The elf nodded, she hung her head for a moment then nodded again.

Alabaster didn't notice as he continued to defend his actions. "And it is my duty to protect her from harm."

Rowan nodded, "It is, and you do this by validating what this man thought?"

Arwen shook his head hard, setting his hair to glint in the sun. "If we don't deny it, then it's true, if we do deny it then it's true. How do you win? She had already started in on him."

Rowan took a slow breath as she calmly explained, "No, she challenged a crowd. When he disengaged himself from the crowd, I would have loved to see how she handled it. Jumping in to save her is not wrong, it is a good thing and something to be proud of. You jumping in to protect her before she needed saving is. You never gave her a chance, making her appear to be less than you, less capable than you, in their eyes."

Chapter 43

Rowan and I walked at the head of the group. Both boys were hanging back. Sliverleaf was on the cart. The lake was only a few days away, and we were already two days into the journey.

"I think my brother fancies you, and I know Arwen does."

I snorted. "I figured he be more interested in you, of the two of us. You're definitely more attractive, at least to me."

"Are you a lover of women Chloe? Does my brother lose you to mine or Sliv's fairness?"

I blossomed crimson so deep I could feel it on my neck and in my ears. I kept my voice even. "Well, I like the look of you, her, and Al for that matter. But no, I don't think I am a lover of women. Honestly though, I haven't really thought much of it. I am much more interested in friendships than sex." The thought of Alabaster and me doing that sent more heat to my face, as did the thought of me and Arwen. That man was something to behold.

This topic had to be changed, now. "So you're a Lady are you?"

"By your standards, yes I am. Mother really does control all of the Kingdoms of Bone. Though to be honest, that is not as ominous as it sounds. The land bridge that separates the fresh water sea and Sea of Mists is known as The Bone. All of its lands are under mother's control. It is more than what you would call three counties, but we divide things a little differently."

"So that makes Al a Lord doesn't it? You two are brother and sister."

"Yes it does. Officially Al's title would still be Lady. When he made the choice to be male he also dedicated his life to the Empresses as a priest. He is white; he is a priest, and he serves the Empress. Technically he is a Handmaiden. Even the male priests have the feminine titles. There was a reason for it once, and no one quite remembers now. The priestesses will tell you that this tradition is still in place to make acolytes think about why they may have been there in the first place. Like the shoes given to higher level priestesses." She smirked, "Trust me they are... interesting."

"I can see why he didn't use Al's title then. It would have given the man something else to harp on."

"That may be why. It might still be kept as a way to show a woman's title is not something to be embarrassed of. That women aren't something to be ashamed of. Remember, the Empress came out of a culture much like yours. They treated women as something less."

I shrugged. I had never really been ashamed of myself. I had long ago stopped worrying about how people saw me as a woman. I would make them take me seriously. As we walked, I had to ask "Does that mean that Al is actually a priestess?"

She chuckled. "What do you think?"

Shaking my head I turned and looked at Sliverleaf. "At any rate, have you ever seen Dragon's Breath?"

"No, but I have heard of the place." She swallowed hard. "Ba'call said it was beautiful, but smelled awful. No one wants to live within a day's travel of it."

***

We traveled for the rest of the day in silence. Our normal banter and discussions of philosophy somehow didn't seem appropriate at the moment. Camp was set up, and the night watches were set. Alabaster did try to apologize to me for what happened earlier, but I told him I found it endearing and left it at that.

We set out the next morning, and I quickly started to notice the difference in the landscape. The plants were more gnarled, and the green of them had more of a blue tint to it.

By mid-morning, Dragon's Breath could be seen from on top of the hill, through the trees and brush. The lake was weirdly blue, vibrantly so, but some darker patches seemed to be in the water. As we got closer, the wind changed, and I learned why most people avoided the place; the reek of brimstone was thick in the air coming from the lake. Plants around the area and trees were stunted. As we got up to the lake, I saw it was ringed with white sand. Further from the water it began to turn blue, and about half way between the water and the tree line the blue sand turned into blue crystals growing out of the ground.

The camp of people wasn't hard to spot. As expected, the slaves were not in the best of conditions; they were filthy, and most of them looked sick. All of them were in strong box style wagons like the ones used by the guard, only bigger.

The thing I found fitting as I watched was that the slavers and guard, of whom I only saw a few, didn't look that much better. When I saw one vomiting, a new idea formed in my head. I ran back to tell the others. With a new plan in mind, we took David and walked right up to the camp.

Upon seeing us, one of the guards ran off calling to someone. Sick men make mistakes. These guys probably just wanted to be away from here so bad that anyone coming up *had to be* who they were meeting. Men like this always believe everyone is like them, so even the LeatherWings, who were known slavers, didn't give the cause for alarm.

Out of a tent a man emerged. He was clothed better than the rest of the rabble, and he looked to be in his mid-thirties. Much like everyone else, his skin had yellowed, and he had a sheen of sweat to him. His eyes were dull and his cheeks were hollow.

"Hail." he greeted, not really looking at us. "Was about to shove this lot into the water and go on. This place is not as clever as I thought." His breath was labored, his voice weak with sickness. He was poisoned, as were his men. "Let's get these wretches turned over to you and be gone from this accursed place." Only then did he look up. I have no idea what he expected to see, but heavily armed adventures with LeatherWings wasn't it.

He called the alarm. His men were sicker than he was. It was how we got this close without them noticing what was going on. Their skin was dried and flaking. Eyes were swollen, red, and cloudy. Whatever was here was killing these men long before we arrived.

There was no fight. Most of them took one look at us, healthy and ready for trouble, and dropped to their knees. Even their leader only gave token resistance. The winds and land of Dragon's Breath had taken its toll on the villains. Now, despite the fact that no sane person would come here, it turned out not to be a good meeting spot when you would have to wait around for days. We rounded them up and went to look after the people they had harmed.

There were twenty-five strong wagons, each made with iron banding and bars, and each held forty or so people. Happily, despite the poor conditions of the slaves, most of whom were starving and dehydrated, the limited air flow and no exposure to the ground of the area seemed to save them from the worst of the poisoning. They were sick, but not as sick as the guards. Some may have called it justice, or the work of the gods, but when you count the fact that not a one of them, slaver nor slave, could stand on their own, I called it neither.

They were sick but not as sick as the guards. Some may have called it justice, or the work of the gods, but when you count the fact that not a one of them could stand on their own, I called it neither.

With the slavers sick and the slaves starved, we let the slaves stay in the wagons for easier transport but broke the locks on all but one of them. Those that could were encouraged to ride on top, and the healthiest we got to help us drive. In the remaining wagon we jailed the slavers. The going was slow as the oxen were not doing well either.

See? No justice here.

It was well past night fall before we dared to stop for fear of the poison of the land.

Alabaster and Arwen tended the sick, both the slaves and the slavers. I went off to find water which was sorely needed, and we simply didn't have enough for all these people. Sliverleaf disappeared into the darkness to find food, any that she could. We had two hundred and thirty mouths to feed this night. Rowan stayed to guard the slavers who were bound with rope tied by me.

She figured if I trusted the rope with my life as I hung from my precarious perches, then she could trust our lives to it with these sick men. I didn't have the heart to tell her I had never really done a lot of second story work, but I knew my rope and was confident.

When I returned, the doors had been taken off the strong wagons, now the people inside knew without a doubt we weren't going to hold them if they didn't want to be held.

Arwen walked over to me. "They fear that we own them now. Given the gruesome stories of the 'demons to the south' being slavers I can understand why. Most of them flinched from Alabaster to start with as we made our rounds. These are all god fearing people. They seem to have been taken from all over." Arwen looked over at my priest. "Some even from the Empire of Five, they have been helping to reassure the others that they are safe. Some come from as far north as Five Rivers. Chloe, some of them come from home, from South Point. One of them used to be a maid in my house; she too is helping calm the others."

"How did they wind up here?"

Alabaster grunted. "They are mostly street people and pilgrims. People who won't be missed, taken from the roads, from the streets and alleys. The ones from our side of the line are those of your people that followed us after the sacking of Unstoma.

They had set up towns and tried to learn our ways, but usually they keep to themselves. A lot of them lived in The Bone."

I winced. It meant that they had been taken from under Vela's very nose. "You said some of them were from home?"

"Yes, and all of them had similar stories. It seems that they all are people that went to the Ca'talls work camps. They were there for a couple of days, and one by one they were moved out, taken from showers, parts of the mines when they were alone, or other such. Since the place isn't a prison and people come and go all the time no one noticed."

My heart dropped. Piper had gone to one of those places. She could have been taken, maybe sold to the Children. My heart seized. "Any other patterns?"

"Apparently a lot of them are children of Waban, sold off for displeasing their fathers or husband. All of those are women."

I hated Ca'talls and his priests, but compared to the followers of Waban, Ca'talls' worshipers were a wonderful people. Waban taught only hate; hate for anyone that they decided weren't people. To them, only first born men were real people. After that came the men that weren't first born. The women and children were called Inferiors. Everyone else was inferior to the Inferiors. The oldest male priest of the cult was the only person of any real consequence, and he ruled with absolute power and authority.

The cult was hated and feared by many. They were fought against by any of the children of the All Father. Waban was the offspring of two of the All Fathers children, Ba'teece and his wife Sou. Their child was the lord of Hate. He is the only one of the Dark Seven to have been born of the light besides Lunavner.

"What are we going to do with all of them?"

Alabaster spoke up. "We will hit Snake's Turn tomorrow, early. We will see if they will take most of them there. I have told them we are going to Cliffport to confront the man who bought them. A few of them have agreed to come with us as accusers and witnesses. We are taking all of the slavers back to Cliffport."

Arwen turned white. "That is a death sentence for these people; you realize that?"

Alabaster turned towards him, "And indefinite imprisonment for them here in your lands. Difference is each of them will get a separate trial back home. They are all guilty of complacency, but some of them might be spared. Can you say that for them here?"

"No." he sighed. "The outrage will condemn them all."

We all looked at each other. This was big, bigger than we had thought. The scope of it was enormous. From The Bone to Five Rivers, they were more than a season apart. Apparently the slavers had connections that far spread. It was sickening. It also meant someone had to set it up.

Rowan broke the silence. "All right then. Once we get back to Cliffport, we turn this over to them, get our guild membership, and then head down to Five Rivers. We are taking Bec home anyway. Might as well see if we can warn them about the slavers. Start trying to figure this out."

We all agreed. We had confiscated all of the money the men had on them. It was being given to each of the former slaves. They would still need to pay for food and such once we got them to Snake's Turn. All in all, I felt miserable. We had saved these people, but I could take no pride in it. They were still sick and hurting.

What did I have to be proud of yet?

That night I dreamed. I dreamed of my mother.

Chapter 44

My mother is a wonderful woman. She told me all about my daddy. Daddy was a Knight of God. He defended me and Momma and the whole town and the land from those that will hurt us.

We were happy.

Then the man came. I didn't see him, but he made Momma cry. She said he was a Cardinal. It is funny; he is a bird man. She told me Daddy had died. That was not funny.

How could Daddy die? He was a Knight of God. He was a hero. Heroes do not die. Daddy wasn't dead; the man lied to Momma.

Daddy had not come home. His shiny armor, I can remember it. I could see my face in it. But it wasn't back. Daddy needs to come back. Momma is sick. She is tired all the time. She doesn't want to play anymore. Daddy will play with me. He always plays with me.

Mommy gets worse. She coughs a lot. She coughs so hard she got to put both hands on the table. I am worried about Mommy. Daddy, come home. Help Mommy like you did me. Put your glowy warm hands on her and make the bad go away.

Mommy is in bed now. Been there for days. The people who help Mommy run the house don't come any more. One of them told me she was sorry, but she had her own little girl to look after.

I can't wake Mommy up.

I shake her, and she rocks.

She is pale like the candles.

Her mouth is dry.

Her eyes are opened.

I poked one.

She didn't blink.

I ran crying to God's House.

They took Mommy away.

Then they took me to God's child house. There are lots of kids here. They are sad. I am sad.

I want to go home. The priest tells me I am home.

I run away soon as I can. I haven't seen Mommy in a long time. I get back home and open the door and run inside. I call out. Mommy doesn't answer. A man I never seen before catches me. He wears a red dress. Says I am in his house. He takes me back, back to the child house.

I get hit on the back with leather straps for running away. This is where God wants me now.

It hurts; it hurts a lot.

I don't try to go back home again. That is wrong; it was wrong to do that.

I make friends with the other kids.

Then a man comes. It is the red dress man. He is now Father. He is here to take care of us.

Chapter 45

As we are coming into town, the guards of Snake's Turn met us on the road. We made a hell of a sight. They opened up their church and their homes to the people. All of them pitched in to help even the man we had the fight with last time helped us out.

He walked up to Arwen. "Brother, I am sorry." He looks at the faces of the people being helped. "Truly this is the work of the Gods. I was wrong. You and your people may be strange, but does the Divine Light not work with the strangest of people to do good upon this land?" Arwen just pats him on the shoulder and then hugs him.

I missed Ba'call. Her words, and help us, her puns, would have helped here. The pain is a bit too much for me to bear. We need a little cheer after traveling for two days with the sick and broken of the slaves and the sullen silence of the slavers.

Most of them seem to be doing a bit better. Of the two hundred slaves, almost all of them were still too weak to move, and the journey here had been a hardship for them. Dehydration, sickness, exposure, all of them had taken their toll. The local Magistrate took writs from them all. We also received a sworn statement of how many there were and their condition to take back with us. We are going to make that son of a bitch pay.

Only one man said he was strong enough to make the journey back to Cliffport. Before being enslaved, he must have been a brute of a man. His shoulders were still broad and his muscles, though much leaner, still looked strong somehow. It was evident that he had been a real problem for the slavers as his back was a mess of old and fresh whip stripes. He had been without food for so long his stomach would only take the barest of a few mouthfuls without voiding its contents. He was one of the ones we all thought might not make it. Guess he is a tough old bird.

He somehow managed to walk over to us and asked to join us and stand before the Judges and Nobles as visual proof.

He had a point when he said, "Paper is sometimes easy to ignore, but the suffering before you never is." I didn't know about the rest of them, but I wasn't going to turn this man down.

***

We took the direct route from Snake's Turn to Cliffport. The road was a straight shot, so I highly doubt even we could get lost. This way on the main road with weigh stations as well as fairly level terrain, we should be back in town in side three maybe four days as opposed to the week the other route should have took us. After all this time, we weren't going deep into the grasslands and hills to meet our doom.

As we went, the boys took care of our captives. As both of them put it in their own ways, *"If we are cruel to them no matter what they have done, we become like them."* and *"They are not beast but men; as men, they deserve our compassion. What awaits them is a fate they have chosen with their actions, but I will not pile more upon them. It is not my way.*" Bet you can guess who said what.

Camp that night saw our new "friends" well fed, even if it was simple fare of breads, cheeses and dried fruit. The former slave, though obviously still weak, insisted on being up and about. He joined us by the fire and sat to listen to our banter. Which to be honest was more picking and teasing of each other than anything else. We had all taken to trying to lighten our moods. Sliverleaf, though she had taken the collar off of her neck and was holding and worrying with it, was being more talkative now than ever before.

I think everyone jumped when he spoke. I did at least.

"A question to ask, if you do not mind. You have freed us, freed me from the slavers, but though they be strips of leather, shackles around your neck you wear, is not it the same thing?"

His mode of speech may have been different, but his words were crisp, as was their meaning. His accent said this was not his first language, but the words were spoken with a precision that said whoever had taught him was a native speaker. Up until now, he had only spoken to us in trade.

We all looked at each other for a moment, trying to decide what to say.

Sliverleaf didn't hesitate. "What is the purpose of a sword?"

He looked over at the elf, considered her for a moment, and then slowly he answered. "A sword is a weapon of death. It destroys those before you be it a good man or an evil one."

"Your sword then, when you still held it before villains overcame you; it tasted the blood of the innocent?"

He straightened. "Was a swords man I was, a knight like your champion. I took many a life, and spared many, but innocence to my knowledge never stained my blade."

"Then you know, a blade is not evil, it is those that wield it?"

"I do." His voice was curt and his words were spoken clearly. "But human life is not a blade; it is not my job nor yours to own another being."

"A point not asked for, nor made, Knight of Five Rivers. You asked if they were the same thing. That is the question I answer first. The difference is this; the philosophy of the sword in the hands of a villain is to impose might to make himself right. The hand of a hero on the same sword is the hand of justice, is it not?"

"Perhaps, though perhaps it is just more bullying. Done for reasons most would agree with, but bullying nonetheless."

"Maybe, but let us take your stance for a moment. The sword is outlawed; no smith will make one ever again, and all are found and destroyed. The sword exists no more. Does this solve the problem that made the sword evil?"

He smiled and continued. "I will follow this. No, it does not. Men will still kill men for the price of an apple. As we have seen with my circumstance, men will still make swords on their own. Or find other ways to do so. Those men will be found and brought to justice, and much less suffering results."

"Oh, yes, let us punish those that use swords much more harshly. You have not solved the problem. Instead where your view of things cannot be seen, men and women see swords each day, but they do not have a name for it. They call them long knives, pig stickers, the long hands of god. The evil men make the victim afraid because they tell them if they tell you that they have seen a sword, they will be punished. Even if the guard believes them, there will be no sword there when they come to investigate the claims of a victim."

"I think I am seeing what you are getting at. So how does what your culture do help these victims?"

"Evil men will always exist. Weapons and words, rape and violence, they will always be here in this world. No amount of good work will eliminate them. Even if you cut an evil completely from the world, someone will rediscover it in the future."

"So the quest for good and right is a pointless one, and we should embrace the darkness in our hearts and do no better?"

Sliverleaf remained calm and spoke clearly. "Not at all. We stop pretending it doesn't exist. Always there will be servants; always there will be poor, always. Because there will never be anyone that can do everything. Power will always belong to the ones who can win someone over to their side. Give everyone equal money, and all things needed to live, and seconds later one will willingly give some to another and that one will now have more. If someone has more, then someone has less. Slavery had its throat cut years ago; the LeatherWings came and slew it, only to have it survive here. You are but a morsel we have pulled out of its mouth."

He leaned forward, his slight frame making his words carry more weight, "A beast you and yours feed, I have not forgotten that."

"Perhaps, but our people, or rather theirs, have no shame in it. When they see abuse, they do not fear to bring it up. When they see wrong being done, they fight it. It is not slavery that is the problem. Call it indentured servitude, an employment contract, or organized labor, it does not matter. Always someone will treat those under them as lesser, worth less than they are, be it by birth, upbringing, or education. You will not stop this by outlawing slavery, or by labeling slavery as evil. Instead, those people will congratulate themselves for not being slavers. If they are not slavers, it can't be evil. You have made the word evil, not the act."

He watched her like a hawk. Almost waiting for a slip up, as if he was hoping there wouldn't be one. "A point it could be said that you have, but we consider the act evil."

She sighed. "True, but you do not define it; you think that the word makes the understanding simple enough. This is not how you stop the evil of it."

He stood straight and tall and looked down on the elf. His expression said what he thought of her arrogance, the arrogance of things people too dumb to not know what slavery meant. "Then how pray tell great one, do we defeat this evil?"

"By leaving it no room to hide." She met the challenge in his gaze with one of her own, "You have forced slavery into the shadows. From there, evil eats at its festering corpse. These men of evil instill fear in the people they prey on: fear of pain, fear of discovery, fear of shame, to keep them in line. To keep them from speaking. Much like the rapist that knows their victim dare not speak for fear of them being blamed." She took a breath and rose slowly to her feet as she continued. "They use obligation to ensure that, since I helped you, now you have to help me. They use that to keep good men paralyzed from helping so that even guards turn a blind eye. Guilt, so any that it has happened to or has done it will never speak of it." She shook slightly as she stood. "For then it will mean they will expose themselves or be seen as weak. Once into evil, evil keeps you there by telling you that there will be no forgiveness, no hope, and nothing but pain. But if you just do what we say, everything will be all right. No one really cares for you out there. At least here, you know the score."

The man spat on the ground. "You could say that the church does the same thing."

"What does that say about your church?" Sliverleaf smiled. "These people help, teach, and let those that are different live their lives. Any there know all they have to do is ask for help, and they will be heard. None are lesser; they do not even have what you would call lesser or less important ranks. They are all servants of each other, and all they meet. There, queens and kings serve the people, and their servants serve them so that they can concentrate on ruling. If the ruler abuses that servant, they simply leave, knowing that their voice will be heard. So though they have slaves, if I can put it in your way of thinking, if the King's slave can leave the King and tell their stories of abuse, then so can anyone else."

"What stops one from lying to get someone in trouble?" His words were low, almost dangerous. I don't know the game he was playing, but I was seeing more of Sliverleaf than I had ever.

"That is seen as interfering with the free will and destiny of the person you slander. An attempt to force them to act in a way they would not. That is death." Her voice remained calm.

"So all you have to say is *go ahead, no one will believe you* then they are stuck."

"Abuse of the system will happen, but when you have a people that actually care about each other? These people expect an answer when they ask you how your day was. They do not say it to be polite. By our ways, they are very strange. They are taught since birth to care for each other and to stand up for themselves.

"And this...this works?" He asked slowly.

Sliverleaf smiled, and I watched her come to terms with something inside herself. "Against everything I was ever taught? Yes. It isn't perfect. They screw up. They assume their pain is less than others more often than not, and they do not always communicate when they are hurting. But it is not because they do not believe that no one will care. It is because they do not wish to be a burden to others. Such mistakes are common from what I have seen." Her gaze settled momentarily upon Alabaster. "But when you are caught doing this, they make sure you do not wallow in guilt, and they always say you are better and encourage you to try harder."

"I had heard that they were bloodthirsty barbarians." His voice was matter of fact.

"They would consider that a compliment. They fight; they love, and they protect will all their heart. They go to war constantly amongst themselves, and all to make sure that different ideas and opinions flow."

Chapter 46

I sat there that night on watch and stared out to the darkness beyond the light of the fire. A few days ago, we'd started this journey. Now, here we were almost at its end.

It seemed unreal to me, like I had been in the grip of some fog. Ba'call was dead and in a box not far from where I now sat. The slavers were in their own slave wagon. The slaves were now freed, and one of them was coming with us to make the case against the man who bought him. Bought and then sold him to the hive for the gems. Gems the Hive didn't want.

That man then cut the gems and sold them to people for more money so he could buy slaves to give to the Hive. Nice little triangle. Since the bugs didn't consider the gemstones worth anything, because even they couldn't eat stone, it meant that our slaves were essentially sold for worthless rocks.

God, that meant that if you looked at it that way...

How could someone do that to a person? To turn them into just another commodity and trade them for something someone else thought of as worthless? My friend died because this man thought of people as *worthless*.

It would have been so much easier on me a few months ago. I could just think of this man as a monster. A villain, a thing that all he was good for was dying. Reduce him to a thing because he had hurt people. To think of him as less than human.

Now, after all this time with Alabaster, Ba'call, Sliverleaf, and the others, I didn't have that luxury. I was so lost in thought that I didn't notice Sliverleaf sit down beside me until she spoke.

"Guard means you watch for trouble my friend. You, however, are watching the fire dance. Speak to me; tell me your troubles."

I snorted. "Shouldn't I be saying that to you?" I turned from the flame to look at her. The fire light had made it so my eyes just saw a blur to begin with. Slowly her face became itself, and her grief was plain to see. "Sliv, I am sorry. This has to be so hard for you. How long were the two of you together?"

Her smile was faint. "Almost two years. I left home to try and find myself. She found me surrounded by the people my race calls Darklings. She had been sleeping in a tree the night before. The tree I found my back against." A single tear glistened in the light of the fire.

"She jumped in to help you?"

"Gods no." She shook her head and smiled. "That would have been unseemly for her, and at the time for me. She watched me fight them. Made snarky remarks on my fighting style or lack thereof, and basically was a smart ass commentator as if my life and death struggle was amusing. When I started taking more than I was giving, I told her to stop being a bitch and come help." She chuckled. "That was all she was waiting on. It took me weeks to forgive her."

She took a deep breath. "She followed me. Always a few steps back. I had picked up a stray. I was going nowhere near where she was going, but she acted like she had nothing better to do."

"What happened?"

"After trying to run her off didn't work, nor yelling at her or throwing rocks, I invited her in by the fire one night. She said that is 'all she had been waiting on'. She spent the rest of the night talking to me, but about me. She knew everything I was feeling, had felt, why I left home. She even knew I preferred women." She blushed deeply.

"The people, Elves, we are completely open sexually. Most of us at one point or the other tries both sexes. For me to have no interest in men...well, it isn't something people discuss. No one would look down on me but..." She looked away. "But Ba'call took one look at me and told me what happened. It wasn't some magic of hers; it was just who she was. She helped me like myself again." She stared out at the darkness, the pain still shining in her eyes.

It took me a moment to get it, to understand what wasn't said. I reached a hand out to her and put it on her shoulder.

She jerked out of my touch. "Don't. Better doesn't mean healed. I can talk now, but there is a reason I am usually distant."

Sliv had always seems so aloof, and now, I understood some of that. Yet with her pain, the pain of losing her friend, here she was comforting me.

I looked at her. "I am sorry, Sliv." Really, what more could I say?

"Don't be. You didn't do this, and she died protecting someone. It hurts that she is gone, but she saved me; she saved you. To me, that makes us sisters." She took a deep breath. "And you are hurting, as am I. My pain is mine, and yours is yours. By themselves, they will drag us into the pit. But if we share them, then we will both know the pain of the other, and that someone cares. Maybe even understands, and that will lessen the weight of the pain. It is the way of my people." She smiled at me, "With that, and what I learned with Ba'call, I think we can be more than hurt. Get past pain." She turned to me. "So speak of your pain with me sister, and let us lift up my love's spirit."

I took a deep breath. "She believed in me, in us. She helped me when I had questions about things with Al. She was familiar with my people, much more so than Al. She gave me a way to get a handle on things, things Al and Rowan take for granted."

She slid in a little closer. "Like what?"

"Like the difference between discipline and punishment, and why yelling isn't always bad, and why soft words aren't always good."

Chapter 47

As we sat talking, I became aware that Sliverleaf's quiet nature was a way for her to deal with things. As she started opening up, telling me about things she and Ba'call had done, she became animated. I smiled when I realized she was a hand talker. The more relaxed she got, the more her hands and arms flew. Don't get me wrong; she was obviously a very serious person which was a good counterbalance for her Mistress, but everything about her was brightening as she talked. Her eyes were wide and sparkling and held laughter.

"So there we were, still weeks north of even here. All the locals knew about the Cats is that they were uncivilized beast men. So we were sitting in the inn with Ba'call insisting on setting everything on the table in its proper place for a fancy dinner party: forks, spoons, water glass, mugs, everything. She even had a linen napkin. I have no idea where she got it, but here is this beast man sitting, as my people say, *'all poshed up'*." She chuckled with the memory. "Every local in the place was staring at us. I was so embarrassed. I asked her quietly what she was doing. I was long past the point where I tried to get her to behave in anyway other than what she decided she was going to do." She trailed off laughing.

"What did she say?"

"Tis the best meal and the best company we have had in weeks. This fine food smells as if the great ones had made it for these fair people and ourselves. Is this not a feast? And is this not one of the finest courts of people we have yet seen on our journey? Why not pull out our best manners for these, the best of peoples?"

She settled back down. "I was mortified. At the time, I thought she was making fun of those people." She turned and looked out at nothing, "But one of them sat down with us and received a greeting as if he was a royal dignitary of, as she put it, 'this fine land we find ourselves in'. Before an hour was out, she had turned the entire place into the fanciest of court functions with everyone down to cook and staff playing along. We were so loud that the guard came, but after a few moments the locals had even them joining in."

"Arona Vale." The strange voice made us both jump. "They still do it once a month. They call it the Feast of the Cat. They elect themselves a Queen to host the party, and the entire point is to have fun. It has become quite a holiday. It brings people in from most of the surrounding area."

I looked back at the voice. Our new friend whom so recently had talked with us about slavery was walking up slowly to join us by the fire. Again, he came to sit with us. Personally, after last time, I didn't think he would. "Please, excuse me. It is still colder than I would like, and I find myself as an old man. May I join you by the fire?"

Neither Sliverleaf nor I were going to deny him. So we made a place where he could sit comfortably.

Looking at him made me remember the start of my new life. Starvation can rob even the strongest of us of something deep inside. It makes you tired and more than just from hunger. It comes with a pain, an ache that is almost forgotten, but always on the edge of notice. I saw in him what I felt in myself just last fall. Feeling old and worn was a good way to describe it. I had only been an adult for a short time, and in some ways I still had the resilience of childhood.

This man was not young. If he was healthy, I would say he was coming up on over thirty summers, maybe half way to his fortieth. His black hair was still matted. It was a long style and was streaked with the white of age. His mountain had snow, but mostly it was still forest. He had dark brown eyes to match his darker skin tone. His body showed the scars of a man who lived by his sword arm. Even sick, his gait and bearing said he was not only a Knight but a guard and at least a sergeant-at-arms. He was old enough to have sired me, which probably meant that he was a father. Depending on how young he made his match, perhaps even a grandfather. If that were so, then his grands were still babes. After we got him comfortable, his sigh of release for being off his feet was more audible than he probably intended.

"My apologies for interrupting you; you sounded as if you were waking. Please do not let me interrupt."

Sliverleaf cocked her head. "My good Sir Knight, we are quite awake."

I smiled. "No Sliv, waking is to remember the dead, to celebrate their life instead of mourning their loss." I turned to him. "You follow Protista. You're a child of nature." He nodded at me and smiled.

I looked back at Sliverleaf. "He doesn't believe in death. Death is only the end of life. It is not punishment nor reward. It is like the forest. For his faith, when people die, you celebrate the good they have done. You wake for them."

His voice was strong despite his frailty. "Quite true, and though I knew not her name, I do know of the incident of the Feast of the Cat. I know of the good it did a town whose heart had died. Before you and your friend went through, the year before, their crops had all shriveled in the sun. They had to ask a local Baron for help. For this, he taxed them savagely. In all, they paid thrice what the food was worth, but they had no choice. After that feast, food and company of the good nobles of the land, as your friend put it, the common people turned the mood in the town from defeat to hope. Add that to your friend's tally of good."

A tear glistened in the fire light as it slid down Sliverleaf's face. The smile was both sad and overjoyed. "I thought she was just being her usual silly self. She probably knew, that is what her people do."

"Possibly, only the gods know." He glanced over at the lonely box. "But I do know that the Cats miss as much as they hit. This time she did well." He looked at the elf directly. "The Cat Men believe life a journey, much like my people. They see death as natural, but if her journey is not yet ended, you will see her again, and you will always carry her in your heart."

Looking at him, I realized he knew the GrassLords. He really *knew* them. "How? How do you know her people so well?"

"Over nine different tribes of them pass Five Rivers throughout the year. It is actually odd to not see them around. Granted, they mostly keep to themselves. They trade with us, but so does everyone else."

He sat back with a smile on his face. "No, their young love to sneak into the city. It's a great game for them. They would be welcomed through the gates, yet still, they climb the walls, sneak in through the water ways, even hide in carts." A soft chuckle escaped his lips. "And once they are in, they cause as much good-natured havoc as possible. Most of the nobility don't like them, but the people do. The Cat Men are the greatest jesters, clowns, and entertainers of folly our city has ever seen. Of course, the guard has to round up the ones that come without signing in and clean up the sometimes massive messes they make. But they also have strengthened our defenses, helped stop slavery in the city more than once, and saved lives. During a fire they came out of the woodwork to help. They are loved, or rued, but rarely hated."

His smile was genuine and very reminiscent of the look some-one gets with a precocious child. "But pray thee, continue. I will add when I can, but I do not seek to interrupt."

Chapter 48

As we sat by the fire, listening to its crackle, the old man looked at us. He had been listening to me telling the tales, to us talking of Ba'call and the ways of the Empire of Five. His face screwed up, and then he spoke.

"I see problems with your story, but I am old enough to know that good ideas often sound like bad ideas. There is evil in this world, and frankly it sounds as if this culture would allow it, rather than stamp it out." He stopped and looked at us. A look of shame crossed his face. "I apologize. It is your time of mourning, not the time for me to interrupt."

I agreed with him. I was all for debate. I prided myself on open discussion and reason, especially since my rebirth.

Sliverleaf had other ideas. "No harm done. Bec would have welcomed it. In her memory speak your mind."

Our charge simply nodded and continued. "It seems to me you allow people to act as they wish with no thought to propriety or decorum, as if the views of your fellow man mean nothing." He stopped and waited.

She nodded, "Please continue. I wish to be sure of what you mean before I react."

"A man walks into a wife's home while the husband is away. They spend time together, enjoy their friend who has not yet returned and nothing untoward happens. They are secluded. The town sees; tongues wag. Though man nor woman has done anything wrong, the husband heard the gossip. He went to his wife and slew her and his friend as well. His town cheered him, for this as it was viewed as right. Though no deed happened, I say to you that both were guilty of leading to evil gossip and their own murder."

I took a deep breath. I had heard such arguments before. We all had. It was proof that what man thought could cause great evil by accident. I never believed such things, but they were after their own fashion true enough. It was always the tickle in my mind as to why things with the LeatherWing could not work in the long run. Hatred and jealousy won out. Man was what man was, evil. To believe otherwise was to be naive.

Sliverleaf waited a moment, considering. Then, "The man is guilty of many crimes, as is the town itself. He acted as a beast, not man. He had no trust for his partner nor his friend. The evil words meant more to him, as did his pride, than the love of his wife." She sighed, "Had he talked to his wife or his friend rather than let the village decide his and their fate, then they would have told him of their fidelity. But the word of gossip meant more than love. He did not trust, did not love, merely possessed. He was not in love with her, but the idea of her. His hatred for her and his friend, jealous that they had something not shared with him. His evil was great, and for those that blame the couple who did no wrong, it is just as evil as if you had been the one to have murdered them."

"If they were not inappropriate this would not have happened. She was to blame."

"What is inappropriate in enjoying friendship, love and joy? Tell me what is there to be blamed."

"They did not take into account the nature of man."

"Man is not a beast, but as long as you treat him as such, that is how he will act."

"How do you mean? You let me explain myself, I can do no less." His smile was genuine; he was enjoying this.

The bastard. He was attacking her world with a tool he knew she could not counter.

Sliverleaf turned to me. "You are a thief, yes?"

Taken aback, my mouth answered my friend before my instincts told me not to speak in front of a guard.

"Uh, yes?" *What are you doing, elf?*

"When you are in a good place, a safe place where you are treated as a person, do you steal?"

My hackles were up. She had shifted the attack from herself to me, bringing my misdeeds out in front of this stranger. But trust was hard earned, and she had earned it. Despite everything that screamed at me, I answered with truth rather than offense.

"Yes, well, no not really. If I am broke, I might lighten a purse or two, but not in the inn I am staying in. It is bad for business. You don't foul your nest. Whether people know you are a thief or not, if you don't steal from them they usually won't turn you in."

His mind went to the same place mine did. Proof of what the LeatherWing had taught me, that there was little difference in the two, guard or thief. "What has this to do with what we speak? You bring up another sin to cover the first?"

"Peace guardsman, all will be clear in a moment." She turned back to me as she spoke. "Now you are in a slack inn, one with the chains on the chairs, where the keeper watches your every move, be it if you did anything or not. What do you do?"

The chuckle escaped my lips before I could check it. I had been in such a pit a time or two. "Same as even the honest men, walk off with anything and everything I can get my hands on. I have seen even the most honest of men brought to theft by such an insult."

"Why?"

"If you expect me to act the thief, to treat me as one, what do I lose by doing simply what is expected of me?" I shook my head. "If I am the saint, still, I am treated as the sinner. If I am the sinner, then at least I deserve the reproach."

Sliverleaf smiled and the older man rankled at my words. He spoke and looked at me sincerely as he did so. "But surely it is better to be virtuous even if men treat you as lesser?"

My elven sister spoke slowly. "But now you forget man's weakness. Not the one you think is there, but the actual one. Expect a lie, and you will be lied to; expect the truth, and you will get it eventually. Both our stories are on how man's view of what you do twists even honest men. In yours, a little trust would have made the difference and stopped a murder; in mine, trust would stop a thief in her tracks. So tell me, adhering to the gods of good, why does my way stop evil, and your way create it?"

"Men will always be evil. Trust will get your throat slit."

"Men will always be evil, but long before my trust gets my throat slit, I will know my sword, my arms, my armor and my shield. I am prepared for man's evil and welcome the world with trust, until it pulls blade upon me. At that point, be they good or evil, I will slay them. If they survive, then I will heal them and attempt to find the why of it. Until then, I will make the world a better place by accepting man on man's terms."

His snort of dismissal was as loud as it was unwelcome in my ears. "And yet in both cases, if they had just behaved as they should, Innkeeper and the man and woman, evil would not be done."

"Behaved as they should by whose standards?"

"The Gods, society, people standards. If you want to be a barbarian, go into the wilds and live as you like. But if you are going to live with others, act as you should, not as you wish."

"The Gods? Oh man of Five Rivers, you have stepped into the mud with those words. I follow the gods of our Father. I am of The Light. And does The Light not teach across every god that a man's tongue is his undoing? Are we not told to forgive and let others live as they will, not as we think they should? To judge the tree by the fruit it bore rather than its thorns and leaves? Or even better, does it not say beware the man that cleans the outside of the cup but leaves the inside stained?"

She took a deep breath. "In your story, people gossiped and slandered. They spoke of things that appeared to be wrong. And thus, the tree was judged by its black leaves and sharp thorns instead of its fruit of loyalty and love. When the man acted, he cleaned the outside of the cup for all to see and threw the wine of love and loyalty away." She smiled at him. "It is the priest, not the Gods that have filled your head with such words. I have read most of the writs, and while I do not know this Forest Goddess of yours, she doesn't sound like the sort to care what man thinks and says, but rather what he does. Your words are not the words of the Gods of the Light, but of Waban, Lord of Hate. You want people to behave as you feel they must. Because it offends you that they do not behave as you do. So, you shame them. But the shame is not theirs, it is yours."

He stood, his legs shook, and it was a pain I knew too well. "Shame is there to show you, that you are doing something you know is wrong. It prevents evil."

"Shame causes man and woman to hide from the light and let evil happen in the shadows. Honesty and acceptance leaves true evil no place to hide." Was her only reply.

The next action happened so fast I missed it for a moment.

She tackled the man. A man of nearly forty winters, starved to atrophy, and she tackled him. I was on my feet to pull her off of him, and it was good that I was. The scarlet bloom of blood spread its petals from the stem of the arrow lodged in her back. She had put herself in the way of the blow.

We were under attack.

Chapter 49

Firelight is bad for night vision.

People that think you keep a fire to see by or use a candle or torch by carrying it in front of yourself, have never stepped outside of their comfortable homes at night. Stage shows do this in darkened theaters and playhouses so you can see the actors' faces. Staring at a fire at night as we had been doing means your eyes aren't adjusted to anything outside of the circle of light. Not to mention the blurs it causes in your field of vision. The ghost of the flames left behind in your sight.

So, I could not see where the arrow had come from. Sliverleaf was just now getting off of the man whose life she had probably saved, so she was no help either. So, I listened.

There, off to the right just outside of the flames light was a blank spot of sound, a place where the chirps of the city of bugs had quieted down. *That way.* I reached behind me into the fire and grabbed a brand. With all my might I flung it towards the silence; at the same time I screamed.

"Arrow! Sliv's hit; we've got incoming."

Picking up the burning log scattered sparks, some of them catching on me, some on Sliverleaf and others on the guy. My hand didn't register the pain for a second but for only a second. The heat didn't leave when the brand did. I felt nothing lick my wrist, so the burn could wait.

A burning arch flew through the air and illuminated the archer. A man, dressed in dark greens, all mottled likened to foliage. A woodsman, probably a full warden like Ba'call had been. He was already moving as it flew along its path, but now his vision was as screwed as mine was. I did recognize him give a signal to someone else in the dark.

Two armored figures came in from the other side of the fire. One breaking one way around it, one the other. The first was headed towards me, the other towards our elf. I had to trust that she could deal with the second.

I feinted to the left, a movement of my body, a flinch to-wards my sword. He moved to intercept. A feint does that. Some people think a feint isn't a movement to what it looks like you are going for. No, a real feint is more fluid, a contest of wills be-tween you and your opponent. You leave yourself open to both possibility if you did it right.

As he went to intercept me and my sword, I brought the leg up I had just taken the weight off of. I swung it at the back of his knee for a sweep. The handle of his hammer had other plans. Kicking a wooden shaft with the tendon on the back of your ankle hurts a lot more than the same kick to a knee, even an armored one. Knees give, oak does not.

Ignore the pain. Move or die. I rolled away. He was between me and my sword. My daggers had other ideas.

Armor protects you. It is meant to. Forget those suits you see in plays or in Lords manors. Real armor moves. It has joints, and it covers all of you in a beetle carapace of steel, complete with giving you a funny looking butt. But you still move a little slower; it is not from weight. Good armor distributes the weight. It does tend to still keeps steps small. This man's armor was worth more than even the gems we had as it was segmented, giving him even more movement.

I hit my ass hard. My scream was of panic. I sold it well.

He came in close to disable me. Never leave an opponent, even a fallen one up again. Even if you don't kill them you can't afford someone running around. He closed in, hammer high, but turned it to ring my bell rather than crush my skull. He was being honorable. I felt bad, but just for a second. That first arrow was meant to kill the old man. Alive may have been an option but only an option.

Both of my daggers were in my hands as I scrambled away from him. Or I made it look like I was; I wanted him close. The current style of plate has a short skirt of over lapping plates over each leg with a cod piece and a buttock guard. I shoved both blades between those plates and prayed I would hit leg. The angle meant the steel and edge would go up.

Blood coursed down my hands before his scream tore its way out of his body.

Behind me, I heard a snarl not that unlike a great cat; my heart seized. Logic told me she was dead. My spirit had still not let go of the hope. I turned, not towards the sound, but towards that forlorn box.

Still closed tight.

Not her, not her.

I turned towards the sound, my grip relaxing on the hilts of the knives. Rowan was all wings, a fury. She had sprung upon another attacker. Neither the Woodsman, nor either of the knights, but a figure in simple clothing whose hands shimmered colorlessly in the light. I watched as her claws stopped inches from the figure's chest, halted by something that flashed brilliant blue when she struck. The mage smiled, but the look was as feral as anything that faced her. I recognized a woman's face and form but didn't know her.

Her body may have been saved from the claw attack, but her neck still took the brunt of Rowan's in sweeping wings, one to either side. Not a lot of damage, but a world of pain and distraction. The shimmer disappeared from around the woman's hands.

The white blur to the left side told me that Alabaster was also tangling with someone, but they were outside my sight. A quick glance told me Sliverleaf wasn't faring as well. The woman on her had pulled her up by her hair and was wiping something black across her face.

No idea what it was, No time to find out.

This man had offered me and mine harm; if he still lived after this was done, I could allow myself to remember he came in for a disabling blow rather than a killing one. For now, I didn't have that luxury. Already on the ground I got my feet underneath me. He batted at me with his hammer. It thunked solidly into my back. I reversed the grip on the handles as I moved. My back screamed in protest. Definitely a bruise, better that than a broken back, I scream at myself in my mind. *And break you he will if you don't move.*

With both of my legs under me I shoved against the earth with all my might. My weight and his made my feet dug furrows into the ground. Dead lifting a man is not something I can do. I don't have the strength, and my blades weren't meant to handle weight, not like this. I felt the handles twist in my hands; they were slick with blood, and the edge bit into him anew. Then, sickeningly, I felt, rather than heard something pop. He became dead weight, legs no longer able to hold him. To my horror the hilts snapped off in my hands. My force up and his weight down was too much for them.

I broke the knife Alabaster had given me.

I had expected a scream, a moan, something to have escaped this ruined man. You would have too, but no, I watched his eyes glaze over as I was face to face with him. A strange grimace came across what I could see of him through his helm slit. But his eyes, his eyes had almost a relief in them. Then darkness...then nothing.

I could not worry about what it meant, would not. Sliv was gagging, crying in anguish. As he fell before me, I was already moving. I did not wish to see how he fell.

Whatever the black stuff was, it was alive. It clung to her face and then started moving on its own. Creeping over her eyes, nose, and sealing her mouth, filling it.

My sword is not meant to take on armor like what she was wearing. It just wasn't. It could cut her, maybe wear her out. If I could keep it up long enough, I might even win if I could avoid her killing me first. No armor is perfect, but a completed suit of knight's armor is pretty damn close. Killing her wasn't an option.

Knights against each other will actually reverse those long swords they carry and use a maneuver they call "The Hammer". They strike with all the force they can muster, bringing the hilt, cross-guard, and pommel down on the helm. It can stagger even the best trained and armored knight. I didn't have a long enough sword to do that with, but I did have a convenient hammer.

I grabbed the discarded weapon, moved behind the woman. She didn't notice me. She was gloating over our elf's form, reveling in my friend's panic. A string of words were pouring forth from her, joy in her voice, joy at the suffering of another. I brought the hammer up as high as I could without over balancing myself. Seriously, pick up something heavy, swing it over your head and you are just as likely to go backwards as be able to hit your target.

My shout of fury was joined by another, a shout of warning. The woodsman had come back into the light and was screaming over the din of battle. Had she not been so intent, she would have seen him before I did. As it was she was turning her head when I brought the hammer down on her helm. Her head snapped around violently. She had no time to react; my blow was well aimed. I didn't get to enjoy my success.

Two arrows hit me back to back. One in my arm making it fall. A numbness hit before the pain. The pain was insignificant for what was happening, not nearly enough. The second flew towards my face. *"Aim small, miss small"* is meant for aiming for buttons on a chest. I turned my face away. It flew by me, but my cheek caught fire! A burst of pain that was again not in proportion to where I had been hit. The world was slowed. I felt the veins, the feathers, as they went through the cut neatly torn into my face. I reached up and brushed my cheek with the back of my hand. The leather of my glove ground into the raw flesh. My cheek was laid open. I had moved and queered the shot, but not enough. A nick, hopefully.

How much damage was done to me would have to wait. The arrow had continued on, so my skull didn't stop it. That was good. One arm down, bleeding, and my world reduced to so much pain.

But alive.

Slowly, too slowly, I looked back over at the archer, the woodsman. His bow was already coming up with a new shaft notched. His aim was true, and I was still moving from the shot that didn't kill me. I screamed at him. All my anger, all my frustration, Piper's hand, Ba'call's death, Sliverleaf's rape and now torture at his friends hands, all my hate, every injustice I ever felt.

It did nothing.

On his face was written much the same. My pain could not impress him, he carried it too. I felt for him, even as I flung the hammer with my good hand, I felt for him. I knew it would not really hurt him, but maybe it would mess up his aim.

I missed completely. I think the handle caught his leg. One of those brushing things.

I was dead. I still hadn't even hit the ground, but it wouldn't be long now.

When I hit, I would roll towards him. Logic said roll away, logic, instinct, call it what you will, you don't go towards the guy trying to kill you, and that is exactly why I was going to do it. If I made it to the ground before he loosed the arrow he would expect me to go anywhere but towards him. It would cause a second of delay.

His arm was almost at full extension; the hammer throw didn't buy me enough time.

My eyes registered it before my mind did. I felt a smile spread across my lips and had no idea why.

He saw the change in my eyes. His face went from grim determination to confusion. Then I have no idea what was on his face anymore; I could no longer see it.

A white blur hit him hard. Arms wrapping around his chest. It knocked him off his feet and straight into the waiting blow of a great sword. You would think that Alabaster and Arwen had discussed this, but they simply didn't have time. Alabaster was still moving. The savagery I had once glimpsed, now set loose, all to protect me and his friends.

I turned my head to survey the field. The Knights seem to be down. The male was still; the female was kind of rocking. The old guard was with Sliverleaf, helping to clean off the black morass from her face and calming her. A bottle from somewhere was in his hand, and he was pouring it on her head. His foot was on the sword of the female knight.

Good, that is taken care of.

I changed focus, already making it to my feet from training not to be on the ground when the guard came kicking. A burst of light shone off to my left; the boys were off to the right. They seemed to have it under control though.

Left it is.

Rowan rocked back on her heels. A second flash of blue fire hit her in the chest plate. It was already scorched. Her eyebrows were gone, as well as some of the hair on top of her head. The woman's neck showed bruising, her clothing was disheveled. I had thought that Rowan had the mage; my mistake.

Behind her was a man on the ground. He was also in robes, gold and red. He was a priest of Ca'talls. Under that robe would be armor; I knew his kind. He was on the ground, but his hands were still outstretched and around Rowan's ankle.

He had taken the opportunity to distract her. Probably when Alabaster rushed to save me. Now it was my turn to save a friend. No daggers, no hammer, but my sword was beside me.

Never fight fair. Just don't do it. If two honorable people fight, it is called a match. It has rules; things you can do; things you can't. Combat has none of that. Granted, some things are still bad form. Picking up a small child to use as a shield is definitely one of them, but if you think that way, rules don't mean a damn thing for you anyway, or at least it shows you to be a bastard and probably evil. At least in my book. If you are in combat, fight dirty. Fight to survive.

Two steps back, reach back grab sword.

Good, it hasn't shifted in the meantime.

Next, kick log into fire, hard.

Noise and sparks draw everyone's attention. Sword is behind back, out of sight.

Still look unarmed, wounded.

Light and sound dazzle.

They all turn, stop watching me. The Priest is getting to his feet. Quickly, I jump through the shower of sparks. My eyes are closed. Once I hit the other side, I run into the darkness. I stumble. Good, that is the edge of camp and most of the light.

I open my eyes. Some of my night vision has already returned. I turn right and head off into the dark.

Now it looks like I have run off. Who can blame me? I am wounded, out of action; I have no weapon, and I just had to have two party members save me. I hope they buy it. I change the way I walk as I run, cutting back behind.

Please, if there are Gods, and any of you bastards care about anyone in that group let me make it back without being seen.

There, the mage, I crept up behind her. Sword reversed for a pommel strike. The priest shouted a warning; she turned.

See, this is what you get when you rely on gods.

I struck fast. Her nose met steel and erupted into a spray of fluid.

"I've got her. Get him." I didn't wait to see.

Always assume your partners are doing their part of the job. If you can't trust them for that, why are they partnered with you? You always want to be aware of your surroundings in a fight; someone might need your help, but Rowan was now one on one. The sound she made sent chills up my spine. This close, it was definitely not Bec's call. I could not imagine fighting more than a few LeatherWings if they all had battle cries like that. I think I would break and run.

Head out of the clouds, girl.

I turned and looked squarely at the mage. She was righting herself, but blood was flowing down her face.

She brought her hands up to start a new spell. I jumped at her. Wrapped my legs around hers waist, my hands around her throat and rode her to the ground. I could feel the invisible force of her "armor", and it kept me from really getting to her. Plus, it was slick; it made holding her hard. It felt like slimy eel skin, rough and slippery all at the same time.

Screw it. I sat on her hips in the most unladylike fashion and bounced on her. I slid around a little, but it kept her down. I then took double handfuls of dirt and dumped them on her up turned face, right into her open mouth. I didn't throw it, just let go and let it slip out from between my finger. It work, she gagged, and started wiping her face. It wasn't an attack, so she didn't react like it was.

Screw decorum, I started bouncing on her like an over enthusiastic lover while picking up more handfuls of dirt and just dropping them in about the right area. She responded like anyone that doesn't want some asshole on top of her dumping dirt on her face.

She started and kept wiping at the dust and bucking to get me off. The slickness of her phantom armor worked in my favor. I wasn't holding her down; I was riding her. She didn't have the strength to throw me off.

After a few more seconds of this, she shocked the hell out of me. She started crying. She just collapsed laid there and balled.

I watched her for a moment for a trick. There didn't seem to be one. I rolled off of her, ready for a fight. She curled up and protected herself. Tightly into a ball like a small child.

Okay. Let's see what's left.

Rowan and the priest were still going at it. His mace glowed faintly as he swung it at her head. She was already ducking the blow and going in for one of her own. Good a place as any, I suppose.

"GET'ATTA WALNASH. HALNART TORATANA. SHI CORRATTA NU FLIVE RULLAS BUALLT WORND ORN AFFARS!" The scream was load and meant to be obeyed.

Authority is a funny thing. Give a man enough and you listen even if you don't know the language. I stopped cold. So did everyone else, especially our attackers.

The old guard was on his feet. Legs were trembling, but he stood proud. In trade he continued. "Healers, you Alabaster and you Cleric of the Light. Start with the knight there. If you do not move soon his life will finish spilling out on the sands."

They both moved without question. I knew why Alabaster did. I could not think why the other guy would.

Who the hell is this guard we had picked up?

"As of right now, by my authority, I am taking both sides prisoner. You will take orders from me by order of the High Council of Five Rivers. Rowan, see to their mage. She might respond best to you at the moment." He and I watched as she moved to obey, then he continued. "Sir Arwen, check all other combatants and take their weapons, their team and yours both, please." He looked around. "Chloe, sit before you fall." With that he reached down and helped Sliverleaf up. "Please, sit by the fire; the Mage Bane is still in your system." He looked at the remainder of the attacking group. "Black Fang Rock. Who leads you now?"

The priest looked up and at the old man, "Kraimer of the Deep." He gestured at the fallen man.

"Who is your second?"

"Me." The woman at his feet answered him. She was sitting now, with her helm off and with her head between her knees.

"I am second, former leader of the Black Fang Rocks, before Kraimer took over."

He turned back towards the woman. "And what was your contract adventurer?"

"To take down the thieves and slavers who had stolen Lord Corbin Shale's latest shipment and to prevent them from selling it in his own town then taking their slaves back to the Empire of Five."

Chapter 50

I stared at the Knight as if she had grown two heads. The allegations were astonishing. "What?" Don't get me wrong. I heard her, but she might as well have just said that we were all butterflies, and she was merely trying to net us.

The old guard ignored my question. Can't say as I blamed him really. It didn't add anything to the conversation. "Go on. Tell us your story. How and when you were hired and what were you told?"

"Lord Corbin keeps a small retainer with the local guild. He likes to hire new blood and give them a chance, but he is also aware that sometimes the groups are less than honest." She was glaring at us still. "We were new to town; just got in when we got offered a job. He explained he had hired a few of the southern demons, an Elven Sorceress, a Beast Woman, and a human girl. He told us it turned out the girl was a slave who needed freeing. On top of that, they had taken delivery of his goods and then went off to meet someone else. They were overdue by a week when he got word that they were spotted headed back this way with a slave wagon with people inside. They were headed back to their monstrous empire." She was looking dead at the slave wagon now.

I squeezed my eyes shut. Their leader had been trying to save me. He had been trying to save me and I had probably killed him, certainly crippled him. I knew I was crying before I opened my eyes.

"How long ago was this?" I had to know.

"Two days. We were met just outside of town by about a day. A messenger with all the right paperwork intercepted us. He said that we needed to be on our way before they-" she gestured at us, "-had a chance to make it to town or change roads. Just stop them before they got to hand off the goods and people."

Her group had lost. Their woodsman was not being brought to the fire and he was not moving. Low moans were finally coming from the knight I had wounded.

Good, not dead, not dead. Let's hope the clerics could get their miracle.

Rowan had gotten their mage up and was wrapped around her, rocking and soothing. Five on five and we had won. Our victory had only cost us one death, and it wasn't one of ours.

A man who had been lied to about who and what we were was dead by our hand. We were all just puppets of the man we were going to bring down.

I hung my head. The old guard looked at me as if reading my mind "You did not murder this man. You were defending yourself. You are not the one that sent him to his doom. That would be the man who was selling me and the others to the Children."

The woman looked at him. "What did you say?"

"These people you were sent after; they saved me. They broke up a slave ring that was to sell me and others to the bugs. That is where your Lord Corbin has been getting his gems. The men in that slave wagon are the slavers, not the slaves. Chloe and company were taking them to Cliffport to stand trial with me as witness. You were lied to."

Her scream of rage shook me. I stood. As I did exhaustion overwhelmed me. My hand hurt; it screamed at me. My arm caught fire and throbbed. Then my head reminded me that it too was hurt. The world swam black; the fire darkened. The night sky came into view before it too was gone. It was all too much.

I'm falling.

Chapter 51

I woke to the feel of a fire near me. A dull ache was present in my body. It took me a moment to realize why. My cheek was the worst of it, followed by my arm. I looked down at it. New skin was pink over the hole the arrow had placed in me. It ached but didn't hurt.

I looked around to get my bearings. This was not where we were. I slowly reached for my knives to find them no longer there. I looked out further. I was still. No need to move as of yet. I saw the female knight tending to the male knight...

Alright, I knew she was alive, and now I knew he was too. Had things turned while I was out? I wasn't bound. Trust first; I am not an animal that just reacts. What was her name? I couldn't remember. Shift gears.

"Water?" I sat up slowly. With my right hand, I keep the covers close to my chest. I curled my hand around the loose soil cupping it firmly. If this went south, or more south I should say, then her face was the target.

She turned and looked at me then spoke in Trade. "I don't speak your north tongue. What do you want?" The venom in her words was plain to hear, but it didn't feel like it was still directed at me.

Alright, good to know. She didn't speak Highlander. Probably also meant she didn't speak LeatherWing. I switched to Trade; communication was better than ignorance here.

"Water." I sat up more bracing myself with the handful of dirt. Quicker to fling it and fall back at the same time. She was already coming over with a skin. "Where is everyone else?"

From behind me came the answer in the voice of the old guard. "Out. You are with me, and technically still my prisoner Chloe. Relax. Your friends are safe. Your Alabaster and Rowan are scouting ahead to see if we have any other surprises waiting. Sliverleaf is looking for herbs to tend to the wounds. Their healer, Maric, is gathering more wood and water. You nearly bled to death young lady. You're a fighter; I'll give you that."

"You also nearly crippled our leader for life, wench." The woman's tone was bitter. I couldn't blame her.

Alright, no love lost there. Blood was inevitable if you were going to be an adventurer. I had gotten into this for money. Now I wonder if any amount of money is worth this.

As I sat up the rest of the way, I surveyed the camp. Arwen was at the edge of the firelight...Sliverleaf, Alabaster, Rowan and now Arwen. My group was mostly intact after our last fight. Looks like I got the worst of it. I brushed the dirt off my hand and winced. Right, I had grabbed the log out of the fire.

Looking at it was a bit of a relief. It was not bandaged and only slightly red, but it was very tender.

As for the other group, their leader was alive, and the armored woman had gone back to tending to him. Their cleric was off getting water. I didn't see their mage, and I knew what happened to their woodsmen. We were mostly intact. Mostly. Two were dead because this man, this Corbin Shale, had lied to all of us. He had lied to me, and I believed him.

I had dealt with liars all my life. I should have known better. No amount of gold was worth Ba'call's life, nor the life of their woodsman.

No, not gold, but we had stopped his plans. Saved people, saved the man who had just saved us. Ba'call died saving me, and I will be damned if I was going to sit and let that man do this again to anyone else. Yes, for me, Ba'call's life, my life, would be worth stopping him and men like him. For Bec, I would be better. As for the money? A girl's got to eat, but if the money wasn't right and the cause was, then screw the money.

I looked back at the guardsman and cocked my head. His eyes were on me intently. I had planned to ask him a question; now a different one sprang to mind. "What?"

With a chuckle he broke eye contact and looked at first ground, then stars. "I was going to be asking about the pain, the blood of your path." His Highlander was still accented, but understandable. "But the look that was crossing your face. I have seen this look many times. My Captain often wears such a look."

Alright, now I definitely needed to ask instead of just wanting to. "Who are you? You stopped their attack cold."

A look crossed his face, one of humility.

My god, an actual humble man.

"I am D'arren Lanshire. I was a 'nobody' noble, but am a Lieutenant to the Captain of the Guard and High Paladin of the Church of Ca'talls in Five Rivers." He shuffled a foot, looking more like a man of only twenty winters instead of well in to his thirties. "It's kind of an important placement I don't feel I've earned completely."

I gave him an eye. "How could you be a 'nobody' noble?" Never had I heard of such a thing."

He swallowed hard and looked at me. "By being the ninth son of a villain, my Lady."

"I'm no Lady."

"But you are. I just watched you count the cost of this little endeavor and find its worth not in gold, but in lives spared and saved. Your face might be hidden to others, but I have seen such looks before. My Captain often wears such a face. He knows both the tragedy and comedy of life, and he counts his worth as you do in lives, not coin. I think he would like you and you him."

I snorted. "A guard thinks a thief a Lady. If this is what your captain teaches you, I might like him after all."

"I have seen Ladies, landed and noble, whom were little more than thieves at the tit of the world, and I have seen thieves being more noble than church nuns. Yes, this is the example he sets, for the people, the guard, and the Church."

I snorted. Time to try that new outlook again. "Ca'talls and his own are a blight upon my land and town back home. I fled to get out from under their grasp. But I have since learned not all churches teach false. If this man leads your church then yes, I will meet him. I was going to Five Rivers anyway."

"Good, I will introduce you to him myself. He will want to meet you I am sure of it. His own..."

The sound of mail on flesh drove the conversation to a halt. My head whipped to the noise fast enough to crack my neck. The woman had just slapped the man she had been administrating to. Their conversation had been in the back of my awareness, but I didn't understand what they were saying. Whatever it had been, now it was a fight.

He was sitting up and looked as if to stand, naked from the waist up, covered by furs from there down. His voice was pitched and broke, betraying a youth his looks did not give. She took exception to what he said and yelled back at him a string of word that was cut off by his insistence of some fact. Then calmer he carried on, firm but not cruel.

To my side D'arren translated. "He is saying you are not to blame, not for his injury nor Calvin's death. She says they should not be here with his murderers nor helping us no matter what my rank is. She said Calvin would agree with her."

I swallowed hard. *Murderers.* That is what she thought of us. Their fight went on, but I knew what he had said that cut her off. Calvin was dead. A man I had never met whose pain was so deep that I saw it across the battlefield, and now, I would never know him.

"He is saying that we are on the side of right; that they were tricked." His words were flying almost as fast as the knights words were. The woman cut him off with a voice so venomous that it made me shudder.

"What is she saying?" I wanted to know. No I didn't, not really. I need to know.

"You won't like it. I know I don't."

She continued on with that same voice, cold, hateful and flowing with rage.

"Tell me."

"They are beasts, like the elf defiler, the demon puppets. Even the real people here are in league with them. After the suffering we have seen, they deserve to die for that even if we were lied to about why." D'arren's face contained not anger or rage but sorrow. Hearing these words hurt him somehow.

I wanted to speak. I think he did too, but the Knight, with bare hands, slapped her across her helmed face. The slap was hard enough that it knocked her down. In a voice bellowing with rage he spoke, no, commanded the prone warrior, for he was not speaking to her as a woman, to leave his sight. No words shared were needed; his gestures and mannerism communicated his full meaning. One of their Knights obviously had honor.

He looked towards me, but my eyes were only for his thighs. Pale pink scar tissue was twisted and knotted from his outer hips down the length of a few inches on the outside of each. My handiwork. The blades hadn't cut so much as has torn the tender meats of his legs. No wonder he passed out. I felt shame and guilt wrack through me. It didn't break until he suddenly reached down and covered himself with the furs.

He had been completely naked under there, and I only had eyes for the damaged I had wrought.

His voice broke through my embarrassment. "Hear me, did you?"

I looked up at his eyes and shook my head. "Women." He muttered to the man at my side. "I said do not take her words to ill. Her and her company had two leaders before. One was her. The other was her husband. The company did fare not so well. Captured and killed was her husband. Elves to who the forest is everything, and humans are less than nothing. Tortured they were, and for a length of time it was great. They took to raiding Elven settlements and putting them to the torch." He sighed

"I step in before too much damage they did. But healing-" he shrugged, "-for my sister in bonds of law, it has not been easy. All not human is her enemy, even now two years hence."

He looked me in the eye again. "Your blades found true marks. Be not ashamed of surviving. Blame you I don't. Blame the man who lied to you and mine. He is guilty of Calvin's death, not you. No guild will work with him after this. And if the Southern..." He trailed off shaking his head. "I am sorry, no other word do I have for them, Southern Devils are as lawful as claimed then he will answer for the death he caused in both our families."

With that he stiff-legged walked out after the woman who had been married to his brother.

Chapter 52

We arrived in town a few days after that exchange. We were as well as Alabaster and their healer York could make us. Sliverleaf had repaired our armor as best she could. D'arren was riding well now with nearly a week's food on the right side of his ribs.

Cliffport's sky bridge was just as impressive as it was the first time I saw it. It brought a smile to my face to see it again and a sting to my heart to know that despite what had happened, the world didn't realize it had changed.

At the first guard post we hit; we told our story. Most of our prisoners were happy to add to it bits and pieces of this tragedy or that. A lot of them were just thankful not to be as sick as they had been.

We were all escorted to the Magistrate's office where we got to tell the tale again and again. Each time, we got to wait, and the Guards with us got asked if it was the same tale or not. Finally, before the bench of the Lords of Cliffport, we got to tell it one last time.

We were asked question after question. We showed them the box of sand with the slave papers in it, as well as the box of gems.

I didn't talk much, mostly just nodded. They had a Warden come in and look over the wounds Ba'call had received.

Seeing her like that made the tears start again.

When we got to the part where we got ambushed, the woman tried to have us brought up on charges for the death of Calvin, their Warden. She was as venomous and hateful as before. I cringed inside with every word she spoke. It was decided that the death was not our fault but the fault of the employer. His punishment for that would be the striking of his name from guild rosters.

As for all the other crimes he was charged with, the course of action was clear. He would have to be brought in, a trial would have to be called, and we were given the honor of going with the guard to arrest him. That was something both groups could agree on.

So, with twenty guards and two groups of adventurers, we went down to his little dock side warehouse. Each of us armored as if battle waited just outside.

The building was just as I last remembered it. It would have three entrances at the front and the large loading ramp and receiving door at the back. We split up to cover them all. We didn't want him getting away. Had it been a little closer to the water, I would have thought about a boat door.

With the main force being me and my crew, as well as half the guards, we took the front while the other half took the back with the second group. We walked into his shop as if we owned the place. The front keeper looked at us as we poured into the shop from every door as if we had grown antlers upon our heads.

"C-Can I help you?"

"We have come for your master by right and writ of the Lords of Cliffport. Stand aside."

He looked at us and back towards his master's office. "Of course, right this way."

He nervously got up from behind his desk and walked us back towards the office door at the back of the show room. What I had admired before in the craftsmanship of the gem work now was just a glaring reminder of the blood that paid for it.

He opened the door and preceded us, announcing us and the guard as if everything was normal despite the circumstance he found himself in.

"Master Shale, the LeatherWing group as well as the guard are here to see you."

Shale surprised me when he got up and came in front of his desk and off his throne to address us. Men like him usually like to have something between him and the people coming to arrest them.

"What seems to be the trouble here?" His tone was light and not at all worried. He settled himself with his hip leaning against his desk; his pose was relaxed. Did he think this would just go away?

The Captain of the Guard stood forward "On behalf of the City of Cliffport and the Nation of the Empire of the Five, I am here to place you under arrest, to take possession of your ill-gotten gains and all your papers."

He nodded. His lower lip was slightly protruding as if con-templating what was just said. He seemed more annoyed than worried. "And what are the charges?"

"Slavery."

He smiled. "Is not slavery legal in the Empire? Is it not one of the so-called *sacred duties*?" He shifted and stood before his accusers as if he had done nothing wrong, as if he was untouchable.

Alabaster broke first. "Slavery is, but what you are doing is criminal and wrong. You hurt them and harm them. You sell them. You gave them to the damn bugs as food and for what? So you can get richer?"

"Be that as it may, slavery is legal."

The letter of it, yes, but he didn't know a few things. I found myself speaking words so very new to my lips. "The Law of Slavery: to masters, it is a privilege to own a slave, and they are your most prized possession. Feed them before you eat. Clothe them before you clothe yourself. See to your needs after you see to theirs. Teach them your way and learn from theirs; mistreat them at your peril." I stopped and looked at him. "You have definitely eaten before they did. You have definitely clothed yourself first. You stand there and say, 'slavery is legal', but by their standards, what you have done is not slavery." I looked over at Alabaster, at Sliverleaf, at Rowan, at the spot where Bec should have been, even at Arwen. "This isn't what you and I call slavery. They call it slavery; we call it family. For them, it is a way to adopt an adult and bring them into your family. To show them a better way." I looked back at the son of a bitch. "You? You just use people."

He nodded. "I see." He stood straight and tall as if accepting his fate. "Now, I will pay the price for my pride, and you will pay the price for your uncivilized laws. You see, James, the man who led you back here, is as culpable under your backwards law as I am. It means his death as well as mine. He has nothing to lose. Do you now, James?"

We are turned to look at the little clerk at the same time. He was standing by the huge glass case that held the golden grubs. "No, Master, I do not."

As he broke the glass, Corbin stomped his left foot onto the floor while we were all looking at James.

The trap door Corbin was standing on gave way and dropped him and the rug concealing it out of sight.

We had bigger problems.

The grubs were moving. They swarmed James, the man who had set it all off. His body quickly became covered in foot long golden grubs. Their bloody needle-like teeth ripped him apart as they swarmed over him. He was still alive and screaming as they ate him. As they gorged themselves on him, his clothing, the wood of the floor, anything and everything else they could get their mouths on, they began to spread out towards us. As soon as their little bodies got fat enough, they would stop moving and excrete a new golden slime covered body which would then start eating and growing.

The creatures came straight for us. Well, some of them did. Some of them were going for the walls, some the chair, some the drapes and other cloth, some the carpets on the floor. Hundreds of them, if not more, seemed to be eating everything in sight.

I lashed out and stepped on the nearest one. It squished under my boot, offering no more resistance than if I had stepped on a rotten plum. I stomped another.

Then another.

But it was like stomping on ants. The creatures stopped their advance only long enough to eat their fallen comrades. Otherwise, they were unfazed as they teemed towards us. I heard the door swing back open, and Sliverleaf started screaming at us.

"Out! Do not look back. Bring oil, torches, anything that burns. If they get out, the town is lost." We ran through the showroom; the bugs not yet following us, but undoubtedly they would be soon enough. Then it hit me. To save ourselves and the town, we would have to burn this place. The fire would destroy all the evidence, including who else was involved and who, if anyone, he had been taking orders from.

I moved, shoving the guard that was between me and the door before me. As my shoulders got even with the frame of the front door I was knocked forward onto my face by the wall of heat from mage's spell.

From the ground, I looked to see her framed in fire as she came out of one of the side doors. Some of her hair had caught as she herself backed out of the door, sending small ball after small ball to explode into the ruins of the floor and surge of the grubs.

For now, we had a bigger problem than evidence. The Children of Am'met were here to feed.

Chapter 53

The building's front was starting to catch. Fire spells, I am told, would not be much good if they caught everything in the area on fire every time you cast them, but if you pour enough of them into a spot back-to-back, you can ignite things. This building was starting to go nicely.

Here's the problem with a building fire in a city...other buildings tend to be around. This causes one and only one reaction out of every good city dweller upon seeing the fire, the bucket brigade.

The guard were running up and yelling for buckets of water and had already started organizing the citizens and dock workers that had sprung into action.

Our guard, on the other hand, was yelling at them to bring lamp oil, fish oil anything that would burn and quickly.

What's more, the people at the back, the other group of our people, had no idea what was going on. They had undoubtedly run in at the sound of spells going off. Now, I was hearing incoherent screaming from the back. They may have just walked into that nightmare, and we didn't have a way of telling them not to before they did.

I screamed a command at any guard I saw, *"Burn it! Burn it down! For your lives burn it!"* I don't think I had ever screamed so loudly in my life, but it was too late. Between the confusion of the bucket brigade and the people who knew what was going on, one of the walls was eaten through, and the creatures poured forth out onto the streets.

I moved as fast as I could and grabbed two of the three children who had been bouncing farthings off the side of a nearby building. Normal stuff, kid stuff. They hadn't moved in the confusion of the fire. The adults would take care of it, and the fire wasn't on this side. It is what made it perfect for the bugs to get through.

One child was left.

I had no more arms. I wasn't strong enough.

I looked back over my shoulder seeing the boy run for all he was worth.

He wasn't fast enough. He wasn't going to make it ahead of the wave of glittering bodies.

Arwen jumped between him and the grubs' hungry needle like mouths. He fell as he did, but he shoved the boy with all his might. I heard the bone in the lad's arm snap as he fell.

Better that than other things. Arwen had thrown him past me. I swung the smaller of the two boys I was caring onto my back. I hoped he would hold on. I learned right then and there; little kids know how to hold on. As I ran past the boy Arwen had saved, I grabbed a fist full of his hair. "Move you little brat. Or do you want to be dinner?"

"But the man?" Despite his protest, my helping hand was all he needed to get off his ass and move. I looked back. Arwen's chain was keeping the bugs at bay; they were having trouble biting through it. They were swarming him, but he was pulling and snatching at their bodies. I didn't know if his God is real or not, but for his sake, I hoped she was.

Keep going; keep on the job. Your partners will do their part, or they won't. Worrying about it won't do you or them any good. I'd kill him later if he didn't survive.

That would show him.

I deposited the ruffians down past the guard's line. Good rule to live by. The good guys? They're the ones running towards the place everyone else is running away from. Today, I was one of those good guys.

I had no bloody idea what I was going to do.

There are certain smells in life you never ever forget. Once, while playing on the docks as a front to pick pocketing, I asked the fishermen how they got the oil off themselves at the end of the day. Most said they didn't, but one gave me a wink and let me smell what he used. He said it was alcohol made from the blood of evergreens. Said it would take anything off. His friends said yes, it would; just don't get it too near the fire.

Evergreen alcohol has one of those smells you never forget. I smelled it now.

I turned, leading with my nose. This stuff cut the smell of the fish, but it was hard to tell where it was coming from. Then I saw it. One of the buildings was being repainted. I felt a wicked smile spread across my face.

I grabbed the nearest guard.

"If you believe in gods, you had better thank them and come with me. I got an idea." I held on to his arm as I headed for the building. In my mind, no god would let the Children exist, let alone let them in a city this size, but if there was such a thing then this would provide believers with proof. To me, it was just cosmic coincidence.

But I would take it.

When the smell hit his nose, he looked at me. "Are you mad girl? That stuff burns hot and spreads quickly. The building won't be salvageable, and it might take the rest of the block with it."

"Better the block than the city. Those things won't stop."

He nodded in grim understanding.

We looked for and finally located the source of the smell, a large oaken barrel with brushes still in it. Problem was it was too big for us to move.

I muttered. "So much for your gods."

"What was that?" He looked over at me.

"Nothing. Find its lid and something to move it with."

"I can call for help."

"Which is quicker, yelling with the other yells and hoping someone figures out that it's for a different reason? Or doing as I say?"

He started looking for the top. I started looking for a mallet. Wooden barrels can be recapped, but you need a good mallet to do it. I found one about the time he came over with a barrel top...to one of the paint barrels. "All I could find miss."

I glared at him. Since we had nothing to lose I tried it. It fit. Not well, but good enough.

"Open the door! We are gonna roll this thing over to the bugs." With that I started knocking the top back on. It was a pain in the ass, and didn't want to go. Or maybe, I had just never actually done this before. Either way, it took me a bit longer than I would have liked. When I looked over; however, the big door was still closed. "Why is the door still shut?"

"It has a padded locked miss; can't seem to find the key."

"The city burning to the ground is the better option of what we face today, and you are worried you can't find the key to a lock easily replaced?"

He looked at me as if I had lost my mind. Then slowly, he blinked.

I don't know what it is actually called, but I have seen that kick used in combat. I had always wondered how effective it really was. I watched him bend forward at the hip and kick back out behind him with his leg. The ring that held the chain in place and the door closed popped out when it reached the end of its length.

"Good point my Lady." He bowed towards the door like some sort of gentleman. "Shall we ma'am?" Was all he said as he came over and started helping me roll the barrel.

The absurdity of it struck me as funny.

Chapter 54

Alabaster saw me as we were rolling the barrel over. He didn't ask what was up; he just jumped in and helped us push it. He yelled at people to get out of the way, and to my amazement, they did. When the way was clear, I saw that Arwen had indeed managed to get the little abominations off of him even though he was covered in blood. Sliverleaf was using that same spell to blast the horde back into the building and try to keep them there.

"All is lost. We should evacuate. They will dig into the rock and wait. If we don't get some oil on them, the fire won't touch them at all." The strain on her face was apparent, and she looked ready to drop. Blood was pouring down her nose and ears. Tears streaked with red lent color to her pale face. She was pushing herself past exhaustion.

Grinning, I called out to her, "I got it covered." And with that I nodded to the guard, and we kicked the barrel into the building. It gathered enough momentum on the down slope to jump the meager lip of the boards and rolled gently inside.

Sliverleaf called over, "You found a barrel of oil?"

"Nope." The guard grinned. "Found a barrel of 'Tine."

I watched the elf's eyes go wide with terror as she screamed "Run. Don't ask; *run*!"

Rule two, when the heroes you saw running towards the danger start running away from it *you keep up.*

I followed her lead, and when she stopped I stopped. She settled behind a wagon that had wound up turned on its side during the commotion.

"What's wrong?"

"When 'Tine gets hot enough and it can't catch fire, it goes up."

"Up?" I looked at her confused. "How up?"

"Very." The shock wave hit first, then the sound. It knocked the cart onto us, breaking the wheels as it did. We wound up flat on our faces, our lower legs were pinned, but it didn't feel like it had its full weight on us.

So, that is 'how up'.

My head rang, as did my ears. How those two things could be separate, I have no clue, but they were. I looked down. The wagon was resting on my legs but not by much. The metal strut meant to keep the cart stable in motion (I have no idea what they are called; they look like iron bows to me) had held. That and the axle had kept almost all the weight of the cart off my legs. Sliverleaf was already sliding hers free. I followed suit. Scraped and bloody but not broken.

That was good.

I stood and looked back at the warehouse fire. It was going now, full and flaming. It looked like every part of it was on fire.

Boards and debris lay radiating out from the door of the place. Some of it was grizzly, but I didn't see any moving bugs.

The town guard were already moving in with what I hoped was oil to put on the first fire and water to put on the others.

I couldn't hear a thing over the ringing in my ears. I looked around to see both Arwen and Rowan running towards us. I looked and found Alabaster limping our way as well. He had a tear in one wing and what looked to be a piece of wood hanging out of it. All said and done, it looked like we were alive.

All of us anyway.

Smiling, I walked over and hugged Arwen, motioned for Alabaster to come over, and was for the moment, just glad to have my new family alive if somewhat broken.

Corbin Shale got away.

Epilogue

A few days later, D'arren, Alabaster, Sliverleaf, Rowan, Arwen, and I were sitting at a table remembering the fallen and planning for the future. We were also telling tall tales. What else do you do after an adventure like that?

The other group had made it through as well. Part of me was a little worried about that.

It took a couple of days of searching to make sure none of the grubs had survived.

We needn't have worried. Apparently, the grubs don't live very long if this far away from the hive because they eat each other.

Who knew?

Still, better to be safe than food.

Arwen had lost an eye saving the kid. One of the teeth of the little monsters had popped it. The patch was going to take him some getting used to. To me, it just added to his charm.

Alabaster was grounded for another few weeks. The rip in his wing was healing. But apparently, it took time to heal properly, and magical healing tended to screw things up.

Not that if you ask me, magical healing was worth all that. I had a few new scars to show off if anyone cared. Rowan had gotten hurt the least, and even she was sporting a new set of lines across her cheek and a puncture wound in her side and more bruises than she cared to complain about. That side one had happened during the other group's assault on us, but I didn't find out about it until after the fight at the warehouse. She had reopened it, it seemed.

That's what I get for passing out after almost every fight. I *am* new to this.

I didn't pass out this last time.

So there we sat. I was warm and comfortable. I might be in the shit, but I was happy. So as the old saying goes, I was going to keep my mouth shut. I think I was just glad to be sitting with my new family. It had been so long since I had one. I like it.

I turned my attention back to D'arren's story. In the time between the warehouse and everything getting tidied up; he was almost in good health again. He was certainly in good humor.

"So, there he was, tied to the table of this cult of the Waban, going to be sacrificed to their dark ways when me and the boys burst in. He was naked as the day his ol' mom first set him ta' tit, and he looks at us and says. 'I seem to be short of sword and long on club. Do me a favor and arrest these bastards.'"

Rowan chuckled, and Sliverleaf just shook her head. The boys rolled with laughter. I didn't get it, and I am not sure I wanted to. He has been talking of this Captain all night, and I for one was glad to see him feeling better.

He cleared his throat and looked at the three of us girls. "Guess you had to be there. At anyway, as Broken says, Broken is one of the Sergeants and he's got worse hero worship for the Captain than I do." He chuckled to himself with that memory.

"As Broken says 'Captain Thunderhammer says do it this way' and we do it..." He went on, but I lost all understanding of the words he spoke.

Thunderhammer. I hadn't heard that name in so very long.

I looked up. Everyone was staring at me.

"Chloe girl." D'arren's face showed real concern. "You okay?"

"What was his name?"

"Broken? Well, it's actually Brak Kohon. He is one of the Sergeants of the Guard, a fine Dwarf."

"No, the other one; your Captain." I stood up. I thought I had done it slowly. I was trying so hard to control myself. I felt the stool topple behind me. Guess it had ideas of its own. "What is your Captain's name?"

"Marcus. Marcus Thunderhammer. Why girl? You're shaking."

That son of a bitch.

He was alive.

"That's my Father's name. He's alive. That Bastard is alive. And he left me and my mom to rot."

Peoples of M'Diro

This section is a description of the various peoples who call M'Diro home. In each book when a new race is brought up for the first time they are described. This section is meant as a handy reference to them.

Humans: They range in adult height from 4 to 7.5 feet (1.22 to 2.13 meters) with most being 5-6 feet (1.5 to 1.8 meters). Human hair and skin tone vary from light to dark with blond and red being the least common, skin tone goes from pale to dark as well, with most being a deep tan. Eye color runs the gamut from green and blue to grey, black, and various shades of brown. Men tend to be larger than women.

Orcs: Larger and stockier than Humans, Orcs are two distinct groups; one being True Orcs, the other being a hybrid of Orc and Human often just referred to as Orc because they are the ones most humans interact with. Orcs as a whole are 5 to 8.5 foot (1.5 to 2.6 meters) with 6 to 7 foot (1.8 to 2.13 meters) being the norm, True Orcs being the ones to top out the range. The visual difference between the two is slight, with True Orcs being somewhat larger overall, and having slightly flatter faces. Orc skin color is slightly darker than Human, with a green tint. The only purely human trait that Orcs got from the mixing is having curly hair.

Liberi: They look completely Human, with one exception: their height. Ranging from 2.5 to 3.5 feet tall (.7 to 1.06 meters) they often pass themselves off as children if they can get away with it in the lands of the "big".

Dwarves: The average Dwarven height is 4 to 5.5 feet (1.22 to 1.37 meters). They are a stocky lot, often seeming as wide as they are tall. Most are a deep brown color in hair, face, and eyes. Blond and black do show occasionally, with black being more common in the mountains and blond down on the plains. Red hair is all but unheard of but, given all known dwarven cultures have a red headed god, being born with your hair already soaked in blood is seen as the sign of a strong warrior. Both men and women can grow thick beards and often do as a sign of age and pride.

Gnomes: These people are a hardy group that prefers to live in wetlands or swamps. Ranging from 3.5 to 4.5 feet (1.06 to 1.3 meters) with the women being taller, these grey-skinned people claim to have rocks in their bones, and they aren't wrong. Far denser for their size than they should be, only their wide feet keep them from sinking into their home terrain. Their hair is usually some shade of brown, with eyes that are bright brown.

Elves: The people known as Elves, much like the Liberi, have another name for themselves: The People. At 4.5 to 6.5 foot (1.3 to 1.98 meters) the most striking features of these people are their hair and eyes. They always match, and they are always the color of gemstones. They do have pointed ears, but they aren't much longer than the Human ears. Elves do not have a great deal of sexual dimorphism as both men and women have breasts and hips with the men's being less pronounced.

LeatherWing: Overall, their morphology is simple: 9 small horns on their head, 3 over each eye and 3 down the middle of the forehead; clawed hands and feet; wings that are usually over 3 times their height; and a tail that, while it can be flattened out in flight to be used as a rudder, when they are firmly on the ground and relaxed looks much like a penis. There are eight different skin colors: Red, Orange, White, Green, Blue, Yellow, Purple, and Black. Each color has all the gradient variations within it. Colors appear to be sex based with Red, White, Blue, and Purple being sex specific to cissexual females, and Orange, Green, Yellow, and Black being cissexual males. Reds and Oranges tend to be larger and stronger, Whites and Greens tend to have better memories, Blues and Yellows tend to be better with logistics, and Purple and Blacks tend to just be more powerful. Height-wise they run the gamut from 5 foot (1.5 meters, uneasily a Purple) to 9 foot (2.75 meters, usually a Black) and everything in between. Hair color usually matches their skin to a degree, but eye color can range from disturbingly human to utterly outlandish. They can fly, for between 10 minutes for a poor flyer and 30 minutes for a strong flyer, though they prefer to glide when they can. They are capable of running on all fours or two legs.

GrassLords: This cat-like people are 4.5 to 6.5 feet (1.3 to 1.98 meters) tall. Depending on their age, they could be much lighter or much, much heavier than they look. Any large cat coloration is normal for them, except the mane of a lion. Eyes are blue to orange to green to grey. The most notable feature is, as felines, they do not have a single set of mammaries, but instead have two sets, giving them four breasts. They are capable of moving while upright, walking or even jogging on two legs, but can't run like that. In order to run they must drop to all four limbs.

SkyLords: An avian species, consisting exclusively of raptors, they stand 2.5 to 3.5 feet (.7 to 1.06 meters) on average. They decorate their feathers in a variety of colors and patterns. They have six limbs: two wings, two arms under their wings, and two legs.

The Heard: Often mistaken as The Herd, these hoofed ruminants are also known as Devil Deer since they are almost indistinguishable from normal deer in every way. The most notable distinguishing characteristic is that normal deer don't wear jewelry, nor trophies from the hunters who failed.

About the Author

R. F. DeAngelis is Trans Woman and activist with a chronic pain condition and dyslexia. She honestly believes that the story will set us free and refuses to give up despite the curve balls life throws at all of us. She has been in a committed relationship for 20 years and is a practice of BDSM as a top with a wonderful family and support structure she loves very much.